P9-CRH-130

THE EXAMINATION

Avelyn glanced toward Paen and realized that she had been so consumed with worry at the "being naked in front of everyone" part, that she had not allowed her mind to continue on past that. Now, it struck her that it was time for the bedding. She tried to swallow, but there was nothing to swallow. Her mouth was as dry as dust. She was also having trouble breathing again, although she was most definitely unbound now.

Avelyn's mother had explained all that would happen this night, as a good mother should. It hadn't sounded terribly attractive or dignified, but her mother had assured her it would be fine. Avelyn found that hard to believe at the moment as her husband shifted to lean over her cringing figure. Her thoughts died abruptly as Paen kissed her. She stiffened under the caress, her lips pressing tighter together as his mouth drifted over hers. She was still and uncertain as to whether she liked the caress. Before she could make up her mind, she felt his hand on her breast through the linen and gave a start of surprise. She opened her mouth on a protest and found it suddenly filled. Avelyn was pretty sure it was his tongue, though she had no idea why he would put it inside her mouth... Unless he was checking to see that she had all her teeth.

Other books by Lynsay Sands:

THE CHASE
TALL, DARK & HUNGRY
LOVE BITES
SINGLE WHITE VAMPIRE
THE LOVING DAYLIGHTS
WHAT SHE WANTS
A MOTHER'S WAY ROMANCE ANTHOLOGY
THE RELUCTANT REFORMER
WISH LIST (Anthology)
BLISS
LADY PIRATE
ALWAYS
SWEET REVENGE
THE SWITCH
THE KEY
THE DEED

The PERFECT WIFE

LYNSAY SANDS

LEISURE BOOKS NEW YORK CITY

A LEISURE BOOK®

October 2005

Published by

Dorchester Publishing Co., Inc.
200 Madison Avenue
New York, NY 10016

ISBN 0-8439-5499-X

The name "Leisure Books" and the stylized "L" with design are trademarks of Dorchester Publishing Co., Inc.

Printed in the United States of America.

Visit us on the web at www.dorchesterpub.com.

The PERFECT WIFE

Prologue

"Oh."

That soft breath of sound made Avelyn turn where she stood on the trestle table. Lady Straughton—her mother—had murmured the noise and now paused in descending the stairs to watch with watery eyes as Runilda fiddled with the hem of Avelyn's gown.

Lady Margeria Straughton had been teary-eyed a lot lately, ever since they had received notice that Paen de Gerville had finally returned from the Crusades and wished to claim his betrothed. Avelyn's mother was not taking the upcoming nuptials well. More to the point, she was not reacting well to the fact that Avelyn would be moving to Gerville soon after the nuptials were finished. Avelyn knew her mother was happy to see her married and starting on grandbabies. It was the moving-away part that Lady Straughton did not care for. But then, Avelyn and her mother were very close. So close that rather than be sent away while young, Avelyn had trained at her mother's knee, taught with patience and love.

"Oh," Lady Margeria Straughton breathed again as she crossed the great hall, her maid on her heels. Avelyn shared a smile with Runilda, then shook her head at her mother and said with fond exasperation, "Do I look so hideous that it would see you in tears, Mother?"

"Nay!" Lady Straughton gasped in denial. "You look lovely, my dear. Very lovely. The blue of the gown brings out the blue of your eyes. 'Tis very flattering."

"Then why do you appear so tragic?" Avelyn asked gently.

"Oh. 'Tis just that you look so . . . so much a lady. Oh, Gunnora! My babe is a grown woman now," she bemoaned to the servant at her side.

"Aye, milady." Gunnora smiled patiently. "And so she is. 'Tis time she married and left this home to build her own."

At the maid's gentle words, Lady Straughton's eyes filled with tears once again. They were threatening to well over her lashes and pour down her face when Lord Willham Straughton—who had been seated quietly in a chair by the fire—stood with a squeaking of leather and the jangle of mail.

"No tears, my love," he chided as he moved to join the women by the trestle table. "This is a joyous occasion. Besides, we had our Avelyn longer than I had hoped. Were it not for Richard and his Crusades, we most like would have lost our girl at fourteen or shortly thereafter."

"Aye." Lady Straughton moved to lean against her husband's side as he peered approvingly up at his daughter. "And I am ever grateful that we were allowed to keep her to twenty. Howbeit I am going to miss her so."

"As will I," Lord Straughton agreed gruffly. He encircled his wife with one arm as he turned to his daughter. "You look beautiful, child. Just like your mother on the day we were wed. Paen is a lucky man. You do us proud."

For a moment, Avelyn was startled to see her father's eyes go glassy, as if he too might cry; then he cleared his throat and managed a crooked smile for his wife. "We shall just have to distract ourselves as much as possible from our loss."

"I can think of nothing that will distract me from losing our daughter," Lady Straughton said dismally.

"Nay?" A naughty look crossed Willham Straughton's face, and Avelyn was amused to see his hand drop from her mother's waist to cup her bottom through her skirts. "I may be able to come up with a thing or two," he said, then urged her away from the table and in the general direction of the stairs. "Let us to our room so we might discuss these ideas."

"Oh." Lady Straughton sounded breathy, and her next words, while a protest, were somewhat weak. "But Gunnora and I were going to count stores and see what—"

"You can do that later. Gunnora may go rest herself for a bit in the meantime," Lord Straughton announced.

The maid grinned, then slipped out of the room

even as her lady protested, "But what of Avelyn? I should like to—"

"Avelyn shall be here when we return below," he said as he urged her up the stairs. "She is not leaving yet."

"If she leaves at all."

Avelyn jerked in surprise at that softly spoken insult from behind her. She managed to keep her perch on the trestle table thanks only to her maid's quick action in grabbing her arm to steady her.

Avelyn murmured her thanks to the girl and turned carefully to face the speaker.

Eunice.

Her cousin looked as mean-tempered as ever. Her narrow face was pinched, and there was mocking amusement in the eyes that raked over Avelyn. "What do you think, Staci?"

Avelyn's gaze moved to the two young men accompanying the woman. Twin brothers to Eunice, Hugo and Stacius had matching puglike faces that at the moment bore cruel smiles. The three of them must have entered while she had been distracted by her parents' leaving.

Grand, she thought unhappily. If Avelyn had been blessed in having loving parents, fate had made up for that kindness by cursing her with three of the most horrid cousins in existence. The trio seemed to live to make her miserable. They enjoyed nothing more than a chance to point out her flaws. They had done so ever since their arrival at Straughton some ten years earlier when their castle had been overrun and their father killed. With nowhere else to turn, their mother had brought her children to Straughton, and they had quickly become the bane of Avelyn's young existence.

"I think"—Staci's thick nose turned up as he dropped onto the bench and tipped his head back to peer over Avelyn in her gown—"once Gerville gets a look at what a bovine his betrothed has grown into, he will break the contract and flee for his very life."

"I fear Staci is correct, Avy," Eunice said with mock sympathy as Avelyn flinched under his words. "You look like a great huge blueberry in that gown. Mind you, I do not suppose the color is at fault, for in red you look like a great cherry and in brown a great lump of—"

"I believe I get the point, Eunice," Avelyn said quietly as Eunice and Hugo joined their brother on the bench seat. The warm glow that had bloomed under her parents' compliments died an abrupt death. She suddenly didn't feel lovely anymore. She felt frumpy and fat. Which she was. Only when her parents were around with their unconditional love and acceptance did she briefly forget that fact. Somehow Eunice, Hugo and Stacius were usually there to remind her otherwise.

"I have ever found blueberries lovely and luscious myself."

Avelyn turned toward the door at those sharp words to find her brother Warin closing the door. She wasn't sure how long ago he had entered, but the way he glared at their cousins made her think it had been a while. She wasn't sorry when the trio scrambled back to their feet and made a beeline for the door to the kitchens.

Warin glared after them until they were gone, then turned to his deflated sister. "Do not let them get to you, Avy. You do not look like a blueberry. You look beautiful. Like a princess."

Avelyn forced a smile as he reached up to squeeze her hand. "Thank you, Warin."

His expression was troubled, and Avelyn knew he didn't believe he had convinced her. For a moment, she thought he would insist she was lovely, as a good brother would, but then he seemed to let it go on a resigned sigh. "Do you know where Father is?"

"He went above stairs with mother," Avelyn told him; then some of the twinkle returned to her eyes and she added, "To discuss methods of distracting her from moping over my leave-taking."

Warin raised his eyebrows, then grinned as he turned toward the doors. "Well, if they come down anytime soon, please tell Father I need a word with him. I shall be down at the practice field."

"Aye." Avelyn watched him leave, then glanced down as her maid tugged at the material of her gown. "What think you, Runilda?"

"I think we might take it in another little bit in the shoulders, my lady. 'Tis a tad loose there."

Avelyn tucked her neck in and tried to peer at herself. Her view of her shoulders was too close and fuzzy to tell how they looked. She had a better view of her overgenerous breasts, gently rounded belly and the hips that she considered to be too wide in the blue gown. A blueberry, Eunice had said, and suddenly the cloth Avelyn had chosen with such care lost its beauty in her eyes. She imagined herself a great round blueberry, her head sticking out like a stem.

Avelyn fingered the cloth unhappily. It was lovely material. But even the loveliest material could not make a silly old round chicken into a swan.

"Milady? Shall I take in the shoulders?" Runilda asked.

"Aye." Avelyn let the material drop from her fingers and straightened her shoulders determinedly. "And the waist as well. And cut away the excess."

The maid's eyes widened. "The waist? But the waistline fits perfectly."

"It does now," Avelyn agreed. "But it shall not by the wedding, for I vow here and now that I shall lose at least a stone—hopefully two—ere the wedding day."

"Oh, my lady," Runilda began with concern, "I do not think 'tis a good idea to—"

"I do," Avelyn said firmly. Smiling with determination, she stepped down from the table to the bench, then onto the floor. "I will lose two stone ere the wedding and that is that. For once in my life I will be pretty and slender and . . . graceful. Paen de Gerville shall be proud to claim me."

Chapter One

" 'Tis damned strange."

"Hmm?" Lady Christina Gerville glanced up from her meal with surprise at those muttered words. Her gaze softened as it ran over the man seated between her and her husband. Paen Gerville, her son. His long dark hair was caught in a ponytail low at the back of his neck, his face was clean-shaven, and he was wearing the new forest-green tunic she'd made for this auspicious occasion. He looked much as his own father had on their wedding day: handsome, strong and just about as grumpy, she noted with mild amusement. Then she recalled what he'd muttered to catch her attention and asked, "What is strange, son?"

"This." Paen gestured around the trestle tables filled with people. Lord and Lady Straughton and all their people surrounded them, all but one. The most important one, in his mind. "Where is my bride? 'Tis damned strange that she is not here. She

8

was not about when we arrived last night either. Something is amiss."

Lady Gerville exchanged an amused glance with her husband, Wimarc, as he turned from his conversation with Lord Straughton to hear the end of Paen's comment.

"There is nothing amiss, boy," Lord Wimarc Gerville assured his son. "No doubt the girl is delayed by . . . er . . . beautifying-type things. Typical female stuff. Women are always the last to arrive," he assured him. Then, catching the way his wife's eyes narrowed with displeasure, the older man cleared his throat and sent an apologetic smile her way for slandering the whole of her gender. "Well, anyway, just refrain from worrying. 'Tis just those wedding jitters I warned you about. They are playing havoc with you."

He concluded this bit of encouragement by giving his son what he considered to be a gentle supportive nudge. That nudge nearly sent his large son flying backward off the bench, but Paen—used to his father's affectionate thumps and bumps—grabbed at the table and was able to save himself from ending in an ignoble heap in the rushes.

Grunting as he settled back in place, Paen picked up a piece of cheese and took a bite, but he was distracted. His gaze was locked on the stairs he expected his bride to descend any moment. He knew his father was right and that he was unusually nervous, but Paen had no idea why. The uneasiness had come upon him suddenly. He hadn't been the least uncertain on the way here. In his mind there had been nothing to be uncertain about. He was merely collecting his betrothed, making her his wife.

True, it was a new venture for him, but 'twas not much different from collecting a new squire, which was something else he had to do on this trip. He planned to marry the girl, spend a few days at Straughton afterward, then head back to Gerville, stopping to collect his new squire along the way. Simple. 'Twas nothing to get all worked up about.

Or so he'd thought on the journey here yesterday. This morning, however, Paen was of a different mind. It had suddenly occurred to him that a wife might be a somewhat different proposition from a squire. After all, a man needn't bed his squire. He also didn't have to live out his life with the squire for however long he should be fortunate enough— or unfortunate enough as the case might be—to live. And, too, he could always dismiss the squire if he displeased him. Unfortunately, one could not dismiss a wife, no matter how bad she was.

On top of all that, he had yet to set eyes on his would-be bride. It almost seemed that she was avoiding him. He found it hard to imagine that was a good sign.

"Suck in your breath a bit more, my lady."

"I cannot, Runilda. This is as much as I can suck in." Avelyn pushed the words out on the last of the air in her lungs, then had to inhale to ask, "How close are we?"

The maid's hesitation was answer enough. Avelyn let her breath out on a defeated sigh. " 'Tis no use, Runilda. I shall not get this gown on, and we both know it. 'Sides, even did I manage the chore, no doubt the seams would split the moment you finished fastening the hooks."

"I am sorry, my lady. I should not have taken it in so much." Runilda stepped around in front of Avelyn, her face a portrait of guilt.

" 'Tis not your fault. I ordered it done." Avelyn sank onto the end of the bed, her mind searching for options. There were very few that she could see. She had not lost two stone in the last two weeks. In fact, despite all her determination and best efforts, Avelyn very much feared that she might have gained a pound or two. The lovely blue gown she and Runilda had worked so hard over would not fit.

On the bright side, she supposed she'd no longer need fear looking like a giant blueberry on this, her wedding day. Unfortunately, that left her with the choice of resembling a large cherry or a pile of—

"Perhaps we could let the seams back out," Runilda suggested doubtfully, but Avelyn knew that was impossible. She'd insisted the cloth be cut away to ensure her success at losing weight. She was an idiot.

If she had at least tried the gown on sooner, there would have been a chance to do something about it. But she hadn't. There had been so much to do to prepare for the wedding and the influx of guests attending it, she hadn't thought of her gown or the

11

fact that she'd asked Runilda to take it in. She was a fool.

Forcing away her misery and self-pity, Avelyn stood and began to struggle out of the dress.

"Well, it shall have to be the red gown then. 'Tis the one with the least wear." She tried not to think of the reason for that. The last thing she needed was to fret over its unfortunate effect of turning her face florid. Fortunately, Runilda was kind enough not to bring up that point and merely murmured a heartbroken, "Oh, my lady."

Hearing the tremble in the young maid's voice, Avelyn stiffened her spine. "Here, now. No crying, Runilda, else you shall start me crying as well."

Avelyn turned away from the maid's tragic face, determined that she would withstand this disaster with all the dignity and aplomb she could muster. She would not cry. Even if Lord Paen Gerville should reject her on sight, she would hold her head high and keep a calm and unaffected facade.

Avelyn moved to her chest and sorted through its contents until she found the red gown in question. Her mouth twisted as she touched the soft cloth. She'd thought it the loveliest material she'd ever seen when the traveling merchant had brought it out of his wagon. Avelyn had imagined the cool cloth cut in simple lines, flowing over her body in caressing waves. Of course, she'd imagined herself lean and lovely in the gown—an image that had stayed in her head even once the gown was finished. Avelyn had felt more than beautiful on first donning it . . . then she'd gone below for the sup.

Hugo, Stacius and Eunice had been quick to help clear her vision. Their caustic comments and cruel words had sliced at her pride and pleasure in the new gown, leaving her feeling large and ungainly. It was Eunice who had pointed out that the color had an unfortunate effect on her complexion. Hugo had laughed and commented that he'd hardly noticed, what with her looking like a large cherry in the gown.

Avelyn had never worn it again. Hence the reason it was like new.

It was to be hoped that Paen Gerville was partial to cherries, she thought with a touch of self-mockery as she lifted the gown out of the chest and gave it a sharp snap.

Most of her gowns—including this one—had been packed away for the journey to Gerville. Avelyn grimaced over its wrinkled state, then shrugged inwardly. She was sure a few wrinkles would hardly be noticed amidst her vast girth.

She tried not to think on how much she'd come to hate the gown. Runilda had just finished fastening it for her when the bedchamber door opened.

"Avelyn!" her mother cried. "What are you doing? You are not even in your dress yet! Paen is impatient to meet with you before the wedding."

"What is he like?" Avelyn asked as her mother hurried to her side. The Gervilles were supposed to have reached Straughton early the day before, giving Avelyn and Paen at least a little time to become acquainted. However, the day had passed with no sign of her betrothed and his party. Most of the

other guests had arrived and been settled in before
a messenger had arrived with the news that there
had been a mishap with one of the Gervilles' wagons and they were delayed. Avelyn had already
been abed when they finally arrived at Straughton.

If she were to be honest, Avelyn had been relieved
at the delay in having to present herself before her betrothed. Her cousins' taunts that he would surely reject her the moment he laid eyes on her had haunted
Avelyn these last two weeks. And each time she considered the possibility, she felt queasy with anxiety.

"He seems very nice," her mother assured her.
"In fact, he reminds me a great deal of your father
when younger. Now, come. We must get you into
the blue gown."

Avelyn forced a smile for her mother. "I have decided to wear this gown instead."

"What?" Lady Straughton stopped, her dismayed gaze traveling over Avelyn. "Nay! But why?
The blue gown looks so lovely on you, and this one
is wrinkled." Her mouth firmed and she shook her
head. "Nay. You must wear the blue."

"It does not fit," Avelyn admitted as her mother
grabbed up the blue gown and approached.

"Of course it does. I saw you in it but a fortnight
past. It fit beautifully. You looked lovely."

Avelyn could not keep the doubt from her expression at this claim, but merely confessed unhappily, "I had Runilda take it in and cut away the
excess. I hoped to lose weight ere the wedding,
but—"

"Oh, Avelyn!" Lady Straughton's hands dropped

14

with disappointment, the precious gown now dangling from her fingers and pooling on the rush-covered floor.

Shame washing over her, Avelyn started to turn away, but her mother caught her arm, drawing her into a warm embrace. "Oh, Avelyn, how I wish you would not fret so over your shape. You are beautiful just as you are. Why do you suffer so over it?"

"Because I am a great cow, Mother, and would have it otherwise."

Much to Avelyn's amazement, her mother hissed a curse word as she released her. When she stepped back there was anger in the woman's eyes and her lips had thinned with displeasure. "I ought to hide Hugo, Stacius and Eunice. Honestly! I know they are behind this. Those three—" She suddenly fell silent and a struggle took place on her face; then she calmed and shook her head. "Never mind. You are no cow, Avelyn. You are pleasingly plump. Men prefer their women that way."

Avelyn snorted, but her mother ignored her.

"You cannot wear the red. 'Tis too wrinkled." Lady Straughton's gaze dropped to the blue gown dangling from her fingers. "I have an idea. But we shall have to hurry. They are ready to start for the church and are waiting only for you. Take off the red gown," she instructed, then turned to Runilda. "Go fetch Gunnora. Tell her to find that length of white linen we purchased from the traveling merchant and hurry back here."

"What are you thinking, Mother?" Avelyn asked anxiously as she shrugged out of the red gown.

15

"We are going to bind you," her mother announced with determination.

Avelyn's eyes widened uncertainly. "Bind me?"

"Aye. If we cannot change the gown to fit your shape, we shall change your shape to fit the gown."

"Oh, dear," Avelyn breathed, not at all sure that this sounded a good idea.

Several moments later she was quite sure it was not. She found herself clutching desperately at Runilda to help keep herself in place as her mother and Gunnora worked behind her, busily tugging and squeezing.

"How much more, Mother? 'Tis awfully tight already," Avelyn gasped, her hands clutching Runilda's shoulders. The maid gave her a half-worried, half-bracing smile, then leaned to the side to try to see what Lady Straughton and Gunnora were doing behind Avelyn's back. Avelyn did not need to see. She could feel it. They had wrapped the linen tight around her waist and were drawing it tighter with each pass . . . and tighter . . . and tighter.

"I know 'tis uncomfortable, but 'tis only for a little while," her mother soothed, then ordered, "Tighter, Gunnora. We are almost there."

Avelyn groaned as the restriction around her waist became unbearable. She could swear her vitals were being pushed upward in search of room as the cloth was bound about her. Unfortunately, those vitals appeared to be taking up room generally used by her lungs. Her breath was suddenly terribly restricted. Avelyn nearly fainted with relief when her mother announced, "There! That is it! Now let us just tie it off."

"We cannot tie it, m'lady," Gunnora protested. "'Twill leave a bulge."

"Oh, aye. We shall have to sew it, I suppose." She sighed. "Well, here. I shall hold it while you sew, but be quick about it please, Gunnora. My hands are already threatening to cramp. I do not know how long I can continue to hold it."

"Aye, m'lady."

Avelyn listened to all this through a growing fog. She truly could not take in more than a slight puff of air at a time. Groaning as her head began to spin, she leaned her face into Runilda's shoulder and tried to hold on to the thread of consciousness for just a little longer.

"There!" Gunnora's announcement drew Avelyn from her dazed state.

"Thank goodness! Oh, my hands," Lady Straughton complained. "Here, let us do up the gown. Perfect."

Avelyn presumed the "perfect" meant that they had managed to fasten the gown. She wasn't sure, however, until she felt herself being turned away from where she leaned against Runilda. Lifting her head, she tried for a smile as she found herself facing her mother and Gunnora.

"Oh," Lady Straughton breathed.

"Aye," Gunnora agreed. The two women exchanged congratulatory glances.

"You look lovely, my dear. Just lovely." Taking Avelyn's arm, Lady Straughton urged her toward the door. "Now let us go below before they come looking for us."

Avelyn managed to cross almost half the room, each step slower and more arduous than the one preceding it, before she was forced to stop and catch her breath.

"What is it, dear?" Lady Straughton asked.

"I . . . nothing, I just . . . need . . . to catch . . . my breath." Avelyn forced a smile even as she strained to draw air into her compressed lungs. "Just . . . give me . . . a moment."

Lady Straughton exchanged an anxious glance with her maid, then murmured, "Aye. Take a moment to catch your breath. Then we may go below and introduce you to your betrothed ere we walk to the church."

The small puff of air Avelyn had managed to draw into her chest wheezed out at the very thought of walking—not just out of the room and down the stairs but all the way to the chapel. The church had never seemed very far away to her before, but at that moment it might as well have been miles away. She could not seem to get enough air into her lungs to breathe, let alone walk. Avelyn was faint and swaying on her feet after crossing only her room; she would never make it all the way to the church.

"I do not think I can manage to walk that far," she admitted, feeling as though she were letting everyone down.

"Oh, dear." Lady Straughton steadied her as

Avelyn swayed against her. "You are flushing, then paling, dear. Mayhap we should loosen the binding just a touch."

"We cannot," Gunnora said. "We sewed it in place."

Lady Straughton looked so distressed at this reminder that Avelyn forced herself upright and suggested, "Perhaps if we move slowly."

"Aye." Her mother agreed with relief. " 'Tis more ladylike to walk slowly anyway. Come, let us try again, but slowly this time."

Avelyn took one struggling step, then another. She could feel her face flushing with the effort, then feel the heat seeping away from her skin, leaving her cheeks pale and cold as the room began to spin around her.

"Oh, dear. This is not going to work," Lady Straughton said unhappily, drawing Avelyn to a halt. She hesitated for a moment, obviously thinking, then suddenly turned to her maid with determination. "Fetch Warin and my husband here at once, Gunnora."

"Aye, my lady."

Margeria Straughton turned her attention back to Avelyn as the maid hurried from the room. Noting the way Avelyn was swaying on her feet, she frowned and pushed her several steps to the side until she stood in front of a chest. "Here, dear; sit here."

"I cannot," Avelyn wheezed, struggling to retain her feet despite her mother's pushing. "I cannot sit! That will make it worse. Please! I need air. I need—"

Lady Straughton's eyes widened in horror. "You are turning blue! Runilda! Quickly, the window!" she cried, and pulling Avelyn's arm over her shoulder, she dragged her across the room in a panic as the maid ran ahead and opened the shutters.

It was a gusty day. The wind whirled into the room, sending the drapes around her bed rippling as Avelyn leaned against the ledge. She could feel the breeze clawing at her hair, pulling several strands loose from the tight chignon she'd had Runilda arrange, but she didn't care. All she cared about was the reviving sensation of the cool breeze slapping her face. Avelyn opened her mouth to the wind and gasped, trying to suck air into lungs that simply had no room to accept more than a bit at a time.

"What the devil is going on here?"

All three women stiffened at that roar as the door burst open. Avelyn glanced over her shoulder as her father stomped in with a concerned Warin on his heels.

"Margeria? What is the delay? First Avelyn does not come down; then you disappear and Gunnora—" He paused abruptly as he glimpsed Avelyn's pallid face. The fire fled his expression, replaced by concern as he rushed forward. "Avelyn? Dear God, you are pale as death. What is the matter?"

"'Tis all right, 'tis—" Lady Straughton began, but paused when Avelyn's fingers tightened convulsively on her arm.

20

" 'Tis just nerves, Father," Avelyn finished for her on a gasp, then paused to suck in another bit of breath. Tears immediately welled in her eyes, as much from the torture of her lungs as from her words as she finished, "I am getting married and leaving my home. I will miss you and I—"

Her words ended on a pained groan as Willham Straughton hugged her tight. "And we shall miss you too. You are a spark of light in our lives, child. But we shall visit often and—Have you lost some meat, girl? You seem smaller to hug."

Avelyn's answer was a gurgling gasp as she clutched her father's tunic and struggled to get her face out of his shoulder to breathe in some much-needed air. She wasn't able to get her nose or mouth free, but she did get her eyes above his shoulder. They were wide and alarmed as they fell on her mother.

"Let her go, Willham!" Lady Straughton cried. "You are suffocating her."

Avelyn found herself released at once. She turned away to fall against the window ledge, gasping at the air smacking her in the face.

"Are you sure 'tis just nerves?" Warin asked. "She does not appear to be at all well."

"Aye. 'Tis nerves," Lady Straughton insisted. Then Avelyn heard the definite sound of her mother sucking in a determined breath. It sounded a lovely deep, bracing breath, and Avelyn moaned as she imagined being able to suck in one herself. Then she heard her mother say, "Howbeit, in this state,

21

the walk to the church would be too much for her. Willham, you shall have to take everyone down to the church. Warin, you shall ride Avelyn down there on your horse."

"Ride her down on the horse?" both men exclaimed.

"But 'tis farther for me to fetch my horse than to walk to the chapel," Warin protested.

"Aye," Lord Straughton agreed. "The Gervilles will think her ailing or—"

"Not when you explain that 'tis considered quite romantic at court for the bride to arrive on a charger," Lady Straughton insisted patiently. "And that 'tis all the rage and all the best noble brides are doing it."

Willham blinked at the suggestion. "Are they?"

"How would I know?" Lady Straughton asked with exasperation. "You hate court and will not take me there."

"Oh." Willham nodded in understanding. "So 'tis lying you want me to do."

"Aye."

"Very well." Lord Straughton grinned and headed out of the room.

"He shall make me pay for that," her mother muttered.

Lady Straughton did not sound overly distressed at the thought. In fact, Avelyn was positive she gave an anticipatory shiver as she watched her husband pull the door closed behind him.

Lady Margeria turned to her son. "Go fetch your horse. We shall meet you at the doors." The moment he nodded and turned to leave, Lady Straughton turned her attention back to Avelyn. "Now—Oh, you look better!" she exclaimed with surprise.

Avelyn managed a smile. "I think I am getting used to it. If I stay calm and do not move about too much, I seem to be well." She took one cautious step away from the window, then another.

"Perhaps you would do better to rest until Warin returns with his mount." Her mother placed a nervous hand out as if to catch her should she fall into a dead faint.

"I needs must be sure I shall not faint taking the few steps from Warin's horse to my new husband," Avelyn pointed out, taking another step as her mother, Gunnora and Runilda trailed, hands out to catch her. She had only taken a few steps ere the room began to sway around her. Avelyn suspected it was wasting breath on speech that had brought the faintness on so quickly this time. It seemed she would have to choose between speaking and walking. At the moment, walking was the more important task, so she merely paused for a moment to allow the sensation to pass, then continued on. Avelyn was not the only one to breathe a sigh of relief when she reached the door.

She paused to lean against the door frame for a moment, then managed a smile at the anxious women and pulled the door open. She stepped out into the hall and paused.

All Avelyn need do was manage the long, *long* hallway and then the stairs. Tightening her lips against the whimper that wanted to slip out at the thought of all those stairs, she straightened her shoulders and started forth, terribly relieved when her mother took one arm and Gunnora the other. Runilda then dropped behind to press her hands to Avelyn's back. The three of them were nearly carrying her, and still Avelyn had to pause often to attempt to draw breath and allow her head to clear.

She'd just paused again to suck greedily at the air around her when Warin appeared on the landing.

"Whatever is taking so long? I have been waiting for—" Her brother paused in front of them, his gaze turning concerned. "This is no mere nerves. Dear Lord, Avy is about to swoon." His gaze turned from woman to woman, demanding answers Avelyn could have lived the rest of her life not giving.

Deciding it was best to make the humiliating explanations herself, Avelyn did so as quickly and plainly as she could, trying not to cringe and flush or stammer. Then she awaited his response. Much to her relief, Warin merely grunted, then said, "Well, 'tis obvious you need help getting to the horse, else we will never make it to the church."

He stepped forward and tried to sweep Avelyn into his arms. Tried and failed. With the tight binding, she was as stiff as a broomstick from the hips up. Avelyn simply did not bend. There was no way anyone could sweep her anywhere. For a moment, she feared she'd have to travel the stairs after all; then her brother half squatted in front of her. He wrapped his arms around her upper legs, then straightened with a grunt.

Avelyn let out what should have been a squeal, but was more of a squeak, and clutched at his head and shoulders. "What—?"

"Be still, Avelyn," Warin said gruffly. "This shall be tricky and no doubting it."

Avelyn remained still. Had she not been so starved for air, she was sure she would have held her breath. As it was, she prayed all the way down the stairs and could have wept with relief when they reached the great-hall floor. Warin carried her out of the castle, with their mother and the two maids following, then hesitated on reaching his mount. He turned with her still in his arms and asked, "How am I to get her on the horse? One must bend to sit a horse."

There was a moment of stunned silence; then Lady Straughton stepped forward. "Set her down, Warin, and give me your knife. Then you shall need to turn your back for a moment."

"What—?" Avelyn began anxiously as Warin set her down.

"Turn around, dear," her mother ordered, then set to work on the lacing at the back of the gown. "We are going to slit the lower part of the binding just enough that you may sit the horse."

"But—" Avelyn's protest died in her throat as she felt the lower part of the binding give way somewhat. It was just the smallest bit and was at the lower part of the binding, around the bottom of

25

her hips, so the change brought no relief to her abused lungs, but still it was a blissful sensation. God, how wonderful it would be when the binding was finally removed, she thought dreamily.

Chapter Two

Dear God, the binding was bursting!

Avelyn wasn't really aware of that fact at first. She noticed that some of her discomfort seemed to ease when they were only halfway to the chapel. They would have been all the way to the chapel and halfway through the ceremony at that point, but her mother had come up with the brilliant idea that she, Gunnora and Runilda should walk in front of the horse, each carrying a basket of flowers which they would strew before Warin's mount as they led the way to the chapel. She had thought it a most romantic idea and had wasted several moments raiding her garden of the finest buds.

Avelyn had thought it rather sweet at the time. But now, as her discomfort eased another little bit, and she realized that the split her mother had sliced into the bottom of her binding was splitting further of its own accord, she decided it had been quite the worst idea ever.

"Whatever is the matter? You have gone quite

8

LYNSAY SANDS

stiff," Warin said as Avelyn straightened before him. Not that she hadn't already been sitting straight in the saddle as they crossed the bailey to the chapel, but Avelyn was now stretching her back out as much as she could. And her breathing, which had been shallow panting really, had now stopped altogether as she tried desperately to make herself as small as possible and prevent the rend from tearing further.

"Avy?"

"Hurry," she gasped.

"Hurry? But—" He glanced toward their mother and the two maids, who were walking before them, then back again, and she saw his concern deepen. "Whatever is the matter with your face, Avy? 'Tis all red and puffy."

Avelyn released the breath she'd been holding and hissed, "Never mind my face. The binding is giving, Warin. I need to dismount. Now."

Much to her relief, he did not hesitate further, but called his mother to them and explained the problem and that they must speed up this procession. Nodding, Lady Straughton hurried back to the maids and held a whispered conference. Then the women set out again, this time at an accelerated pace. In fact, they went from a slow meander to an almost jog, rushing along, strewing flowers at a slightly frantic speed as Warin urged his mount to follow on their heels.

They had gone perhaps another ten feet when Avelyn became aware of a definite easing of the

28

binding. This time she could hear the cloth tearing beneath her dress. Warin heard it too.

"Faster," he called softly to the women. Then as the rending sound came again, he simply hissed, "Move!"

Lady Straughton glanced around with dismay, then hurried out of the way as her son urged his horse into a trot. The three women scampered after them, tossing flowers at their backs as they raced forward. Avelyn could not say for sure which of them was the most relieved when Warin finally drew his mount to a halt. She wasn't surprised to find that every last wedding guest gathered in front of the chapel was agape at this display.

Warin slid off his mount and turned to find Avelyn following in a flurry of skirts, alighting with indecent haste in an effort to prevent the rend in her bindings from going further.

She stood very still then, hardly breathing as she waited to see if all would be well or whether she would burst out of the gown like a grape escaping its skin.

"Is it all right?" Warin asked anxiously.

"Aye. I think so," Avelyn murmured. Certainly, the binding was firmly enough in place that she still didn't seem able to breathe much.

"Is all well?" her mother asked breathlessly as she caught up to them. Gunnora and Runilda, also out of breath from their run, were on her heels.

"Aye. I do not think it went very far. How do I look?"

29

Her mother looked her over critically, then reached up to pinch her cheeks. "You are a bit pale, but otherwise lovely."

Avelyn stood still as her mother tried to bring some color back into her skin. The attention to her cheeks, however, reminded her of one of the insults Hugo had tormented her with some years back. He'd said she had chubby cheeks like a squirrel with nuts in its mouth and had followed her around for a whole week screaming, "Chubby cheeks! Chubby squirrel cheeks!" Now, Avelyn imagined herself looking utterly ridiculous with her forced trim body and bloated chubby cheeks.

"There." Her mother stepped back and offered a bracing smile. "You look lovely. Can you walk the rest of the way?"

Avelyn cast a quick nervous glance over her shoulder at the distance to the church steps. Warin had stopped sooner than she would have liked, but she thought she could manage the distance if she went very slowly.

"Aye." Avelyn sucked in her cheeks, trying for a less squirrel-like look as she turned to face the church.

The guests parted like the Red Sea for Moses, leaving a path for her to walk. Avelyn started slowly forward. Very slowly. So slowly she was hardly moving, and still she was panting and fighting a woozy feeling after only a handful of steps.

"Dear God, she looks like a fish!" Wimarc Gerville gasped in shock, then grunted when his wife's elbow found its way into his gullet. "Sorry . . . but she does," he muttered with chagrin, then shook his head. "Wife, I do not recall her cheeks being all puckered and her lips all pursed like that when we saw her as a child and agreed to the contract. Do you?"

"Nay." Lady Christina Gerville focused on the girl walking toward them. Dear God in heaven, the chit was moving so slowly and laboriously, one might have been forgiven for thinking she was walking to her death rather than to her betrothed. Lady Gerville's gaze narrowed on Avelyn's puckered face, and then she relaxed somewhat. "I believe she may be sucking in her cheeks."

"Whatever for?" Paen finally joined the conversation as he watched his bride draw near. If his mother answered his question, Paen was too distracted by his concern over his bride to hear her response. It was not her looks that worried him. True, her lower face was rather squinched up at the moment, making her look a bit fishlike, but even so he could see that her lips were soft and full. She also had a straight nose, and large, clear blue eyes. And her hair was a lovely chestnut brown, scooped up with little tendrils left to soften her face. He suspected that if she released her cheeks, she would be more than passably pretty.

Nay, it was not her looks that concerned Paen at the moment, it was the way she walked. She was as stiff as a soldier with broken ribs and moving at an extremely slow pace that he would expect only from someone weak or ailing. The very last thing

Paen wished for was a weak or ailing bride. He'd been rather hoping for a robust, healthy wife who would offer comfort and strength through the trials life would no doubt have in store for them.

There was little Paen could do about the matter now, however. If she was weak or ailing, he would find out soon enough and have to make do. This betrothal contract had been drawn up in his name when he was just a child, and his honor allowed no choice but to stand by it.

It took a nudge from his father to make Paen realize that his betrothed had reached his side and that—rather than turn to face the priest—he was still standing with his back to the man as he surveyed her with displeasure.

Rocking under his father's not so subtle reminder, he grunted a greeting and offered a smile to the girl.

Avelyn closed her eyes, then blinked them open again and sent up a silent prayer of thanks to God when Paen de Gerville smiled at her. For one heart-stopping moment she had feared that the horrible binding and the cheek-sucking she was doing had all been for naught. She'd been sure that he would do as Eunice and her brothers had suggested and reject her outright.

Legs weak and trembling, fear seeming almost to eat away her strength, Avelyn didn't turn to the priest at once, but instead stared up at her betrothed.

Her mother had not been lying when she said he

was handsome and strong. The man was both. His looks were not the first thing she noticed, however. It was the sheer size of him. He was extremely tall, with shoulders almost as wide as the chapel door behind him. And yes, he was handsome. But, more important to her, he was obviously kind, for though his initial expression had given him away and shown his disappointment with her as his bride, the smile that he was now gracing her with assured her that he would not refuse this marriage. Aye. He was incredibly kind, she decided, and fell a little bit in love with him on the spot for not turning her away.

A throat-clearing by the priest brought Avelyn back to the situation at hand. She turned to face the holy man. His expression made her realize that while she had been busy ogling her betrothed, he had commenced with the wedding and was now awaiting some response from her.

"I thoo?" she offered, flushing at the way her words were mangled by her effort to keep her cheeks sucked in. She had to hold them in place by gently biting on them with her teeth. No one commented, however, and Avelyn forced herself to relax and breathe in some much-needed air. Only there seemed very little air about for her to breathe. The crowd of people pressing in on them appeared to be hogging it greedily for themselves. Trying a little harder to drag air into her lungs, Avelyn grabbed unconsciously at her betrothed's arm and told herself not to panic, but the priest's face was wavering before her, his voice growing louder, then fading in her ears. *Oh, no*, she thought unhappily, *this isn't good at all.*

Paen's concern over the state of his bride's health grew as the ceremony proceeded. She had grasped his arm moments ago. This was not so unusual in itself, but the desperate, clawlike nature of the grasp was. Now, as the long ceremony continued, he became certain that she was starting to sway on her feet ever so slightly. Then when it came time for her to repeat her vows, her voice was breathy and faint.

Paen watched her with concern, so distracted that he wasn't at first sure why his father had nudged him when he rocked under his elbow.

"You may kiss the bride." The way the priest said the words suggested that it wasn't the first time he had done so.

Paen turned to fully face his bride, frowning at the way she was breathing. She was taking quick shallow breaths, almost panting. She was also looking terribly faint. Suspecting that this might be a short marriage thanks to her obvious ill health, Paen bent to press his lips to hers. She tasted of honey mead. Her lips were soft and warm and . . . gone?

Paen opened his eyes with amazement as the crowd around him let out a collective gasp. He was just in time to catch his bride's falling form. She had fainted.

Paen gaped at his unconscious bride, part of his mind in shock, the other part noting that she was indeed passably pretty. More than passably pretty now that unconsciousness had stopped her from sucking in her cheeks. In fact, other than her unusual pallor, she was lovely.

"What's the matter with the girl?"

It was Paen's father who asked that question. His words acted as something of a spell-breaker for everyone else. The mob broke out in immediate chatter even as Avelyn's family rushed forward to surround Paen where he stood holding her against his chest.

"What is going on? Is she all right?" Lord Straughton bellowed, sounding alarmed. Paen had to take that as a good sign. It seemed to suggest that the girl wasn't taken to fainting and that this might be an unusual occurrence. That was encouraging.

"She is fine," Lady Straughton assured everyone even as she and two maids crowded forward to fan Avelyn's face.

"Here, perhaps I should—" Warin Straughton, the brother, tried to wrest the girl from Paen's grasp, and that was when Paen's own shock passed.

Scowling at the man for trying to do what it was now *his* duty to do, Paen elbowed him aside and swept Avelyn up into his arms . . . Sort of. His new bride wasn't very sweepable. In fact, from hips to neck she was alarmingly unbending. She ended lying flat across his arms like a board, with her head and knees hanging off like trailing ivy. It was most disconcerting.

Grunting, Paen moved forward, quickly losing the fanning women as he forced his way through the chattering crowd.

His gaze dropped several times to his bride's face as he crossed the bailey to the keep. The fact that she was pretty should have cheered him. After all, no man wished to bed a fish-faced wench, but even her fairness was not enough in his mind to make up for her obviously weak constitution. In truth, he would rather have a healthy homely wife than a pretty but ill one.

Paen's years on campaign had filled him with certain hopes when it came to a wife. He had spent many—too many—years fighting battle after battle, living in mean tents that leaked when it rained and did nothing to keep out the night chill.

At first, it had been a grand adventure. He'd enjoyed the camaraderie of his compatriots. But as battle had followed battle, and man after man had fallen at his side, leaving him knee deep in blood and death, the grand adventure had begun to pall. Paen had found himself yearning for the comfort of a dry bed, a warm hearth and the soft breast of a good wife to lay his weary head on. Only his fealty to his king, and his desire to protect and watch over his younger brother Adam, who had followed him to battle and was slower to lose his enthusiasm for it, had kept Paen from leaving the war trail and returning home. But when Adam died, a Saracen sword through the chest, Paen lost his heart for battle. Seeming to recognize this, King Richard had given him leave to take news of his brother's death home, and had suggested that Paen might wish to tend to his wedding now. Paen had returned at once with the sad tidings. After allowing a short time for the grief to pass, he had then sent news that he wished to claim his betrothed.

All the while he had been hoping, expecting even, that his bride would be comfortingly plump and strong. A woman he would not crush when he bedded her and whose full, soft breasts could be a cushion for his head on cold winter nights.

"Ohh."

Paen left off his thoughts at that moan. His bride was coming around. He suspected it was the fresh breeze slapping her cheeks that revived her. When she lifted her head and peered at him weakly, he tried to adjust her to a more upright position in his arms, but she still did not bend.

He didn't get to ponder that fact and what it might mean for long because she began to struggle in his arms. Well, that was a kind description. Stiff as her middle was, what she was doing was more like flopping her head and lower legs across his up-raised arms.

"Pray! Let me stand!" She was both out of breath and seemingly terribly embarrassed by the whole ordeal.

Trying to soothe her, Paen offered a reassuring smile and said, "Rest."

* * *

Avelyn stopped her struggles and lay still when her new husband grunted that word. She couldn't tell if he was angry or not. He didn't sound angry, but his expression was a grimace. She supposed he was somewhat put out by her fainting. She hadn't made a very good show of it at the wedding, what with her lisping and fainting and all.

Recalling her lisp when she had said her "I do's" made Avelyn realize that she was no longer sucking in her cheeks. She quickly did so now, hoping he hadn't noticed her chubby face. She then peered past his shoulder to see that the entire wedding party was following them some distance back. He was walking very quickly despite the burden of carrying her, and left the others further behind with each step. She sighed unhappily. This was all terribly embarrassing. It also could not be good for her husband to carry her so far. Warin had carried her down the stairs, but really this was a good distance further than that.

"Pray, my lord," she tried again, releasing her cheeks briefly to speak. "Put me down ere you do yourself an injury. I am too heavy for you to—" She paused uncertainly. Her new husband had stopped walking and was now staring at her in amazement. Even as she noted his surprise, he suddenly burst out laughing.

After a moment, he shook his head and said, "I shall hardly injure myself carrying a little thing like you. Women!" He said the last in a tone of exasperated bemusement and continued to walk again, seemingly oblivious to the fact that Avelyn had flushed an even deeper shade of pink. She was hardly a "little thing" but gave up her protests and suffered the rest of the journey in silence.

It was a great relief to her when they finally reached the keep and entered. It was even more of a relief to be set on the trestle-table bench. Avelyn busily straightened her skirts and avoided meeting the gaze of the man now positioning himself on the bench beside her. She was so nervous that it was almost a relief when the keep doors opened and people began bustling into the great hall.

Lady Straughton was at the head of the crowd rushing to fill the room. She moved quickly to Avelyn's side, her expression concerned. "Are you well, dear? Have you recovered?"

"Aye," Avelyn answered.

"You look much better," a woman she could only assume was Paen's mother commented, coming to a halt beside Lady Margeria.

"Aye. You do." Lord Straughton paused at her side and patted her shoulder awkwardly. Then he shook his head and told a man who looked very much like an older version of Paen, "This is most distressing. Avelyn has never fainted a day in her life. It must be all the excitement."

Avelyn closed her eyes, wishing everyone would just sit down and let the matter go. It was all terribly embarrassing.

"I am sure it is just the excitement," someone said, and Avelyn opened her eyes to peer at the speaker. The woman was about her mother's age, with graying pale blond hair and a pretty face.

"Aunt Helen is right," a petite blond girl agreed. "My cousin was like that as well. She was ever the most stalwart of women. She never fainted a day in her life . . . until she got with child. Then she would faint at the drop of a feather."

"Diamanda!" the older blonde, Aunt Helen, gasped with shock.

"I did not mean that Lady Avelyn is—Of course she could not be with child," the girl said quickly. She was flushed and looked horrified that her words had been taken so. "I just meant 'twas the strain of child-bearing that—And 'tis most like the strain of the wedding and everything . . ." Her voice faded away as she peered helplessly around at the horrified gazes of those around her. Diamanda's expression suggested she might like nothing better than to simply disappear on the spot.

Knowing that feeling well, Avelyn felt pity stir in her for the girl. She knew how uncomfortable it was to be the cynosure of all eyes. She detested it herself, and it was even worse when you were at the center of attention because of something silly you said or did. Forcing a smile, she braved that very thing to aid the unfortunate girl.

"Of course you did not," she said gently. "This is all very silly, really. I have been working hard to help arrange everything. Then, too, I was nervous and haven't been sleeping well. And it *was* quite stuffy there in front of the church with everyone crowded around, was it not?"

"Aye," her mother agreed quickly, trying to help her diffuse the situation. "Come, we should sit.

Cook has been working for days on this feast and planning it for even longer. She is most likely eager to start serving it."

Much to Avelyn's relief, everyone began to settle at the table. She let out a little breath of relief at that and glanced shyly to the side, only to drop her eyes at once when she saw her new husband peering at her.

"Thank you."

She glanced back to him with surprise at those softly spoken words. "For what, my lord?"

"For not getting offended by Diamanda's unfortunate choice of words, and for helping to defuse the matter."

Flushing, Avelyn gave a small shrug and began to absently smooth the white cloth her mother had insisted be laid over the head table. "I am sure she meant no insult."

"She's a child still and awkward at times," he said, then added with a wry twist to his lips, "and, I fear, a bit spoiled. Mother always regretted not having a daughter and showered Diamanda with affection when she arrived to train at Gerville. Mother will be sorry to see her go."

"Is her training done, then?" Avelyn asked.

Paen shrugged. "She trained at Gerville because she was to marry my brother Adam. Now that he is dead, her father is looking for an alternate husband for the girl. He had decided she should return home while they make the search, and her Aunt Helen came to collect her, but mother is trying to convince him to allow Diamanda to stay until she has to marry. A note has been sent to her father, and Helen is staying on until we get a response." His gaze slid along the table to the girl. "I fear Mother will be disappointed."

"You do not think her father will let her stay?" Avelyn asked with surprise, and he shook his head.

"She is a pretty child. I suspect her father may already have made a match for her and will want her home to prepare for marriage."

"She looks to be at least sixteen, my lord. Hardly a child."

"She is fourteen," he corrected.

Surprised, Avelyn glanced along the table to the girl in question. Diamanda did have a young face, clear skin, pixie features. Avelyn supposed she had been misled by the child's figure. While she was small in the waist and in height, she was also extremely well developed in the bust area. Still, at fourteen she was old enough for marriage and not considered a child. Avelyn thought no more of the matter as the door to the kitchens opened and servants began to file in carrying platters of food. The first of the servers moved to the head table, while the others spread themselves among the lower tables. The food smelled delicious, and Avelyn smiled at the girl who stopped before her and Paen to serve them. Paen began to pile food onto the trencher they shared, leaving Avelyn to concentrate on her misery.

She was still finding it difficult to breathe. It was bad enough when she stood, but whilst sitting she felt as if there were a great band around her ribs, crushing them. Which, of course, there was. Avelyn could not even imagine being able to swallow any of the food Paen was piling onto the trencher. If there wasn't room to suck in something as ephemeral as air, there certainly wasn't room for food . . . which seemed like some form of torture to Avelyn, for she was quite hungry. She had been too nervous to eat the day before as they'd awaited the arrival of her betrothed and his family. In fact, Avelyn recalled now, she'd been rather nervous the night ere that too and had merely picked at her food, so it was nearly two days now since she had actually eaten. And here was she, all trussed up like a turkey and unable to eat.

To make matters worse, she was also hot and sweaty, and becoming uncomfortably itchy where the binding stopped below her breasts. The top of the cloth seemed to be chafing the undersides of her breasts, irritating the tender flesh there mightily. Avelyn tried stretching out her backbone in an effort to find some relief and perhaps a bit of air, but the effort appeared to do little good.

"Eat."

"Hmmm?" Avelyn glanced distractedly at the man beside her. He had apparently finished piling their trencher and had already dug in. Paen gestured to the meal and repeated, "Eat."

When Avelyn peered at the food with secret longing, but did not move to take any, he sighed and said, "I had hoped for a healthy wife, with a healthy appetite."

The disappointment in his voice was enough to make Avelyn pick up a drumstick from the selection on the trencher and lift it to her mouth. She didn't bite of it, however, but merely held it under her nose and before her lips and breathed in. The succulent scent of the roasted meat nearly had her swooning with pleasure and longing, but she knew positively that there was no way the food would fit into her presently constricted stomach. It would most likely lodge itself somewhere between her breasts and add to her discomfort.

" 'Tis good, is it not?" her new husband commented, apparently searching for conversation.

Avelyn nodded at once, and took a bite since he was watching her expectantly. Unfortunately, he did not turn his attention back to the trencher as she'd hoped, but continued to watch her, and Avelyn was forced to chew . . . and chew. Dear God, it tasted like manna from the gods. Still, she feared she'd choke on it if she swallowed, so she chewed the meat into mash in her mouth as he watched, then chewed some more.

"I think you have chewed enough," he commented at last with amusement.

With little else to do, Avelyn swallowed the bite of meat. Much to her relief, the food did not lodge in her throat as she had feared, but found room in her squeezed stomach. Avelyn was just breathing a sigh of relief when she heard and felt the binding give way a bit. Alarm filled her at once and she stiffened where she sat, straightening even further to try to prevent more tearing of the cloth, but it was to no avail. The rending sound came again.

"Did you hear something?" Paen asked.

"No," Avelyn squeaked, the bite of chicken churning in her tight belly.

"No? Hmm." He glanced around. "I am sure I heard something, though I am not sure what it was or where it came from."

Afraid to move or even breathe, Avelyn dropped her arms to press her elbows against her sides in a vain effort to hold herself in.

"There it is again!" Paen glanced around sharply, first looking at her, then past her in an effort to find the source of the sound. Avelyn did not look around. She knew the source. She could feel her lungs expand a bit with each rending sound, and where seconds ago she had been afraid to move and possibly make the situation worse, she was now almost desperate to leave the table ere she learned what true humiliation was. For one moment she desperately searched her mind for an excuse to leave, but as the rending came again, she gave up bothering with an excuse and lunged to her feet.

Her timing was bad. A servant had just stopped behind her and Paen, bearing a tray holding a huge ham hock. Avelyn managed to jostle the unsuspecting man as she stood, sending the ham hock sliding off the tray as it tipped in his hands. Acting on instinct, Avelyn bent to catch the large hunk of meat. It was a bad instinct. There was no mistaking the loud rending sound as she did so. She stilled at once, hands on the ham hock that lay in the rushes.

"Avelyn?" her mother asked uncertainly. Avelyn closed her eyes and began to pray. So far it was just her binding that was gone. The gown she wore was holding her in, but she knew its seams would not last long. *Please, God, let me make it above stairs*, she prayed, then straightened.

God appeared to be engaged elsewhere. Avelyn had barely straightened completely when the seams of her gown began to split. She instinctively clutched the ham hock against her chest, trying to hide behind it as her gown burst like the skin of an overripe grape. The ham hock wasn't big enough to hide her. That was obvious from Paen's expression as he gaped at her.

"Avelyn!" her mother gasped with dismay in the sudden silence as all eyes turned to her.

Tears of humiliation welling in her eyes, Avelyn bit her lip and shook her head as her mother rose to move to her side.

"I am sorry, my lord," Avelyn managed to say without her voice cracking. "I wished to look nice and . . . my gown would not fit and . . . Mother and Gunnora bound me up, but the binding has split and—" Her voice died abruptly as Eunice let loose a shriek of laughter. She was quickly joined by both Hugo and Stacius. The three were nearly falling off the bench with their amusement. No one else joined in the laughter, though a giggle did escape Diamanda before her aunt shushed her. Otherwise, the guests and the people of Straughton were all eyeing Avelyn with sympathy and pity, but that merely completed her humiliation.

Mortified, she dropped the ham hock and turned to flee the great hall, racing up the stairs to her room as quickly as her legs would carry her. Now that she could breathe again, that was rather fast.

Chapter Three

Paen stared after his bride in amazement as she fled up the stairs. She moved rather quickly for one who had fainted during the wedding ceremony. He was marveling over this when her mother recovered from her shocked state and chased after her daughter. A pair of women servants followed. Lord Straughton then muttered a word to his son and also rose. Paen noted with some satisfaction that the man paused to give a dressing-down to the rude trio that had laughed. Once the man continued on upstairs, Paen relaxed back on the bench and peered about, rather perplexed by what had just happened. His bride had popped her gown because of some binding? That made little sense to him.

"I do not understand, do you?" he asked his mother at last.

"Aye. I do. The poor dear." Lady Gerville stood and waved her maid Sely over. Then the pair followed the growing parade making their way above stairs, leaving Paen just as bewildered. A glance at his father's expression showed that the older man had no more understanding of the situation than himself. If anything, Wimarc Gerville looked even more perplexed than Paen felt. Still, Paen asked him, "Do you understand what just happened? What did she mean about binding?"

Lord Gerville shook his head, apparently as bewildered as his son. Paen was beginning to feel a bit frustrated when the trio further down the table began to laugh again. As Paen recalled from the introductions when he had first arrived, these three were cousins to his bride, and the woman trying unsuccessfully to hush them was their mother and her aunt. He was about to snap at them to shut up when one of them, the one named Hugo, laughingly explained, "The silly sow had them bind her up. But no binding could hold in her belly and the binding burst. Her poor dress followed suit."

"Why ever would she do that?" Paen asked with true bewilderment.

" 'Cause she is a cow and she wanted to look trim and attractive for you," the one named Stacius said as the trio burst into fresh gales of laughter.

Paen wasn't amused. Expression turning thunderous, he got slowly to his feet, his hand moving to his sword. That brought the trio to immediate silence. Still, Paen scowled at them, debating what to do. He supposed it wouldn't be a good idea to kill his in-laws on his wedding day. On the other hand, they really appeared to need to be taught a lesson. Their behavior showed a complete lack of respect for anyone, including their beleaguered-looking mother, their cousin his wife, and even for the uncle who had taken them in when they had no home. Aye, in his mind, they needed to be taught a lesson, but perhaps another day. Not killing them today would be a bridal gift to his wife.

The silence in the room seemed deafening as Paen had considered the now nervous-looking trio. Letting his hand drop away from his sword, Paen glanced toward the stairs, then hesitated. After a moment, he looked at his father, then to his new brother-in-law. The man had remained silent throughout, watching him closely. Now Paen asked, "What do I do? Should I go above too? She is my bride."

Warin Straughton considered the matter, then quietly suggested, "Best leave go for a bit. Avy is terribly embarrassed."

"Aye. And who would not be, with family like that?" He looked with disgust at the cousins. "I shall have to let her know that I do not hold her responsible for her cousins' oafishness."

Much to Paen's amazement, Warin suddenly smiled and said, "I believe you shall be good for her, my lord."

Paen stared at him in bewilderment, then shook his head and stepped over the bench to head for the stairs. Despite what the brother thought, he would go to her. She was his bride. It was his place to soothe her when she was upset, and he was going to soothe her, dammit.

* * *

"Poor darling," Lady Straughton cooed, rubbing Avelyn's back as she sobbed into the fresh linens on her bed.

"I am an idiot," Avelyn cried into the linens.

"Nay. You are brilliant and lovely, and you fared beautifully at the wedding."

"I fainted!" Avelyn raised her head to cry, and Gunnora and Runilda arrived then, sliding silently into the room. Avelyn took one look at their pitying expressions and dropped her head to the bed again.

"Aye, you did faint." Her mother sighed, then stood, and there was a rustle as she moved across the room. "Come, we must get you changed and return to the feast."

"Changed!" Avelyn sat upright on the bed, horror covering her face. "I cannot return to the feast, Mother! I humiliated myself!" She groaned as she recalled the horrible ordeal. "Dear God, I think I shall die of embarrassment."

"Nay," her mother assured her as she picked up the red gown they had discarded earlier. She began to shake it out. "It just *feels* like you shall die of embarrassment. This is one of those inopportune moments in life. There shall be many more. All you can do is hold up your head and walk with pride." She started back across the room with determination, the two maids falling into step behind her, obviously prepared to help force Avelyn into the gown if necessary. The three of them stopped at the foot of the bed and eyed her grimly. "Now, this is your bridal feast, your celebration. You shall have only one . . . God willing and your husband doesn't die. And you *shall* attend it."

Avelyn stared at the red gown her mother held, considered rebelling, and then supposed she may as well return below. She would have to face everyone sooner or later. She supposed it was best to do so now and get it over with. Heaving out a quivering breath, she straightened her shoulders and slid off the bed to strip the remnants of her ruined gown.

It was at that moment that Lord Straughton arrived and stormed into the chamber.

"Father!" Avelyn squealed and crossed her arms over the thin chemise she wore as she lunged for cover behind her mother and the maids.

"Is she all right?" Lord Straughton demanded.

"Father!" Avelyn cried again, raising her head enough to glare at him over Runilda's shoulder.

"Do not 'Father' me! I am your father!" Willham Straughton bellowed, then paused to frown at his own words. Sighing, he shook his head, then espied traces of tears on the portion of face he could see. Expression softening, he strode around the trio of women to clasp Avelyn's upper arms. Ignoring her obvious embarrassment, he said, "You looked lovely, Avelyn. But you look lovelier still now that you are no longer trussed up like a turkey."

"Oh, Papa." Avelyn bit her lip, then fell against his chest with a sniffle.

"There, there. 'Tis not the end of the world," he soothed, patting her back awkwardly.

Avelyn nestled into his chest, feeling as coddled and safe as she had when just a child as she bemoaned, "Why could I not be more . . . graceful? Only I could burst my binding in front of everyone like that."

"Well, that would be my fault," he sighed, thumping her a little harder in his distraction. "Aye, you got it from me."

"You?" Avelyn pulled back to peer at him with surprise.

"Mm-hmm." He nodded. "See this scar?"

Avelyn followed his gesture to the scar beside his right eye. It had been there as long as she could remember. " 'Tis the one you got in the battle of Belville."

He looked a bit chagrined. "Aye. The battle of Belville. But I never told you exactly how I got it in the battle of Belville, did I?"

"Nay."

"That is because 'tis a tad embarrassing. I fear it was a matter not dissimilar to your own. I'd had a pair of new braes made. I wanted to impress your mother. The damn things were too small. They did not fit at all, but I was too proud to say so and have the tailor make new. I would make myself fit into them." He grimaced at the memory. "Well, I donned them and headed for Quarmby to woo your mother. I came across the battle at Belville along the way. Belville was a friend, and I thought I would help him out and enjoy a bit of sport on my way, so I stopped and joined in the battle. It was

53

near the end of the battle when the seams on my braes burst." He shuddered at the memory. "I instinctively reached to cover my bollocks, and Lord Ivers got in a lucky blow."

He rubbed at the scar on his face with remembered disgust. " 'Twas damned embarrassing, I'll tell you. And that bloody Ivers talked about it for the next six months. He laughed his arse off in the telling every time too. The man rubbed my face in it at every turn until I finally killed him in the battle of Ipswitch."

Avelyn winced. "My cousins shall be laughing about it forever."

"Aye." Willham looked displeased at the mention of his niece and nephews. " 'Tis a shame we cannot kill *them*."

"Wimarc!" Lady Straughton reprimanded, but with little heat.

Her father merely shrugged, looking unrepentant, and Avelyn bit her lip to keep from laughing. The man was no more fond of the trio than she. He made it more than obvious that he felt himself plagued by their presence in his home and tolerated them for his wife's sake only.

A shuffling sound drew Avelyn's attention to the fact that Lady Gerville and her maid had entered at some point. Avelyn's new mother-in-law now stood looking both sympathetic and uncertain of her welcome.

Managing a smile for the woman, Avelyn stepped out of her father's embrace and reached for the gown her mother held. Paen chose that moment to burst into the room, and all the humiliation that her father had soothed returned in full force. Scrambling around her father to hide, she leaned her head against his back as he turned to confront his new son-in-law.

"Here now! What is this, my lord? You do not—"

"Is she all right?" Paen interrupted impatiently.

Avelyn felt her father's back ease at the obvious concern in the younger man's voice. "Aye. She is fine."

"Avelyn?" Paen queried, obviously not going to be reassured until he saw for himself. Sighing, Avelyn quickly pulled her gown on over her head, tugged it into place and stepped out from behind her father. Much to her relief, Runilda rushed up behind her at once to do up the laces of her gown. Hoping her face wasn't all red and blotchy from crying, she lifted her chin and forced herself to face him. She would have to eventually anyway—might as well get it over with.

"I am fine, my lord," Avelyn said with quiet dignity. "A tad embarrassed, but fine."

"Aye. Well. These things happen," he assured her, then added, "And I want you not to worry. There is naught for you to be embarrassed about. I'll not judge you by your cousins' behavior."

Avelyn paused, feeling confusion swamp her. A quick glance revealed that her parents shared her confusion. "My cousins, my lord?"

"Aye. While their behavior is unpardonable, I would not have it distress you to the point that you flee your own bridal meal."

"Oh. Er . . . well, actually, my lord, it was not their cruel taunts that sent me from the table, I am quite used to those," she assured him uncomfortably, so embarrassed to have to explain that she didn't note the way his eyes narrowed. "I retreated to repair my . . . to change out of . . . surely you noticed the seams of my gown split?"

"Oh, that." He shrugged mildly. "As I said, these things happen. I feared you were taking so long due to distress over those cousins of yours."

Avelyn stared at him. He was shrugging away as inconsequential something that moments ago she had been sure was the end of the world.

"These things happen?" she got out on a gurgle.

"Aye. I am forever splitting the seams on my tunics. Diamanda has made me one for every birthday and Christmas since she came to train with my mother, but she makes them too small in the shoulders. They are fine whilst I am at rest, but the moment I take up my sword and flex my muscles, the damn things rip wide open." He shrugged again. "Hardly worth worrying over."

His gaze slid over her now in the red gown, and Avelyn bit her lip, afraid that without the binding he would be displeased. She was doing her best not to flinch when he announced, "You look much better now. There is color in your cheeks, and you are no longer all sucked up and fishy looking."

"Fishy looking?" Avelyn gasped with dismay.

"Aye." When he pursed his lips and sucked his cheeks in to show her how she'd looked, Avelyn felt herself flush again. She hadn't realized how

56

ridiculous she'd appeared. And she had imagined herself looking better! Then she noticed with some unease that he had begun to frown. He was displeased with his bride after all, she thought with distress. Avelyn was all prepared for him to verbalize his displeasure when he stepped forward and reached for her hair. Within seconds he had tugged out the thong Runilda had just begun to put in.

"You have lovely hair. I like it better down. You shall wear it down for me," he announced with a nod, then snatched up her hand and strode toward the door. Avelyn tripped after him, beaming over her shoulder at her parents, Lady Gerville, Gunnora and Runilda.

"He likes my hair. I must wear it down for him. Remember that, Runilda," she cried, then was out in the hall and running to keep up with her husband's much longer steps. Much to her relief, Paen stopped at the top of the stairs. He turned as if to speak, then suddenly frowned as he caught sight of her flushed and breathless state.

Avelyn forced her gaping, gasping mouth closed and sucked air in through her nose. She would not normally have been so out of breath from this little jog, but suspected she had still not fully recovered from the binding.

"I am sorry, wife. I forget you are such a little thing. I must get used to measuring my steps to yours."

"Little?" Avelyn nearly wept at the word. No one had *ever* called her little.

"Aye. Well, not as scrawny as most women, thank God. I should fear your getting ill, or my crushing you, were that the case. Fortunately, you are well rounded and have some meat on your bones, so I will not lose you in the linens. But you are still much smaller than I, and I shall have to learn to walk slower with you."

Paen was busy drawing her hand through his arm as he spoke, so she knew he was not aware of the many expressions that flew across her face. Avelyn was not sure how she should feel after this proclamation. Well rounded and with some meat on her bones did not sound all that complimentary, but at least he did not seem repulsed. Before she could decide if he was genuinely pleased with her or was just making the best of things, he had finished anchoring her to his side and started down the stairs.

Avelyn was fine for the first few steps, but then the great hall came into view with the trestle tables and celebrating throng, and she began to slow. Paen noticed at once and was quick to guess the reason for it.

"You are not to fear your cousins," he ordered. "They shall not trouble you again."

Her gaze slid over his firm expression curiously, but she did not question him on how he could assure that. Instead she took a deep breath and stayed close to her new husband as they entered the hall. The silence that fell over the tables as their return was noted was discomfiting. Avelyn felt herself flush and very much feared she was most definitely resembling that cherry in her red gown. As she took her seat at the trestle table, she cast a nervous glance in the direction of her three cousins, but they were silent, eyes fastened firmly on their trenchers. It appeared they would not bother her again, she realized with something close to awe, and had to wonder how Paen had managed it. No amount of threats or beatings by Warin or her father had achieved it, yet somehow in just a few moments before chasing upstairs after her, Paen had managed to silence the terrible trio.

That realization made Avelyn peer at her new husband with eyes shining with gratitude. Not that he seemed to notice. He was busy filling the trencher they were sharing with fresh food. Avelyn watched with renewed amazement as he piled it on until it was a heaping mountain of food.

Avelyn was just fretting over the possibility that he had concluded from her size that she must eat like a pig, when she was distracted by the return of her parents and Lady Gerville. She smiled at them all a little nervously, then turned her attention back to the trencher. The man was running through the food like there was no tomorrow. Almost half the pile was already gone. It would seem it wasn't a comment on her size. She took in his muscular physique with new respect and was caught staring when he suddenly stopped eating to glance at her.

"You are not eating. Are you not hungry?"

Avelyn tore her eyes away from his legs and

raised her head to nod swiftly. "In truth, I am famished, my lord. I have not eaten since the day before yesterday."

He shook his head. " 'Tis no wonder you fainted, then." Glancing about, he raised a hand to get the attention of several servants, who immediately scurried forward. Within moments the trencher contained another mountain of food.

"Eat," he ordered the moment the servants moved away, and even held a piece of cheese to her lips. Flushing with an odd mixture of embarrassment and pleasure at this romantic gesture, Avelyn opened her mouth to take a bite of the cheese and nearly choked when he popped the whole thing into her mouth. The moment she'd managed to swallow the cheese, he had more at her lips. Avelyn soon realized that this was no romantic gesture. Her husband was feeding her as if he feared she would not feed herself. The man was either blind or daft, for anyone else who looked at her would assume that she ate too much, though they would be wrong. Avelyn often skipped meals and went without—it simply didn't seem to make much difference to her size.

Paen continued to feed her until she finally protested with a laugh that she could not possibly eat another bite. He grinned at her tinkling laughter and set down his latest offering with a nod.

"You did well," he offered as if praising a child. Avelyn shook her head with bemusement, then glanced to the side at a touch on her arm. Her mother and Lady Gerville stood at her back now.

Runilda, Gunnora and Lady Gerville's maid, Sely, were with them.

" 'Tis time for the bedding."

Avelyn's amusement vanished and she swallowed thickly at her mother's announcement. She had been so busy with one worry or another since the ceremony that she had completely forgotten about this part of the wedding. Feeling the heat of a blush enter her face, she avoided looking at Paen and rose reluctantly to be led above stairs.

Avelyn glided through the preparations in a fog. She felt rather like someone heading for their own hanging—knowing it was coming, knowing it would be unpleasant, but helpless to prevent it. They would all see her naked. To Avelyn this was the most horrible event that could ever take place, and her brain was completely flummoxed at the very idea that it would happen and she could do naught to prevent or avoid it.

"Are you all right, dear?" Her mother's concerned voice made it through the fog shrouding Avelyn's mind. Knowing she wouldn't be able to speak, she merely nodded in answer and slid naked under the bed linens Lady Gerville was holding up for her. She had barely settled there when the sound of male voices and laughter sounded muffled through the door. Avelyn unconsciously clutched the linen close as the sound drew nearer. Then the door crashed open and a tangle of male bodies burst into the room. Paen was deep in their midst, already half naked and beset by nearly half a dozen

61

pairs of hands stripping away article after article of clothing. Within seconds of their entering the room, the bed linen was briefly torn away. She was exposed only long enough for Paen to be thrust into the bed beside her, but Avelyn died a thousand deaths in that time, those seconds lasting an eternity as she felt her body scoured by all those eyes.

"Oh, aye, ye lucky sod!" someone cried. "She'll make a fine pillow for yer head of a knight."

"Aye, and keep ye warm during long cold winters too," someone else said. Then Paen was in the bed and Avelyn quickly tugged the linens back to her neck.

The room emptied out as quickly as it had filled, the women following the men out, until Avelyn and Paen were left alone, though Avelyn hardly noticed. She was in something of a dazed state as she marveled over the fact that not a single rude comment about her size had been made. In fact, the men had sounded truly congratulatory toward her husband, as if he had gained himself a prize. She enjoyed that for a full moment before some part of her mind suggested that perhaps not only her cousins had been intimidated by her new husband.

"Wife?"

Avelyn glanced toward Paen and realized that she had been so consumed with worry at the being-naked-in-front-of-everyone part that she had not allowed her mind to continue on past that. Now it struck her that it was time for *the* bedding. She tried to swallow, but there was nothing to swallow. Her mouth was as dry as dust. She was also having trouble breathing again, although she was most definitely unbound now.

Avelyn's mother had explained all that would happen this night, as a good mother should. It hadn't sounded terribly attractive or dignified, but her mother had assured her it would be fine. Avelyn found that hard to believe at the moment as her husband shifted to lean over her cringing figure. Her thoughts died abruptly as Paen kissed her. She stiffened under the caress, her lips pressing tighter together as his mouth drifted over hers. She was uncertain whether she liked the caress. Before she could make up her mind, she felt his hand on her breast through the linens and gave a start of surprise. She opened her mouth on a protest and found it suddenly filled. Avelyn was pretty sure it was his tongue, though she had no idea why he would put it inside her mouth. Unless he was checking to see that she had all her teeth.

He tasted of the whiskey he'd drunk at dinner, which was rather nice. She waited for the examination to be over, sure he must be pleased to learn that she did indeed have all her teeth, but it was a lengthy investigation and stirred some rather odd sensations in her. Avelyn had the overpowering urge to suck on that tongue, and perhaps to examine his teeth as well. Deciding the sucking part might be an aberration while the examining of his teeth would probably be acceptable, she left off the sucking and slid her own tongue forward to move it tentatively around inside his mouth.

She didn't get to feel much in the way of teeth.

The moment her tongue moved in, his began to wrestle with hers. This stirred another whole passel of feelings inside her so that Avelyn did not notice that he was tugging the linen away from her breasts until it was almost gone. She made a quick grab for it, but it was too late. Avelyn supposed she shouldn't be embarrassed to find herself naked in bed with her husband. After all, he had surely seen her when they had whipped the linen away to place him in bed. On the other hand, that had been a quick glimpse and surely he hadn't seen much? She had no interest in his seeing more.

Avelyn had barely come to that realization when Paen began to pull away from the kiss. She knew at once that he would wish to peer at the breasts he had exposed. Embarrassed and ashamed at their very large size, she promptly slid her arms around his neck and pulled him back, kissing him with an earnestness that had been missing earlier. She even gave in to the urge to suck on his tongue as she had wished to do earlier. Anything to distract him from looking at what his clever hands had revealed.

Avelyn sensed his surprise at her aggressive behavior, and was surprised in turn when his own kiss became more intense. She felt his hand at her breast again. This time she did not start at his touch, but arched into the caress as her body demanded. His actions were having a most odd affect on her. Avelyn's nipples were suddenly quite sensitive and tingling as he fondled and pinched at them, something she had never experienced before. She had never thought of her breasts as being capable of such pleasant sensations. She had only ever thought of them as something God gave women to feed babes, but it was most definitely pleasure swelling and zinging from her nipples outward.

After several moments in which her entire body became a mass of wanton pleasure, Paen again attempted to break their kiss. Swamped by the pleasure he was creating in her, Avelyn almost let him, but then fear reared inside her. Afraid that he would be repulsed if he saw her naked and that he would surely turn away from her then, she tightened her arms around his neck. He stilled, then returned to caressing and kissing her, apparently ready to woo her a bit more, but Avelyn knew that she could not keep him so for much longer. For a moment, she was at a loss as to what to do; then a brilliant idea popped into her mind. She would put out the candle. He would not be disgusted if he could not see her. Removing one of the arms holding him to her, she reached blindly up and to the side, trying to find the candle her mother had left burning on the chest at the head of the bed.

Avelyn couldn't find the candle at first and was so distracted with her blind hunt that she didn't notice her husband's hand creeping lower until it reached and cupped the apex of her thighs. She jerked beneath him, a moan slipping from her mouth into his as all the pleasure he had been stirring suddenly coalesced there. Her search for the candle became a bit frantic then, her hand sweeping across the surface of the chest a tad wildly. She definitely felt it when her hand hit the candle holder . . . hard. The soft thud that followed had an ominous tone to it.

Avelyn then broke the kiss herself, glancing desperately toward the chest. The candle was nowhere in sight. She had knocked it clear off the chest. Yet the room was still light. Avelyn was about to twist in bed to look and be sure that it had gone out when Paen's mouth suddenly latched onto one nipple. She stiffened in bed and peered down at the top of his head with combined pleasure and horror. Had he seen her naked? Dear God, that felt good. And she had thought his hand caressing her breast pleasurable! Should he be doing that, though? Babes were the ones who were supposed to suckle at a woman's breast. What had he seen before lowering his mouth to her breast? Had he . . .

Her scattered thoughts died abruptly as his hand slid beneath the linen still covering her hips and found the core of her again.

Her mother hadn't mentioned this part, Avelyn thought vaguely as her body began to hum. She was quite sure she would have recalled her mother mentioning this. Nay. She hadn't mentioned it. Avelyn was so overwhelmed with the sensations he was raising in her that it took her a moment to realize that his head had risen and he could now see her naked. At least from the waist up. . . . and he was frowning.

Disappointment immediately doused the pleasure Avelyn had been experiencing. He was disgusted with her. He abhorred the very sight of her. That realization was just sinking in when he suddenly leapt from the bed, bundled her up in the linens and charged for the door.

What was he doing? she wondered in horror. Surely he would not take her below and humiliate her before all? Much to her relief, he did not cart her below to publicly humiliate her, but merely dumped her in the hall like a bedpan needing emptying, moved to lean over the railing and bellow something to those below, then left her standing there and charged back into the room.

Avelyn stood in the hallway, clutching the linen about her and staring after him forlornly as her heart began to break. Then her eyes settled with disinterest on the flames licking their way up the bed drapes.

"Fire," she breathed. Her eyes widened as her rather slow and stunned brain realized that was exactly what he had yelled to those below. Fire. He wasn't dumping her like so much trash. He might not even have been horrified by what he had seen of her. He was setting her out in the hall to keep her out of harm's way while he fought the fire her candle had obviously started.

Oh! He was so brave and gallant!

And he was at risk of being burnt, she realized as she watched him snatch up his braes and bat the fire with them. Drawing the sheet more securely around herself, she tucked the end between her skin and the linen, then raced in to his aid.

Chapter Four

Snatching up his tunic, Avelyn joined her husband in batting at the flames. She had barely begun to do so when Paen snatched her up in his arms and hustled her out of the room.

"Oh, but I wish to help," Avelyn protested as he set her down in the hall.

Paen merely grunted and shook his head as he rushed to the head of the stairs to bellow "Fire!" once more. Then he raced back into the room.

Avelyn watched him battle the flames, but her mind was somewhat distracted as the fire cast its golden glow over his naked muscular body. She'd known he was tall and large. That much had been obvious even dressed, but naked she saw just how large he was. There was no padding in this man's clothing to impress people. He was solidly built, his legs as strong and muscular as a horse, his chest wide and barrel-like, and his arms as big around as her thighs, but much firmer.

Avelyn's eyes were just dropping to his behind

when Paen grabbed the burning bed drapes and turned away, ripping them free to fall to the floor. It was then she recalled her water basin. Runilda had anticipated her hot and sweaty state after the embarrassing binding incident and had possessed the forethought to bring up a basin of water for her to have a refreshing and quick wash before sliding naked into bed. The used water had not been removed and still sat on the chest by the fireplace.

Ignoring his order to remain where she was, Avelyn raced into the room, snatched up the basin and rushed toward Paen with it. She had nearly reached him when her sheet began to unravel from around her. Before she could grab at the falling cloth, it tangled itself around her feet, tripping her up. Paen turned at her strangled cry as she tumbled toward the floor. He grabbed her arm in an effort to save her. While he managed to prevent her falling on her face, Avelyn ended up crashing to her knees, the water in the basin splashing everywhere as her damp face was suddenly mere inches from an alien part of his body. Her mother had described this appendage while preparing her for her wedding night, but Avelyn had never seen one. She was certainly seeing his now, and in rather close proximity.

She found herself frozen in place, her wide eyes fixated on his staff. Her mother had said very little on the matter of the appearance of this appendage other than to describe it as similar to a finger. "But larger, one hopes," she'd added in a mutter. Avelyn suspected she hadn't been meant to hear the added comment. Paen's was certainly larger than a finger, but it looked nothing like one to her. A rather lumpy sausage perhaps, she thought faintly, then blinked as a drop of water dripped off the end of it, drawing her eye. She was gaping at the odd end of it, an opening that seemed almost to be growing, when Paen made a sort of choking sound that drew her attention upward.

Avelyn peered at his face to find it dripping as well. The water appeared to have splashed all down the front of him. But that didn't explain the odd expression on his face as his gaze slid from where she knelt to his groin. Avelyn followed his gaze and was surprised to see that his staff had grown larger still, and was emerging from itself like a mole poking its head out of its hole. She had just noticed this when she found herself bundled up in his arms again and transported quickly to the hallway.

"Stay," he ordered gruffly, then was gone again.

Biting her lip, Avelyn moved to lean against the door jamb, watching anxiously as he battled the blaze. The curtains he'd ripped away from the bed had fallen across a chest, which had caught fire and was now burning merrily. Paen was attempting to beat out those flames with the braes in one hand and the tunic she'd used earlier in the other. As she watched him, Avelyn recalled her father's comments about this man as they'd prepared for the wedding. Lord Staughton had spoken of him often. She supposed he'd been trying to allay any worries she may have as the day approached. Her father had thought he knew much about Paen. Avelyn supposed that he'd known all that a man might think important, but it had seemed very little to her.

According to her father, Paen had the unusual skill of being able to wield a sword in both hands. It made him a formidable opponent. To add to that, he was also said to be relentless. He, like his father before him, was considered a fearsome warrior. That had been the selling point in her father's contracting the betrothal when Lord Gerville had approached him on the subject. They did not live far apart, and even then as a young lad, Paen had been large and strong for his age and had shown every sign of following in his father's fearsome footsteps. Lord Straughton had wanted his daughter's husband to be able to care for her and keep her safe.

Watching her husband battling the fire in their bedchamber, Avelyn began to understand why. The flames were licking out at him like tongues of poisonous snakes, yet he did not shrink. His strong arms whirled in a constant, unflagging motion. Still, she feared that his determination would not be enough. It seemed that the flames were dancing around him, moving one way and then another, as if they had a mind of their own and played peeka-boo games with him.

Wincing as a sliver gouged into the tender skin of one finger, she glanced down to see that she had clenched her fingers on the door frame in worry. Letting go of the wood, she started to step forward into the room, then paused and glanced toward the stairs instead. She was amazed that no one had noted the fire yet or heard Paen's call for help. Surely the smoke had reached the great hall by now, she thought, then realized that instead it was traveling up the tower. Of course, the celebrations below had grown boisterous and loud. It seemed they had not even heard Paen's shouts, or someone would be here with pails of water. Pushing away from the door, Avelyn ran for the stairs.

She tried shouting from the top of them as Paen had done, but went unheard once again. Avelyn grabbed up the hem of her sheet and hurried down the stairs, shrieking at the top of her lungs. She was nearly at the bottom before anyone heard her, and they all seemed to hear her at once, for the noises died out as all heads turned her way.

Avelyn waited for some reaction—a sudden rush of feet, alarmed shouting for water, a surge of rescuers rushing her—but instead there was sudden and complete stillness as all gaped at her. Unaware of the picture she made with her lush curves and full round breasts attempting to push their way up out of the damp and clinging sheet she wore. Unaware her hair tumbled about her pretty flushed face in glorious chestnut waves that billowed over her shoulders and down to her knees. Unaware those who had thought her merely pleasing or too plump in her dark, dowdy gowns and with her hair pulled starkly back from her face, were now reassessing their opinions and seeing her as a luscious, sensual feast. Avelyn's bewilderment gave way to impatience. At that moment, her husband was upstairs battling alone to save the castle, yet here they all sat like bumps on a log.

"Are you all deaf?" she cried in amazed fury. "Will you let the castle burn down around you? The bedchamber is afire!"

Warin was the first to move. Bounding to his feet, he belatedly bellowed for water as he rushed toward her. But he did not fly past her and race up the stairs as she'd expected, instead pausing before her, blocking her from the view of those below.

"You had best retire above stairs, sister. You are awakening appetites here that were not fed by the feast."

Avelyn stared at him in bewilderment, then noted his eyes skating uncomfortably downward, then away. She peered down at herself, realizing only then that not only was she clad only in a sheet, but that it was damp and clinging indecently to her curves. She sighed inwardly at making such a pickle of herself yet again, but then, what was one more humiliation? So long as Paen had aid, she thought, relieved when the door to the kitchens swung open and several servants rushed out, pails in hand, splashing water as they ran. The clangor and rustle of at least a hundred men rising and rushing forward to claim those pails reassured her. They would not all get one, nor could they all fit upstairs, but at least they intended to do something about the fire.

"Form a line to the well!" She heard her father roar in an attempt to bring some order to the chaos. Shaking her head, Avelyn turned and hurried back upstairs, aware that her brother was hard on her heels.

The smoke had thickened while she was gone, and Avelyn's heart lodged in her throat when she reached the room and couldn't spot Paen. It was as if a thick fog had drifted in the window and obscured the room. Whatever was in the chest had caused a black smoke thicker and more blinding than any she'd before seen.

"Wait here." Warin pushed her to the side, then took the pail off the first man to arrive and charged into the room. Avelyn stood to the side of the door, trying to stay out of the way yet unable to keep from trying to glimpse into the room every few seconds, eager to see that Paen was on his feet still and had not been overcome by the smoke. But her attempts to see into the room put her in the way of the men rushing up with water. She found herself urged to the side by man after man, each of them smiling at her in one manner or another. These smiles seemed odd to Avelyn. She had never been the recipient of them before. Her father's men were always pleasant to her, but these smiles seemed different somehow.

She had little time to puzzle over the matter. Her mother was suddenly there, grasping her arm and leading her away through the flow of men to her brother's room. Avelyn found herself subjected to an examination as her mother checked for injuries, then explained how the fire had started, though she only admitted that she'd knocked the candle to the floor, not that she'd been trying to cloak her body in darkness when she'd done it. She also left out how Paen's kisses had been distracting her, but suspected that her blush and her mother's common sense were enough to give her a general idea of the situation.

Lady Straughton patted her hand reassuringly and was murmuring something along the lines of "accidents happen" when the door opened and her father led a smoke-streaked Warin into the room. Avelyn rushed to his side.

"Is Paen well? He was not injured, was he?" she asked anxiously.

"Were you injured?" her mother asked almost in the same moment, reaching Warin and beginning to examine him much as she'd done Avelyn.

"I am fine, Mother," Warin assured her quickly, then turned his attention to Avelyn, who was struggling with guilt for such a poor showing of concern for a brother she loved dearly. "As for Paen, I think he burnt his hands. And he took in a lot of smoke. I think he—"

"Where do you think you are going, young lady?" her father growled as she started for the door.

"I . . . Warin said Paen burnt his hands and I thought to—"

"Lady Christina will see to him," her mother assured her, taking her shoulders to turn her away from the door.

"But—"

"Nay. No buts, my girl," Lord Straughton said firmly. "You are hardly dressed to be flitting about the castle. His mother is tending to him in the room they were given. We will see he comes here once she is finished." He ended his stern words with a pat on the shoulder, then turned to his wife with a new concern. "The room did not fare well. Avelyn and Paen cannot stay there tonight. We shall have to make alternate arrangements. At least for tonight. Hopefully, tomorrow we might repair it enough to be habitable. I—"

"They can take my room," Warin interrupted. "I can sleep in the great hall this night."

Lord Straughton turned a concerned gaze on his smoke-streaked son, but nodded with relief at this easy solution to his problem. "I shall have a bath put in our room for you so you might clean up," he announced, steering him toward the door with a hand on his shoulder.

"Mayhap you should have one sent to Lord and Lady Gerville's room for Paen as well, husband," Lady Straughton suggested.

Avelyn's father paused and glanced back, his gaze landing on his wife and daughter. His lips quirked up fondly. "Aye. And one for our girl too," he assured her.

Avelyn glanced down at herself as the door closed behind the two men, surprised to see that the white linen she'd been running about in was now a gray-black mess, as were her arms and shoulders and probably her face as well. She was sure she had not been in that condition when she'd run below—her linen had been damp but still white when she'd peered at herself below. She could only think that standing in the door of the room as the thick black smoke had billowed out had covered her in the stuff. She definitely needed a bath.

"You did a fine job on your hands."

Paen grunted at his mother's wry statement as she tended to his injuries. He was trying not to think on the matter too much. His hands were paining him terribly. He felt as if he were holding them in a vat of boiling oil.

His gaze slid to the door of the room and he wondered where his bride had got to. She had tried to help him, he knew, but had been more of a hindrance at first. At least until she'd fetched the others. That had probably saved his life. The smoke had not been so bad with just the bed curtains burning, but once the fire had reached the chest, something inside had made the smoke thick and acrid. It had filled his lungs like a black mass, choking him to the point that he'd become woozy and lost his footing. He'd tumbled to his hands and knees amid the fire, his hands landing on the burning bed curtains.

The bite of the fire had roused him quickly and he had struggled back to his feet just as Warin had rushed into the room with a pail of water. The first pail of water had done little good, but the arrival of several more pails and even more men had put out the fire and aided in removing a good deal of the smoke from the room. Still, it had been a relief for Paen to finally leave that room. He'd spent the past several moments half bent over choking up black bile. He hardly recalled being led into this room and still had no idea where his wife had got to.

"Where is—"

"I believe she is up the hall," Christina Gerville murmured.

Paen cast a discomfited gaze his mother's way. The woman had always seemed to be able to read his mind. It sometimes left him feeling wary around her, as if he must guard his thoughts.

"Aye. She is," Wimarc announced, catching the question and answer between his son and wife as he entered the room. "Straughton says her mother is seeing her cleaned up. They are sending a bath up for you as well. Her brother has given up his room to the two of you." He paused at his son's side and grimaced on seeing his damaged hands. "Not that it would appear that privacy will be needed this night. You can hardly do aught with those." He raised an eyebrow hopefully. "I do not suppose you were able to manage the bedding ere—"

"Nay," Paen said miserably, for truly he had been all ready for the bedding. Avelyn had been as warm and soft as he'd anticipated. She'd smelled sweetly of summer flowers and been as passionate and responsive as a man could wish. Truly, he was resenting the fire's interruption. Were it not for that, he would no doubt be buried deep in her moist warmth by now. Paen heaved a little sigh of disappointment. His sigh was echoed by his father.

"How did the fire start?" Lord Gerville asked after allowing a moment to grieve for a lost opportunity.

Paen shook his head in bewilderment. "I am not

sure. I think a candle got knocked to the floor, though I am not sure how."

"Hmmm. Oh, here is your bath," Wimarc said as a knock sounded on the door before several servants entered bearing the necessities.

"I shall stay and help you," Lady Gerville announced, drawing Paen's alarmed gaze. He'd not been bathed by his mother since . . . well, he could not recall ever being bathed by her. There had always been nurses and servants to see to the task as a child. As an adult, he certainly had never considered accepting her help, and had no intention of starting now.

"I need no aid. I can manage on my own," he said firmly. She did not appear the least impressed with his stern tone. In fact, she merely smiled with amusement. This was the trouble with parents, of course. Such was his reputation on the battlefield that men had been known to quiver at the very mention of his name, yet his mother had not the slightest fear of him.

"Manage on your own, will you?" she asked dryly, drawing his attention from his silent griping. Noting the meaningful look she cast down at his hands, Paen followed her gaze and nearly gasped. The pain had stopped shortly after his father's arrival, when she'd smeared a cool, soothing balm on it. He'd paid little attention to what she was doing after that, his mind taken up with the fact that he'd not managed to bed his bride. Now he saw that while he'd been bemoaning that lost opportunity, she'd been bandaging his hands, and bandaging them. Dear Lord, his hands were now linen-covered stumps. There wasn't a finger or even a thumb to be seen. It seemed he would need help to bathe.

His mind had barely begun to rebel at that thought when he realized that not only would he need help bathing, but the state of his hands had put an end to any hope of bedding his wife this night, or the next night for that matter. He stared at his bandaged stumps with dismay. There was no way he could caress her to the point of excitement, or even hold her with them. To manage consummating the wedding right now, he'd have to have Avelyn either seat herself on—or bend over—something at his hip level so that he need only drive his staff home. Such an act would be humiliating and painful for his new bride without any caresses to prepare her and excite her, and he had no desire to cause Avelyn either humiliation or pain. It seemed the bedding had to be delayed . . . indefinitely.

Avelyn opened her eyes and stared blankly at the dark bedclothes overhead, confused for a moment as to how her light blue bed draping had been switched for these dark red ones without her waking. Then she realized she wasn't in her own bed. Full recollection quickly followed, and her head shot to the side, her eyes finding the man asleep beside her.

Her husband, Paen Gerville.

The man was sound asleep, but even in sleep his expression was pained. Her gaze dropped to his bandaged hands and she sighed. Avelyn had hardly believed her eyes when he'd first entered the room last night. His bandaged hands, along with the pained expression on his face, had been enough to convince her that the bedding wasn't likely to take place. She'd been right. Paen had looked at her long and hard where she lay naked under the bed linens, his eyes seeming to devour her; then he'd heaved a sigh and moved to the bedside, only to pause and stare from his hands to the bed linens with frustration.

Realizing that he wasn't able to lift the linens himself, Avelyn had quickly pulled them aside for him to get into bed, then tucked them around him, biting her lip when she noted the embarrassed flush on his face. Once she'd finished and lain back on her side of the bed, he'd sighed heavily, closed his eyes and gone to sleep.

That had been it for their wedding night. Sighing herself, Avelyn had turned on her side away from him and forced herself to sleep. It had taken a while. Her mind had been awhirl with guilt at causing the fire that had injured him, as well regret that she wouldn't experience what would have followed the exciting kisses and caresses her husband had lavished upon her.

Now it was morning, but judging by the pained expression on her husband's face even in sleep, Avelyn was sure it would be best to let him rest as long as he was wont to. Her mother had always said that sleep was the best cure for any illness or injury.

Easing from the bed, Avelyn released a small relieved sigh as she managed to gain her feet without waking the man. Leaving him there, she scurried to the chest her father had brought from her old room. Her red dress had gone up in flames, along with the others she'd left out to wear in the next few days. She would have to raid her chest for another gown. Very conscious of her nudity, Avelyn donned the first gown that came to hand, a light brown one she often wore while working around the castle. She frowned over its wrinkled state as she smoothed it down, but all of her gowns would be wrinkled from being packed away.

Giving up on the wrinkles, Avelyn glanced toward her husband to be sure he still slept, then eased out of the room and made her way down to the great hall. She paused on the stairs, a small sigh slipping from her lips when she saw that the rest of the castle was already apparently up. There wasn't a single guest or servant asleep on the hall floor. The only people in the room were her three cousins, seated at the trestle table. Avelyn nearly turned around and started back up the stairs, but where would she go? She wouldn't risk waking her husband, and all the other rooms were occupied.

Realizing there was nothing for it, she straightened her shoulders and continued down the last few steps. Avelyn crossed the hall to the table with her head high, hoping her proud attitude would hide her reluctance to be there.

"Well."

Avelyn stiffened at the long-drawn-out word from her cousin Eunice.

"You do not look any different," she finished and Avelyn couldn't resist glancing her way with surprise.

"Different?"

"Aye," Eunice said dryly. "I gather your husband couldn't bring himself to bed you . . . as we feared. Else surely you would look different."

"Nay, of course he didn't, Eunice," Hugo said while Avelyn silently wondered how she would look if she'd been bedded. "Else the proof of her innocence would even now be hanging from the stair banister."

Avelyn did not need explanation of this "proof of her innocence." She knew her cousin referred to the bloodied sheet that would have resulted from her husband's breaching her maiden's veil. Avelyn had attended the wedding of her neighbor and witnessed the rituals and ceremony there.

"My husband's hands were injured in the fire," she said with all the dignity she could muster. "He was unable to complete the deed for now."

"Is that what he told you?" Eunice asked with pity even as Hugo laughed and said, "'Tisn't his hands he needed to complete the deed."

"Aye," Staci grinned. "Was his piffle burnt in the fire as well?"

Avelyn ground her teeth as her dignity deserted her and she found herself swamped with uncertainty. Her cousins must have spotted the flicker of her expression, for—like wolves spotting a weak deer on the edge of a herd—they surrounded her and began to tear away at every bit of esteem she had.

83

Chapter Five

Paen was dreaming he was fighting a fire. In his sleep, he had nothing to use to combat the flames. Out of desperation he began to beat at them with his bare hands, forcing himself to ignore the agony as the roaring fire licked at the flesh of his fingers and palms. The pain was excruciating and finally forced him awake.

Paen sat up with a gasp and raised his hands before his face to stare at them as the fiery pain followed him into wakefulness. He stared blankly at his bandaged hands for a moment, then let them drop into his lap and fell back on the bed as he recalled that he had indeed burned his hands. He stared hard at the cloth overhanging the bed, trying to block out the throbbing pain as his mind went over the events of the night before. His wedding night hadn't been what he'd hoped for.

The thought made Paen glance to the side, only to find the bed beside him empty. His wife had already risen and left, it seemed. Scowling, he kicked the linens aside with his feet, then sat up again. It seemed he would have to discuss a few things with his wife when he found her. He wouldn't be too hard on her, Paen assured himself. She was new to being a bride, after all, but Avelyn needed to learn the things that would make her a good wife. Things such as that a wife did not leave the bed until her husband was up and about as well. What if he'd wished to finish what they'd left incomplete the night before? Not that he could do a proper job of it with his hands as they were, but still . . .

His thoughts ended as he stood up beside the bed and stared around the room, slowly becoming aware that he didn't have anything to wear. All his clothes, every last stitch, had been destroyed in the fire the night before, both those that he'd been stripped of by the men on the way in the door, and those in his chest, which had gone up in flames. Paen had worn only the linen his mother had used to dry him after his bath.

The memory of that humiliating bath made him now scowl at the linen in question. Being bathed like a baby and by his own mother had been somewhat distressing. Not that she'd seemed upset by the ordeal. She'd simply rolled up her sleeves and set to the task as if bathing one of those dogs of hers at Gerville. Then she'd ordered him out of the bath, quickly dried him, then wrapped the linen around his waist and sent him down to this room.

Paen shook his head at the memory, then turned his attention to contemplating the linen on the floor. It was apparent that there was no way he'd be able to pick up the bit of cloth and wrap it about his waist again. He toed it briefly, wondering if he couldn't get his foot beneath it and lift it enough to catch it on one of his bandaged hands. Then, of course, he would have to maneuver it around until he had it about his waist—

Who was he kidding? Paen wondered with irritation. There was no way he could get the linen fastened around his waist by himself. As unpleasant as it was to acknowledge he needed help, he did. He needed to borrow clothes from someone, and he needed help in donning them.

If his wife were here, he could have garnered her aid in dealing with the problem. But she wasn't here—another reason he would have to talk to her about not leaving the bedchamber before he was up and about.

Irritated all over again at her absence, he crossed the room to the door, hoping that his parents were still in their own room and could assist him in the matter. The latch gave him a bit of trouble, but in the end he managed it and made his way out into the hall. He was halfway to the room his parents had been given at the opposite end of the hall when the door across from it opened and Lord and Lady Straughton stepped out.

Paen stopped abruptly, as did the older couple. For a moment, the three of them were frozen in place; his new in-laws gaping, he dropping his bandaged hands to hide himself as best he could. Then the door to his parents' room opened and Wimarc Gerville stepped out. Paen grunted at the sight of him, the small sound drawing his father's gaze his way.

"Son!" Lord Gerville roared, his gaze shifting from Lord and Lady Straughton to his nude son. "What the devil are ye doing standing about the hall bare-arsed?"

Sighing, Paen merely shook his head, pausing when he glimpsed the open door beside him. It was the door to Avelyn's room. The damage hadn't been as bad as it had seemed last night, he realized with surprise. The fire appeared to have been confined mostly to the bed. The smoke had still been dense last night when he'd been led from the room, and he'd been sure the whole room had gone up. He'd been wrong.

Hope rising in him that his chest may also have escaped worse damage, Paen turned abruptly and entered the room, forgetting all about the trio in the hall until he heard his father's gruff apologies on his behalf.

Ignoring the sound, Paen walked around the ruined bed in search of his chest. Any hope died the moment his eyes landed on the charred mess. The top of the chest was missing altogether, leaving the blackened bottom and sides, and a few black ashes in its bottom. There would be nothing he could salvage from there, he acknowledged with a sigh. Then his gaze shifted to the smoky remains of his clothes from the night before. In his desperation, he'd used his tunic and braes to beat at the flames last night. Now the bits of clothing lay in two crumpled piles on the floor.

Grimacing, Paen toed each lump of material. They had been doused with water when the men had rushed in with the buckets, but were now dry. Very dry. They seemed to have almost hardened in the shape they'd been left to lie in.

"Dear God! What a time you have had of it here!"

Paen glanced toward his father as he entered the room. The older man shook his head and closed the door, then leaned heavily against it with a sigh. When Paen made no comment, Wimarc Gerville frowned and moved forward.

"You need clothes, of course. I should have thought of that. It was not until you turned into this room that I realized why you were wandering around naked."

"I have clothes here," Paen said, then admitted with no little reluctance, "I need help donning them, though."

"Well, of course I shall help you, son. What clothes have you . . . ?" His voice trailed off when he followed Paen's gaze to the stiff little bundles on the floor. "Dear God! Surely you do not intend to wear those? They are a ruin!"

Bending, he managed to lift the pile that appeared to be what was left of Paen's tunic. As he peeled it off the floor, it made a tearing sort of sound and stretched straight as a board as he held it up. "You cannot wear this. I shall fetch you one of my tunics and—"

"Your tunics will not fit me."

Wimarc paused halfway to the door and turned back with a frown. His shoulders sagged as he took in his son's size. "Aye. You have outstripped me. When did you grow to be such a large lad?" He scowled briefly, then shook his head and waved the hardened cloth. "But you cannot wear this. Perhaps Warin—"

"I'll not go begging for clothes. My own clothes will do me until we reach home," Paen insisted grimly. "Just give the shirt a shake; it will soften up with wear."

Wimarc opened his mouth as if to argue, then shook his head again and started back. "Warin's clothes probably would not fit either. 'Tis the truth, you have six inches in height on every man here."

It took more than a bit of a shake to make Paen's clothing wearable. His father had to pull the cloth out of its set position and beat it energetically before it was suitable for donning—if suitable could be said about clothing that was smoke-stained and full of holes. But while Paen's tunic and braes smelled of smoke and were marred with holes and stains, they covered all the important bits, and Paen decided they would have to do. His hands were aching, his head now hurt, and he had no patience for searching out clothes that might be free of stains and smells but would tear at the first movement he made. He would just have to see that they returned home at once. While Paen wasn't much concerned with the latest looks in clothing, and usually kept only two outfits so that he always had one to wear while the other was being cleaned, his brother Adam had been of a size with him and had been more of a follower of fashion. There were one or two outfits in his brother's room back at Gerville. Paen could make do as he was until they got home.

Paen doubted that his mother would be pleased at the need to travel at once. The intention had been to rest here for a few days so that Avelyn could become better acquainted with them all before they returned home. That had been his mother's idea. Paen didn't understand what made her think the girl would need time to get to know them better. She had the rest of their lives for that. However, his mother had insisted, and he and his father had agreed to please her. Now, however, necessity had changed their plans. Or at least, his plans, Paen thought as he followed his father into the hallway. His mother and father could stay behind if they wished. But he and his wife would be leaving as soon as he'd broken his fast. They would go fetch his new squire, then—

"Oh, there is your mother."

Paen glanced along the hall to see his mother speaking to Lord and Lady Straughton.

"Go on below and we shall catch up," his father suggested.

Nodding, Paen continued to the stairs as his father moved to join the trio.

Avelyn was the first person he spotted on reaching the great hall. His wife was seated at the table. She

90

wasn't alone. Those cousins of hers were with her, and, judging by her unhappy expression, he guessed the trio were being rude again. Paen reached instinctively for his sword, grimacing when his bandaged hand bumped against its hilt. He couldn't use it.

Left weaponless, Paen was reduced to glaring at the trio as he approached. Fortunately for his mood, the three of them were cowardly enough to flee the table even without his sword to back up his irritation. Releasing a satisfied grunt, Paen dropped to sit on the bench beside his wife, bringing her surprised face his way.

"Husband, you are up."

Paen didn't comment on her surprise. He also showed what he considered to be great restraint in not rebuking her for coming below on her own and leaving him to fend for himself. Instead, he asked, "What were your cousins saying to make you so unhappy?"

Much to his interest, his bride flushed with embarrassment and refused to meet his gaze, but instead stared at her goblet of mead as she answered, "Nothing worth repeating, my lord. In fact, I have already forgotten." Clearing her throat, she said brightly, "Are you hungry, my lord husband? Would you care to break your fast with me?"

Paen was sure she was lying and considered explaining to her that wives did not lie to husbands about anything, not even insignificant little things like whatever bothersome words their cousins might say, but the bright smile she turned on him was rather dazzling and her soft voice addressing him as "my lord husband" was music to his ears. When she held out a bit of bread for him, he found himself forgetting his irritation and reaching for the offering, only to pause when his bandaged hand rose between them, a fat, round stump that was as useless as it looked.

Sighing heavily, he let the hand drop and turned to the table, finding that he was now the one embarrassed.

"I could feed you, my lord," Avelyn offered gently, understanding the problem.

"I am not hungry," Paen lied grimly, refusing to subject himself to the humiliation of his new wife having to feed him like the veriest babe. He glanced to the side to see Avelyn peering at him with something dangerously close to pity and growled, "Eat."

She hesitated, and Paen was about to again order her to eat, when a servant hurried up with a goblet of mead for him.

Relieved that here was something he felt he could manage, Paen carefully lifted both bandaged hands to hold the goblet between them and lifted it to his mouth. Relief coursed through him as Avelyn finally turned her attention away from him, and Paen lowered the goblet a little and swallowed as he glanced at her. She was lifting a bit of cheese to her mouth, and he watched, suddenly dry-mouthed, as she bit off a piece and chewed it slowly. The action raised yet another hunger in him he was incapable of satisfying, and Paen felt his insides turn over with despair. He couldn't eat, couldn't dress himself, and couldn't even bed his wife. Married life was falling somewhat short of bliss for Paen. In fact, it seemed to more resemble hell. Once he had his new squire with him things would be better, he assured himself, watching Avelyn take another bite of food. At least then he would have the boy to help him dress and eat. It would still leave him unable to bed his wife, but—

Paen's thoughts died and he swallowed hard as his wife poked her pink little tongue out and ran it over her lips, both upper and lower, catching and cleaning away any little crumb she'd left behind. In his mind, Paen could almost feel her licking *his* lips . . . and things further south on his body, parts that had not been burned and didn't really care that his hands were.

The sudden clang as his goblet hit the table and the cool splash of liquid down his chest and into his lap drew Paen's attention back to reality. Getting to his feet with a surprised roar, he stared down at the mess he'd made and felt embarrassment paint his cheeks a bright red as his wife gaped up at him.

She opened her mouth to speak, but it was a voice behind them that spoke with concern. "Son, are you all right?"

Turning slowly, he felt his shoulders sag as he watched his mother and father as well as Lord and Lady Straughton hurrying across the great hall toward them. It seemed there had been witnesses to his embarrassing show of ineptitude.

Paen closed his eyes briefly, then shook his head as he opened them and announced, "Avelyn and I are leaving in an hour for Hargrove to collect my squire, then continue on to Gerville. You may accompany us or remain behind as you wish."

Ignoring the startled gasps this announcement invoked, he turned on his heel and strode out of the keep in search of the stables to see his horse readied. It was the only possession that remained intact after one night of marriage. Paen hoped this wasn't an omen of things to come.

"I am sorry, my dear. The original plan was to visit here for a bit after the wedding so that you could get used to us. However, I fear that Paen—" Lady Gerville sighed, then explained, "He has only the clothes on his back to wear; everything else went up in the fire. And with his hands injured as they are, he cannot eat without aid . . . or dress . . . or anything else really. Having his new squire with him will be a great aid I am sure, and—"

" 'Tis all right, my lady," Avelyn interrupted gently. "I understand. I am not upset."

Her gaze slid to her mother's face, and Avelyn knew the same could not be said for that lady. Margeria Straughton was obviously upset at the idea of her daughter leaving so soon. She was also obviously biting her tongue on the subject. Avelyn was sure that Paen's mother was aware of the other woman's distress, and that it was propelling her need to excuse her son's sudden decision.

"I suppose I should go see that everything is packed and ready to go," Avelyn said calmly. "Mother? Would you like to accompany me?"

"Yes, dear." Margeria Straughton caught the hand Avelyn held out and grasped it almost desperately as they walked toward the stairs. She held on as if she would never let go. Avelyn knew the next hour was going to be the hardest of her life. She was about to leave her mother, her father, her brother—everyone and everything she had ever known and loved. She was about to follow her new husband, a man she hardly knew, across England to her new home—a place she had never seen, full of people she'd never met and didn't know. Avelyn had never expected that growing up could be so hard and painful. It seemed to her that men had it easier. Warin, when he married, would bring his wife here, and would never be expected to make a new place for himself somewhere else. It didn't seem fair.

Chapter Six

"Please, Paen, ride in the cart. You will cause further damage to your hands if you—"

"I will not ride in the cart like an old woman or an ailing babe. 'Sides, there is no room in the cart, what with the maids and everything else in it. My wife appears to be taking half of Straughton castle with her."

Avelyn and her mother paused at the foot of the castle steps and exchanged unhappy glances. They had seen him pull himself up into the saddle as they started down the stairs, using his bandaged hands despite their injury, but now they were close enough to see the results of this effort. Paen was a sickly pallid color, and sweat had broken out on his forehead and upper lip. This spoke more clearly of the pain the action had caused him than if he had screamed aloud in agony.

Still he sat stiff and straight in the saddle, pride holding him erect as he struggled to get the reins wrapped around his bandaged hands.

Giving up on him, his mother turned and moved to join Avelyn and her mother at the steps, concern tracing deep lines on her face. "He will do himself more injury with his foolish pride than the fire did."

Avelyn bit her lip and nodded. Her eyes shifted to her husband's stubborn expression, and she considered what to do. Margeria Straughton had not raised a fool. Avelyn took after her mother—a frightfully intelligent woman—and as such, had listened well to all her mother's training. Lady Straughton had not thought it necessary to only train her in how to run a household, or how to deal with staff. Margeria had thought it important to train her daughter in how to deal with men as well. The first lesson she'd taught her was that men were the most stubborn, pigheaded, proud creatures God had created and that a woman had to be smart and quick-thinking to keep them from killing themselves with that pride.

This, in Avelyn's judgment, was one of those times her mother had warned her about. She hadn't a doubt in the world that her husband would insist on continuing their journey despite his injured hands, risking infection and death simply to deny weakness. Life with her father and brother had taught her that men did tend to be foolish that way.

"Father—mayhap you could help me—" Paen said, fumbling with the reins.

When she heard Paen ask his father to wrap the reins around his bandaged hands and tie them so that he could control his horse, she decided that this was one of those times when a smart wife had to act to save a husband from his own pride.

"Oh, dear," she gasped loudly as she rushed forward to stand at her father-in-law's side, distracting him from doing as his son had requested.

" 'Oh, dear'?" Wimarc Gerville eyed her with what she suspected was hope. Her husband merely looked leery as he stared at her.

" 'Oh, dear,' what?" Paen asked, expression grim.

Avelyn batted her eyelashes at her new husband and forced an uncertain smile. "I fear I do not know how to ride."

"What?" Both men peered at her blankly.

Avelyn shrugged mildly. "I have never needed to know. I have never traveled from Straughton. I had expected to ride in the cart, but I underestimated all the things that Mother intended to send with me."

Paen stared at his young wife. She was fresh-faced and rosy-cheeked and smiling brilliantly up at him. She was as lovely as a spring day, but she was also turning out to be the most helpless of creatures. She'd fainted at their wedding, proved herself clumsy enough to start a fire on their wedding night, and now admitted she could not ride. It did seem that Avelyn was not the strong, skilled bride he'd hoped for.

His gaze slid to his father's face, but the man was looking back at the women by the step. His mother was looking concerned, but his bride's mother was looking merely bewildered. Before Paen could puzzle that out, Avelyn captured his attention again. "Mayhap you could teach me to ride?"

Paen noted the way the confusion on Lady Straughton's face cleared at this suggestion, but had no time to ponder the matter, for his mother was suddenly rushing forward, a beaming smile on her face.

"Well! What a marvelous idea! You shall ride with Paen and he shall show you how to ride. It should only take a couple of days. Why, by the time we arrive back at Gerville, he shall have you an expert rider. Lovely."

Paen shifted in the saddle, feeling as though he'd rather missed something. Everyone seemed so damned pleased, he was sure there was something amiss, but could not figure out what. He was frowning over the matter when his wife grabbed her brother's hand and dragged him forward. "Help me mount, please, Warin."

"I can help you to . . ." Paen's voice faded away. It was too late to make such a protest—Warin had already set her on the mount before him.

She turned her head to smile over her shoulder at Paen with a sweetness that somehow made him suspicious. Shrugging the uncomfortable feeling away, Paen grumbled under his breath about wives and women in general, then reached around to try to take the reins, but she grabbed them up instead and asked innocently, "If you are to teach me to ride, should I not hold the reins?"

Paen hesitated, reluctant to give up control of his mount, then sat back with a sigh. "Very well."

He didn't feel any better when she beamed at him. He wrapped his arms around her waist almost reluctantly, felt her snuggle into him, and suspected it was going to be a long journey home to Gerville.

Avelyn was terribly pleased with herself. She finally felt that she'd done something right as a wife. She may have made a muddle out of the wedding ceremony, the celebratory meal and the wedding night, but here today she'd taken her first right step. She'd outsmarted her husband and tricked him into saving his hands further injury.

Avelyn frowned at her own thoughts. Dear Lord, she was proud about tricking her husband, about using sly lies to let him think she couldn't ride horseback so that she would have an excuse to ride with him and take the reins. This was truly a sad day, she decided and sighed heavily, then glanced down at her mother as the older woman put a hand on her knee through her gown.

"You will do well, daughter," she said in reassuring tones as if having read Avelyn's thoughts. She squeezed her knee. "We love you and will visit soon."

Avelyn felt tears well up in her eyes and blinked in an effort to stop them, but they would not be stopped. She was leaving Straughton, the only home she'd ever known, and riding off into the unknown with a man she barely knew. It was a terrifying step to take, terrifying and painful.

"I love you, Mama," she whispered, then was relieved when Paen grunted something of a good-bye and put his heels to his mount's sides, urging it to move. Blinking away her tears, she tightened her hold on the reins and paid attention to directing the animal out of Straughton's bailey.

Avelyn had not told a complete lie when convincing her husband that she should ride before him. She'd lied about not being able to ride—she'd ridden horseback since she was very young and was quite good at it. However, she hadn't been on long journeys. There had never been any need to leave Straughton. Avelyn supposed she'd imagined that they'd ride for an hour, stop to rest and refresh themselves, then ride a bit more and stop for a nooning meal and another rest, then head out again. She thought wrong. They ate their noon meal in the saddle—fruit, cheese and bread that Paen had her retrieve from a bag dangling from the saddle. Or, that was to say, *she* ate. His hands bandaged as they were, Paen had been unable to eat. He'd made the attempt, trying to hold a hunk of cheese in one bandaged paw, but had barely managed a bite or two before the cheese had tumbled to the ground. She'd offered to feed him, but Paen had shaken his head and growled that he wasn't hungry.

Avelyn's heart had ached for him. The man was too proud to accept her help and so would go hungry. She would have thought him a complete idiot, except that surely this was no worse than her nonsense with the dress. She supposed pride made fools of everyone.

For the most part, they rode in silence throughout the day. It was a relief when they rode into a clearing in early evening and Paen announced that they would stop there for the night. Avelyn dismounted quickly and eagerly—too quickly and eagerly. Her feet hit the ground and nearly collapsed beneath her. She was forced to clutch at her husband's leg and the saddle to stay upright.

"Are you all right, Avelyn?" Wimarc Gerville was at her side at once, taking her arm to help her remain upright.

Avelyn managed a smile and nodded, too embarrassed to peer up at her husband as she released his leg. She allowed her new father-in-law to lead her to a fallen tree at the edge of the clearing and settled there to begin stretching her legs as he returned to help his wife dismount. Much to Avelyn's relief, Lady Gerville was not completely unaffected by the length of time in the saddle either and leaned on her husband's arm as he led her to join Avelyn.

"You ladies rest a bit while we see to camp," Lord Gerville instructed.

Avelyn and Lady Gerville watched him walk back to join the men now dismounting and seeing to the horses. Both women sighed as one, then shared wry smiles.

"Are you as sore and weary as I am?" Lady Gerville asked with self-deprecating amusement.

Avelyn nodded, adding, "Thank goodness it is not just me. Not that I am happy you are sore too," she added quickly.

"I understand, my dear," Lady Gerville assured her gently.

Avelyn relaxed.

"I am just sorry that all of this has conspired to force you to leave Straughton earlier than planned. I had hoped you would have the chance to get to know us all better ere having to leave your family."

Avelyn glanced away and swallowed the lump in her throat, then forced a shrug. "We can get to know each other on the journey and once at Gerville."

"Aye, and I hope that we will become close. My one great sorrow was that I had no girls with my boys. While I love my sons, I envy your mother having one of each, and am pleased to welcome you as my daughter."

Avelyn smiled and reached out to squeeze the woman's hand, then turned her attention forward as the other women joined them. Lady Helen and Diamanda had also ridden on horseback, and Avelyn wasn't surprised to see that they were just as stiff as she and Lady Gerville. She was, however, surprised to note that the maids following them were also moving stiffly. It seemed that riding in the cart had not been much better than riding horseback.

"Lord Gerville is having the men set up the tents first so that we might ready them while the men finish with the other chores to make camp," Diamanda announced as she dropped onto the log on the other side of Lady Gerville.

Paen's mother murmured something of an acknowledgment of this information as Helen settled next to the girl; then they all fell silent as they watched the men produce tents and begin to unroll the heavy cloth to set them up. There were two tents, one larger than the other. Avelyn knew that a traveling tent was an unusual luxury, and supposed that the fact that they were traveling with two of them was a sign that her husband and his family were very wealthy. That was nice to know, but Avelyn had a more immediate concern. She had a serious and somewhat urgent need to relieve herself, but was rather embarrassed to bring the matter up. Bodily functions were not something girls were encouraged to discuss, and she'd been trying to ignore the necessity, but it was getting to the point where she could no longer ignore it.

Avelyn felt sure she was about to burst when a pair of legs were suddenly in front of her face. Raising her head, she peered up at her husband with a combination of relief and question.

"The tent is up," he announced and held out a hand to help her to her feet.

Avelyn hesitated, then ignored his bandaged hand and got stiffly to her feet on her own, sighing when her unwillingness to cause him further injury to his bandaged hands brought a scowl to his face. He was doing his best to pretend he wasn't injured, and apparently didn't appreciate her not playing along.

Shaking her head, she took his arm and listened as he led her across the clearing to the larger tent.

"This will be our tent," he announced, surprising her. "I have assigned two men to unload whatever you want to outfit it. They are already starting on the bedding, but if there is aught else you want, you must tell them."

"Aye, husband," Avelyn murmured, glancing behind them and relieved to note that Runilda was following. She had no idea how to outfit a tent and doubted Runilda did either, but hopefully, between the two of them, they could work it out.

"Do you have any preference as to where we arrange the bedding?" Avelyn asked as he lifted the tent flap for her to enter.

Paen shrugged as she released his arm and stepped past him into the tent. "The back right corner should do well enough," he suggested. "Is there anything else ere I help the others?"

"Aye." Avelyn felt a blush rise up her cheeks and stared at the corner he had gestured to as she admitted, "I have need to use the garderobe, my lord. And a bath after the dusty journey today would not go amiss." With the embarrassing part of the request out of the way, she turned toward the tent flap saying, "I realize that both are out of the question out here, but . . ." Her voice died as she saw that he was no longer standing in the tent-flap entrance.

Frowning, she walked to the opening and looked out. Her husband was quite tall, a good head above most of the men. Avelyn had no problem spotting him, but was bewildered to see that he was on the other side of the camp, talking earnestly to his mother and father.

"A garderobe? She truly asked about a garderobe and a bath?" Wimarc Gerville shared his son's obvious horror.

"Aye. What do I do? Should I have the men dig one and—"

"And what? Prop your tent over it? Dear Lord." His father shook his head at the very idea.

"I hardly think she expects you to dig a garderobe for her, Paen," Lady Gerville interrupted with some exasperation. "If the girl has to go now, she would hardly be willing, or even able, to wait about for hours while the men dig one for her. No doubt she was asking what sort of arrangements were used out here while traveling."

"Oh. Aye, she may have been," Paen agreed with relief. "She was asking about a bath too, to get rid of the dust from travel, and must realize that I cannot possibly present her with one of those."

"Aye. Just so. So . . . find her a nice secluded spot by the river where she may tend to both matters," his mother suggested gently.

"Aye." He nodded, obviously relieved to have the crisis resolved.

Lady Gerville shook her head as she watched him return to his tent. "He has spent much too much time on Crusade."

"Hmm." Wimarc nodded his agreement, but was grinning as he did. "He likes her. The boy is eager to please her."

106

"Aye, he does." Lady Gerville joined him in grinning. "Aye. He does. We chose well."

"*You* chose well, my love." Wimarc gave credit where it was due. "Though 'tis still beyond me how you knew when she was a wee babe that she would grow up perfect for the boy."

"That is easy. I imagined you with her mother."

"What?" Wimarc Gerville turned on his wife in shock. "You what?"

"Well, 'twas obvious even then that Paen would grow up to be just like you. He was very like you even as a small lad. And Avelyn resembled her mother very much. I simply tried to imagine how you and Lady Straughton should have got on were it not for Lord Straughton and myself, and it did seem to me that the two of you would have got along rather well."

"Well, we . . . I . . . she . . . She is a fine woman, but . . . But I love you, my pet."

Lady Gerville grinned at her husband's discomfort. "Aye. But it would not have been hard for you to love her as well. And that was what decided me on Avelyn for our son."

Wimarc opened his mouth, then clamped it shut again, smart enough to let this topic die without further comment. A man eventually learned which topics were dangerous, and which were safe to discuss with his wife. This was definitely one of those dangerous ones.

"Wife?" Paen stuck his head into his tent, relaxing when he spied his wife busy with her maid arranging the furs that were to be their bed for the night. It had occurred to him that if she had to "visit the garderobe" urgently, she might not wait about while he ran off to discuss the matter with his parents. He was relieved to see that she had not been so impulsive or foolish as to head out on her own. An obedient wife was a smart wife, and a smart wife was a good wife in Paen's book.

"Aye, my lord?" Avelyn left Runilda to the bed and approached him at once.

"Come," was all he said, then turned and started away, waiting until they had left camp before he wedged his bandaged hand under her arm to help her keep her balance as they traversed the uneven ground of the woods. He was quite pleased when she did not barrage him with questions as to their destination. In his mind this was further evidence of her obedience to him.

Momentarily satisfied with his parents' choice of bride and his life in general, he began to whistle a tune as he walked. The habit, one he indulged whenever alone, was so ingrained that he was not even aware he was doing it. He led her down to the river's edge, then along it for a ways before he was satisfied that the spot he'd chosen was out of the way. Then he turned to face her and hesitated.

Paen wasn't sure what to do now. They were married. She was his wife. However, they hadn't consummated the marriage. Did that mean he could stay and watch her bathe, or did chivalry insist he allow her privacy? The baser side of him, the lower half really, was urging him to stay and watch. The upper half—only a very tiny portion of his head—was urging him to do the chivalrous thing. She had proven herself shy on their wedding night. He'd had quite a struggle relieving her of the linen she'd clasped so tightly to herself. Then the fire had rather ruined his view. In truth, he didn't get much of a look at all, but that was beside the point. She was obviously still shy around him, and he really should allow her privacy while she bathed.

Paen wasn't terribly pleased with this dictate of his conscience, but salved his lower half by assuring himself that he would see her soon enough. As soon as his hands had healed and he was able, in fact.

"My lord husband?"

Husband. Paen smiled at the word. He was a husband now. Her husband. He had realized that, of course, in some abstract sort of way, but having her call him *husband* somehow made it more real to him. It made him feel rather proud and puffed up. He was a husband. He belonged to someone as his father and mother belonged to each other. He had a wife of his own. It made him feel . . . well . . . warm inside . . . and a little older actually, he realized with surprise. He felt kind of grown up.

"Husband?"

Pushing his thoughts away, Paen turned his attention to his little wife. "Aye?"

"What are we doing here?"

"You said you wished to bathe and tend other matters. This seems a suitable spot."

LYNSAY SANDS

Avelyn glanced around with new eyes, then sighed, "Oh, dear."

Paen frowned. "I realize 'tis a bit rough, but 'tis the best I can do whilst we are traveling. Surely you realize I cannot present you with a proper bath and—"

"Oh, aye. Of course, husband. I am quite pleased. This is lovely," she interrupted to assure him.

"Then why the sigh and 'Oh, dear'?"

"I . . . It is just that I wish you had explained where we were going when you collected me. I might then have thought to bring something to dry myself with and—" She stopped and bit her lip when he cursed. Then he used one bandaged hand to urge her around and kept it at her back as he hustled her back the way they'd come.

Avelyn was flushed and out of breath by the time they broke back out of the trees and into camp. He hurried her to their tent.

"Fetch what you need. I shall wait here," he instructed, then took up position outside the tent flap, standing straight and stern, arms crossed over his chest.

Avelyn peered at him for a moment, trying to decide if he was annoyed with her for being such a bother, then decided that dallying would no doubt annoy him more and ducked quickly into the tent. She returned moments later with a bag holding what she would need, and found herself relieved of the bundle. Paen caught it up between his bandaged hands and hurried back the way they'd come, leav-

110

ing her to run after him. Avelyn was beginning to feel a bit like a horse on the bit, but remained silent as she ran to keep up with her husband. It seemed he'd forgotten that he needed to measure his steps. She was not going to remind him.

He led her back to the spot he'd first chosen, but stopped dead on stepping into the small clearing. Directly on his heels and unprepared for the sudden halt, Avelyn stepped on his heels and nearly raced up the back of his legs before she caught herself, then muttered an apology and steadied herself with a hand on his back. When there was no response to her apology, she stepped around her husband to see what held his attention. Her eyebrows rose somewhat at the sight of Lord and Lady Gerville kissing in the clearing. Avelyn had thought the affection her parents shared was rare. It appeared it wasn't as unusual as she'd thought.

Muttering something under his breath about stealing their spot, Paen turned on his heel and started back out of the clearing, Avelyn following once again. Much to her relief, they moved a little slower this time, and it was only a couple of moments before he found another spot he was satisfied with.

"I shall be just on the other side of that bush do you need me," were his parting words; then he set her bag down and left her alone in the clearing.

Avelyn stared at the spot where he had disappeared back into the trees and felt her heart swell with gratitude at his consideration in allowing her privacy. It hadn't occurred to her that he might expect to stand watch and . . . well . . . watch, but she realized now that he would have been well within his rights to do so. She was terribly grateful he hadn't . . . until she pondered why he might not want to.

Of course he wouldn't want to. Who would wish to see her naked? Having thoroughly depressed herself with her own contrary thoughts, Avelyn sighed and set about undressing herself, not in the least uncomfortable that he was on the other side of a bush from her. She had no fear he would look. She was as safe as if she were in her own room with the door barred. Paen would never bother trying to catch a glimpse of her.

He was going to look. No, he wasn't. Aye, he would. Nay, he would not.

Paen argued with himself repeatedly as he listened to the soft rustlings of his wife undressing a few feet away. *He really* wanted to look. He was going to. She was his wife. His property. He had a right to look.

But it was terribly unchivalrous, and really rather childish behavior. It would be reminiscent of a stunt he and his brother had pulled when young striplings, peeking through the bushes at a bathing village lass. Aye, it was beneath him to peek through the bushes at his naked wife like some lusty lad, he told himself.

A soft plop sounded. Something hitting the

ground? Her dress mayhap? Or was it already her shift? Was she standing there all creamy skin under the waning sun? He could almost picture her with her soft brown hair falling over her full plump breasts and brushing over the tops of her rounded hips. Paen licked his lips at the image that formed in his mind. He had to look. He just *had* to. It was killing him. He *was* no better than a lusty lad. He—

Was supposed to be guarding her. He was to make sure that no one absconded with her, and that she came to no harm like being attacked, or taken away, or drowning. His ears picked up a soft splashing sound, and he stiffened. Was that a "bathing away the day's dust" sort of splash, or was it a drowning-type splash? It could be either, he reasoned, turning to face the bushes that stood between him and his naked, wet wife.

Naked and wet. The words ran through his head, and he decided that he really should just check. Just a quick peek to be sure she was all right.

Of course, his conscience argued, he could call out to be sure she was well and never look.

"Shut up," Paen muttered to his conscience and used his bandaged hands to shove the branches of the bush aside to peek through.

"Tsk, tsk, tsk. Peeking at her like an uncouth youth."

Paen released the bushes so quickly at those amused words that he slapped himself in the face with the branch. Cursing, he straightened and turned to glare at his father. He managed to infuse some self-righteous indignation into his voice. "I was just checking to be sure she was all right."

Wimarc Gerville arched one eyebrow at that claim and grinned as he settled to sit beside Paen. "Then I raised you wrong. I would look if it was your mother. Hell, I would be in the water with her."

Paen smiled at his father's disgruntled tone, then asked the obvious. "Then why are you not in the river with Mother?"

"I would be if you had not come along. I was getting ready to when you interrupted us. Your mother decided we had best behave if you two were so near." His resentment was obvious.

"Sorry." Paen was having trouble sounding sincere. It was good to know that he wasn't the only one suffering. "I had not thought you even noticed us."

"Oh, aye. Your mother noticed. You know she has eyes in the back of her head when it comes to you boys." The last word had barely left Lord Gerville's mouth when a pained look followed it.

Paen felt guilt swamp him as it always did when his thoughts turned to his dead brother. He felt guilty for not having been able to save him, guilty at being the one to survive. He was silent for a long moment until his father cleared his throat and distracted them both from the subject of Adam's death. "So? *Was* she?"

"Was who what?" Paen asked in bewilderment.

"Was young Avelyn all right?"

"Oh, aye." Paen sighed heavily. "She was frolicking neck deep in water."

Wimarc laughed at Paen's rueful voice, knowing that his wife being up to her neck in water had not been what he'd hoped to spot while peeking through the bushes. "Mayhap you should check again. 'Tis a tad quiet now on the other side of the branches."

Paen hesitated, then shifted onto his knees on the boulder and pushed the shrubbery aside again to peer through. The sight of his wife floating on the water's surface, still and pale, drew an abrupt curse from him.

"What is it?" Wimarc asked, catching his son's alarm, but Paen was too busy scrambling to rescue his wife to answer.

Chapter Seven

The water had been cool at first, but Avelyn had adjusted to it quickly. She had always enjoyed swimming. When she was a child, her parents had often taken her and Warin on picnics by the river. Avelyn had always looked forward to those trips, but then Aunt Isidore had arrived with the cousins. They, of course, then had to be included in the picnics and had ruined them for Avelyn with their taunts about her being a great whale floating in the river. These things were always said far enough away from the adults to be sure they were not overheard. Avelyn had taken less and less joy in swimming until she'd refused to do it at all. At least she'd not forgotten how. She'd swum for a bit, and was now floating happily in the water, completely relaxed in the knowledge that her husband would be sure no one disturbed her.

Avelyn had barely had that thought when she was suddenly caught under the arms and lifted out of the water. Avelyn almost screamed, but a glance down showed a pair of bandaged stumps poking out from under her arms and she realized it was her husband. As quickly as that, those linen-covered stumps shifted her about and she found herself clutched to his massive chest. Stunned and confused, she heard her husband shouting rather incoherently about drowning and devils as he ran out of the water with her.

Avelyn tried to figure out what he was trying to tell her. Had his mother or father drowned just upriver as she'd bathed? Or had they been attacked and killed by some devils as she lay floating obliviously?

Horror consumed her at the thought of either possibility befalling her lovely in-laws. Avelyn lay still against her husband's chest as he raced out of the water and began to crash through the woods. There was no mistaking the tension in the arms holding her tight to his chest. Her husband was in a panic. Paen did not seem the sort to panic easily, so Avelyn knew for a certainty that something was gravely wrong.

The fact that he had not even paused to let her collect her gown was another sign of the gravity of the situation. It made her think that they must be under attack, for if the matter had to do with one of his parents drowning, she was quite sure he would not be racing through the woods carrying his rather large and heavy, naked wife.

Avelyn could have asked him what had occurred, but he had gone silent since dragging her out of the water, and she feared he might be trying to keep their whereabouts a secret if they were under attack. It did seem that she should not slow him down by making him attempt to talk while running, so she forced herself to remain still and silent in his arms.

When they reached the campsite, Avelyn was suddenly mortified by her unclothed state. She noted the startled reactions of the men as Paen charged through with his naked bundle. It was obvious they had no idea what was going on. When Paen finally began to slow, Avelyn decided she might now ask what had occurred to cause this uproar, but before she could, Paen had lifted her and she was slammed down on her belly across the back of a horse, knocking the air out of her. A bare second passed before her husband was on the horse with her. One bare knee was inches from her face, the other brushing her legs and buttocks as he set the beast into a run.

Any possibility for Avelyn to regain her breath died as she found herself slammed repeatedly into the horse's back. She was grunting with each jolt, when she became aware of something pressing down firmly on her backside. It took only a moment for her to realize that it must be her husband's bandaged hand placed there to hold her in place as he rode them to safety.

Avelyn groaned between grunts as she realized her husband was riding her around in circles, with her bare bottom up and in full view of the men. At that point she determined that if their men did not kill whoever had attacked and caused all this up-roar, she would surely do so herself.

Avelyn soon became aware that her husband was speaking again. He was talking in low tones. Her head was closer to the drum of the horse's hooves than to his mouth, but still she could make out some words. They sounded like a cross between a curse and a prayer, or perhaps a plea and a rant. He was talking of someone named Adam and telling whomever he was addressing that he couldn't take Avelyn like he had Adam. He was threatening whomever he was speaking to with dire consequences, and Avelyn was just beginning to think her husband mad when she caught the word *God* and realized it was their Maker he was addressing.

It was then that things began to jell in her head. It occurred to her that riding someone around strapped to the back of a horse was a common method to try to revive a drowning victim. Avelyn began to think that she may have misunderstood things. Perhaps Paen had not been shouting about his mother or father when he'd pulled her from the water. Perhaps he'd thought she had . . .

Dear God! Her husband had mistaken her float-ing for drowning. He was trying to save her life—wasn't that just the sweetest thing in the world? That thought ended on an "oomph" as Paen sent the horse leaping over something and she suffered a particularly nasty jolt to her stomach. He appar-ently heard the whoosh of air leaving her lungs for the hand on her derriere tightened, squeezing her cheek as he urgently called her name. Then he began to slow his mount.

Avelyn considered matters for the few brief moments it took for the horse to slow to a stop. If, as she began to think, her husband was attempting to save her life, she didn't think he would appreciate looking the fool if she explained she hadn't been drowning. There was also the fact that she was presently stark naked, butt-up on her husband's horse. A most humiliating situation to find oneself in. Truly, Avelyn began to wish she *had* been drowning. She was still trying to decide what to do when the horse came to a complete halt and Paen managed to lift and shift her onto her back in his lap, no doubt further damaging his poor hands as he did so.

Avelyn kept her eyes closed. She did, however, manage to drape one arm strategically across her naked breasts while the other dropped down to allow her fingers to flop over the patch of curly hair at the apex of her thighs.

"Avelyn?"

For a moment, she was torn as to what to do, and then she decided to go with the nearly-drowned pretense, or at least not to deny it. She blinked her eyes open and then let them drop closed, trying for a weak-nearly-drowned-and-oblivious-to-the-fact-that-I-am-naked attitude. She was rather hoping that if she pretended she wasn't naked, he might not notice.

"Avelyn?"

"Paen?" Avelyn opened one eye, rather proud of the tremble she put in her voice. It made her sound weak and nearly drowned.

"Thank God," she heard him breathe. She opened both eyes to see that despite her hopes, now that the crisis was over he was apparently becoming aware of her naked state. Avelyn cringed inwardly as his gaze drifted over her exposed body. She could feel the heated blush following in the wake of his eyes and shifted uncomfortably, trying to manage a fetal position on his lap.

Her action seemed to make him aware of her distress, and Paen suddenly dragged his eyes back to her face. He cleared his throat and sat up a little straighter, then suddenly dismounted, taking her with him. Avelyn found herself set gently in the grass and took a moment to hope there were no bugs or worms under her bare bottom as she drew her knees up and clasped them to her chest in an effort to hide as much of herself as possible. She glanced up to find Paen removing his tunic, and felt a thrill of alarm ring through her. Surely he didn't plan to consummate the marriage here? Had the very sight of her nakedness impassioned him so that he had to have her now?

That thrilling possibility died in her as he finished removing his tunic and slid it over her head. He was merely trying to cover her up, Avelyn realized, oddly disappointed. She should have expected as much, of course. She just wasn't the sort to impassion anyone, Avelyn thought as he dropped to

121

his haunches to draw her hands into the arms of his tunic, dressing her like the veriest child.

"How do you feel?" he asked anxiously once she was covered.

"Er . . . fine . . . thank you," she murmured, then became aware that his gaze had dropped and an odd expression covered his face.

Avelyn glanced down to see that his tunic was in worse shape than she'd realized. Paen had had little choice in wearing the tunic and braes they'd used to put out the fire. The smoky, holey tunic was all he'd had to wear, but Avelyn had not noticed until now just how damaged his clothes had been. The tunic smelled of smoke and had several holes where the fire had burned through. One of them just happened to be placed such that it allowed her breast to poke through.

Oh, dear God, Avelyn thought, blushing when Paen reached out and attempted to push her breast back inside the hole with one bandaged hand. Handicapped as he was, it was an impossible effort.

Brushing his hands away, she took over the task herself. Avelyn slipped her breast back inside the tunic, then shifted the cloth so that the hole wasn't in quite such a dismaying spot. She then kept her head lowered, too embarrassed to raise it and meet his gaze.

Her downward glance left her staring at his bandaged hands, and Avelyn sucked in a startled breath as she actually looked at them. As thick as the bandages were, there was blood showing through the cloth on both hands. It looked fresh.

This little rescue attempt had apparently not been good for him.

"My lord!" She snatched at his hands, only to release them abruptly when he drew in a hissing breath. Avelyn raised her eyes to his and shook her head slowly, amazed that he had been able to carry her through his pain. "We must get you back and tend to them."

Paen's answer was a dismissive grunt, but he did stand. When he offered one bandaged stub to assist her, Avelyn grasped his arm above the wrist and got up as well, no longer caring how she must look standing there in naught but his tunic, her damp hair falling in snaky tendrils down her back. Now she was wholly concerned with her husband's well-being. Taking his elbow, she urged him back to the horse, then hesitated and faced him.

"Shall I help you mount?" she asked with concern.

Paen snorted at the possibility and merely caught her under the arms with his bandaged hands, neatly tossing her up onto his horse. The action was quick, but not so quick that she did not catch the pained grimace that briefly tightened his expression. Biting her tongue to keep from berating him for his prideful behavior, Avelyn sat quietly as he mounted behind her and grabbed up the reins to turn the mount back toward camp.

Lord and Lady Gerville came rushing forward as soon as they re-entered camp, but Paen did not stop his mount by the other horses. Instead, he rode straight to their tent. Relieved that she wouldn't need to cross the campsite in her skimpy attire,

Avelyn quickly slid off the horse. Out of the corner of her eye, she spotted Lord and Lady Gerville rushing forward and heard their concerned questions as to her well-being. Not eager to stand around any longer than necessary in her holey tunic, she left Paen to answer and ducked into the tent.

"Oh, my lady!" Runilda rushed forward the moment Avelyn entered, anxiety on her face as she grabbed her arms and looked her over. "Are you all right?"

"I am fine, Runilda. Truly," she assured her when the maid's concern did not ease.

"Oh, thank the good Lord!" she said at last, relaxing. "I near to died when Lady Gerville said you had drowned. Thank God Lord Paen was able to bring ye back around." She was bustling Avelyn across the small tent to the makeshift bed they'd built of furs and linens. The maid had been busy, Avelyn saw; the tent was now as comfortable as it could be. There was even a flickering candle set on the chest, adding light as evening darkened the sky.

"Now you get out of that wet tunic. We must get ye warm and bundled up else ye may come down with the lung complaint," Runilda ordered.

"I will not get the lung complaint," Avelyn assured her, but quickly stripped Paen's tunic off as the maid moved the candle to the floor so that she could open and dig through the chest. When the maid then held out a strip of linen for her to dry off with, Avelyn waved it away. Her ride on the horse had seen to drying her. Other than her hair she was no longer damp. She was, however, eager to get dressed before Paen returned.

"Find the bag of herbs and fresh linens we packed away to tend the injured, Runilda," Avelyn instructed as she pulled on a fresh shift and then accepted the black gown the girl handed her.

"Were you injured?" Runilda asked with concern as she started hunting for the required items.

"Nay, but my lord husband did his hands little good with all this carting me about and such."

"Oh. Aye. Sely, Lady Gerville's maid, said that his hands were mightily burnt," the girl murmured, her head deep in one of the chests. "She thinks 'twill be a couple weeks ere he heals, and that is only does he not do them more harm with this journey."

Avelyn frowned. She hadn't been fully aware of how injured he was, but had suspected it wasn't good when his mother had been so concerned about his riding on the journey back to Gerville. She would be glad to get the chance to see the depth of the injury to his hands when he returned to the tent.

Avelyn had a long wait. She was just beginning to think she would have to go after him when the tent flap was pulled aside.

Relieved that he had finally arrived, Avelyn stood, a bright, welcoming smile on her face that faded when she saw that it was Paen's mother and not Paen himself.

"Oh." Aware that her smile was fading, she tried to rescue it, and then explained apologetically, "I was expecting Paen. His bandages need repair."

"I already took care of that," Lady Gerville assured her as she straightened inside the tent. "He suffered little damage, thank goodness, and does he give them the chance to recover, shall be back to himself in a couple of weeks."

"Oh." Avelyn sagged somewhat, disappointment surging through her. She was feeling rather redundant as a wife. She didn't appear to be needed for anything that a wife normally did. She'd been wedded, but had yet to be bedded. She'd not even seen her home yet, so hadn't taken on any wifely tasks there, and seriously doubted she would be allowed to since his mother was still alive and well and no doubt firmly in charge at Gerville. And now she wasn't even allowed to tend to his injuries as a good wife should. It began to look as if she wasn't really needed at all.

"I am sorry, Avelyn," Lady Gerville said. " 'Tis your place to tend him now. I fear it shall take some time for me to get used to the fact that my son now has a wife for such things."

" 'Tis all right, my lady," Avelyn sighed, dropping to sit on the furs. "I fear I am something of a failure as a wife."

"Oh, nay, child." Lady Gerville moved forward, dismay on her face. "You are a lovely wife, and perfect for Paen."

"I believe you may mean perfect for *pain*," Avelyn said dryly. "So far I have set my parents' castle on fire, getting Paen burnt as he tried to put it out, and increased the injury by making him think I was drowning so that he had to—"

"Making him think?" Lady Gerville interrupted on a gasp. "You were pretending?"

"Nay, of course not, but he misunderstood. I was just floating on my back. Then Paen was suddenly dragging me out of the water and lugging me around naked as the day I was born."

Lady Gerville gaped in horror. "Why did you not say something?"

"I . . . well, at first I was too startled, and then I thought perhaps we were being attacked. He was shouting something about drowning and devils, and I was not sure what was happening. I thought perhaps someone had attacked and drowned you or Lord Gerville or . . ." She shrugged helplessly. "By the time I realized what was really amiss; I was bare-bottom up on the back of the horse." She shook her head. "I could hardly embarrass him by letting him know he had erred, so I let him think he had saved me." She fell silent, positive that Lady Gerville would be horrified by her stupidity. The woman did gape at her in a rather horrified manner for several moments.

Ducking her head in embarrassment, Avelyn was grateful that Runilda had gone out to join Sely by the fire and so wasn't there to witness this most humiliating confession. As far as she was concerned, it was just another failure on her part. She stiffened, then raised her head at a muffled sound from the older woman, then stared at her mother-in-law with disbelief as it came again. A sound very like a giggle had slipped muffled from behind the hand Lady Gerville had raised to her mouth. In the next

127

moment, the woman gave up the obvious struggle she was waging and burst into gales of laughter.

Avelyn smiled uncertainly and waited for her amusement to fade.

"Oh, Avelyn," Lady Gerville sighed at last. Easing down to sit beside her on the furs, she put an arm around Avelyn's shoulders and briefly hugged her close. "You poor dear, 'tis not you I am laughing at, 'tis all of us. The last few days have been one calamity after another. First there was your fainting at the wedding, then the fire, now this drowning that was not a drowning."

"Aye. I appear to be something of a clumsy oaf."

"You? Nay. Not you, child. Your mother told me 'twas her idea to bind you for the gown for the wedding. As for the fire, you may have knocked the candle over, but Paen was the one who tried to put it out with his hands. Were it not for you running below to fetch help, his pride probably would have seen him expire in that fire. Then today, the man misconstrued the situation, mistook your floating for drowning and carted you about like a madman. None of that was really your fault. 'Twas . . . well . . . fate, I suppose. But fate does seem to be working against you at the moment."

"Against me?" Avelyn glanced at her with surprise. "I am not the one getting injured by these incidents. Paen is."

"Aye. But . . ." Lady Gerville hesitated, and then admitted ruefully, "I spent the entire time I was bandaging Paen's hands listening to him fret over

128

the possibility that his bride may not be what he'd hoped. That you appear fragile, unskilled and accident prone."

Avelyn frowned over this news. She was anything but fragile. She was also well trained and terribly efficient . . . usually. As for being accident prone, she didn't used to be. "What do I do?"

"Well . . ." Lady Gerville briefly pondered the matter. "I suppose we could tell him that he was mistaken in thinking you had drowned," she offered, sounding doubtful.

Avelyn shook her head. "Then he would feel a fool for trying to rescue me. Nay, I could not do that. A wife should protect her husband's pride."

"Aye. Well . . ." Lady Gerville thought for another moment. "I suppose you could admit that you really do know how to ride horses."

"You knew I could?" Avelyn asked with surprise.

"The night of the feast, your mother was telling me of your accomplishments. Riding was among them. I knew at once that you were claiming an inability at the skill to prevent Paen's taking the reins and damaging his hands further."

Avelyn nodded. "Aye, and if I admit to that skill now he shall insist on taking the reins for the rest of the journey," she muttered unhappily. "And he shall do them more damage."

"Aye. He may do. Men are so foolish in their pride." Lady Gerville sighed again. "Well, then, perhaps the only thing to do is to let things go and show with your future behavior that you are capable. And I shall help by not stepping in and taking over your duties in future," she assured Avelyn apologetically. " 'Tis just that I am used to tending such things. If I forget in future, pray tell me and I shall step aside."

Avelyn nodded solemnly, though she knew she probably wouldn't say anything. It was enough for her to know that her mother-in-law wasn't deliberately setting out to undermine her place in her husband's life. She had no wish to nag the older woman should she forget and act like a mother to her own son.

"I know you are embarrassed at having been seen unclothed by everyone, but when you are sufficiently recovered, come join us by the fire. Dinner should be ready soon." Lady Gerville patted her shoulder affectionately, and then slipped from the tent.

Chapter Eight

Avelyn had just built up her courage to the point where she was willing to join everyone around the fire for the evening meal when there was a sudden throat-clearing outside the tent and a tentative, "Avelyn?"

"Aye?" She glanced curiously toward the flap as it lifted and Diamanda peered in uncertainly.

"May I come in?" the younger girl asked.

"Of course." Avelyn smiled at her in welcome, her curious gaze moving to the meat the girl held on a bed of leaves.

"The men roasted some rabbits they snared, and when you did not come out to join us, I realized you must be too embarrassed after the spectacle earlier, so I thought you might like me to bring you some."

Avelyn blinked at the meat she thrust forward, and then lifted her gaze to the girl's face. Diamanda was pink-cheeked with embarrassment, and Avelyn knew her own face was sporting a blush after the

girl's blurted speech. She'd been so embarrassed at
the men seeing her, she hadn't even thought of Diamanda's and the maids' reaction. Burning humiliation now coursed through her at the thought of the
undignified picture she must have made.

Realizing that she was being rude, Avelyn forced
a smile and accepted the food. "Thank you, Diamanda. It was thoughtful of you to think of me."

Diamanda smiled widely. "I just know that *I*
would have died if it had been me carried through
camp as bare as the day I was born for everyone to
see, and I'm not even as big as you." She smiled reassuringly. "I know your cousins were mean to you
about it, but you will be happier at Gerville. Paen
and Lord and Lady Gerville will never make fun of
how you look, like your cousins did. The Gervilles
are such wonderful people and accept everyone, no
matter how big or ugly they are."

Diamanda blinked as she heard her own words,
then said quickly, "Not that you are ugly. I just
meant that *if* you were, they would . . . or would
not . . ." Obviously confused and embarrassed at
the mess she'd made of what she'd meant to be a
reassurance, Diamanda clucked and turned quickly
away to open the flap. "I should get back to the fire
ere Lady Gerville wonders where I got to."

She was gone before Avelyn could say anything,
though she wasn't sure what she would have said.
Part of her felt as if she should have again said
thank you for the girl's thoughtfulness, but her attempts to reassure her had managed to make Avelyn feel even worse about herself.

Sighing dispiritedly, she settled onto the make-shift bed of furs and contemplated the meat the girl had left. It was a full leg and smelled delicious, but in truth, Avelyn wasn't very hungry. Not that she had been before Diamanda's visit. After the beating her stomach had taken on the back of the horse, the last thing she'd been interested in was eating. But Avelyn knew she should eat. It had been a long day in the saddle and would no doubt be again tomorrow, and after learning that Paen was worried that she wasn't the strong and competent wife he had hoped for, she was determined to keep her strength up.

Grimacing, Avelyn picked up a bit of meat and took a small bite, managing to bite her tongue as she did. Muttering under her breath, she spat the meat out and rubbed her tongue over the top of her mouth, trying to soothe it. She hadn't thought she'd bitten down that hard, but her tongue was tingling. Shaking her head at her suddenly clumsy tendencies, she sighed and forced herself to take another bite of the meat, but found no pleasure in it. Her tongue was tingling, and her stomach began to roil the moment the first mouthful hit it. It was not pleased with the beating it had taken that day and was in full revolt at her daring to try to put anything in it.

Avelyn gave up on the food after just a couple of bites and set it aside, then lay back on the furs. She closed her eyes and tried to relax, hoping her stomach would settle given the chance, but once she lay quiet and still, there was nothing to distract her from her body's complaints and Avelyn was simply more aware of the tingling of her tongue and her upset stomach. She also started to feel a bit crawly, as if ants were racing across her exposed skin.

Frowning, she rubbed her hands up her arms and over her face, then sat up abruptly as her stomach went into full revolt. Covering her mouth with one hand, Avelyn pushed herself to her feet and hurried out of the tent, rushing around behind it and dropping to her knees just in time for what she'd eaten to come catapulting out. There was no heaving, little warning, just a sudden violent expulsion of the food.

Gasping for air once she was done, Avelyn sat back on her knees and pressed one hand to her stomach, reluctant to get up until she was sure her ordeal was over. Fortunately, she hadn't eaten much, and the moment it was out, her stomach mostly settled down, pleased to be empty again. It seemed she wasn't going to be eating tonight.

Avelyn ran her fingers slowly over her stomach, pressing softly and wincing at the tenderness there from the bruising ride. A tingling tongue and tender tummy—she was a mess. The fates did seem to have it out for her at the moment.

Shaking her head at her own fanciful thoughts, Avelyn stood cautiously and waited another moment to be sure she wouldn't be sick again, then made her way back around to the front of the tent, her gaze sliding over the people around the campfire as she did. No one appeared to have noticed her sudden run from the tent. Nor did they notice her slipping back inside, thank goodness. The last thing she needed was for her husband to know she'd thrown up. It would just reinforce his concerns regarding her hardiness.

The sight of the food resting beside the bed made her grimace and her stomach rumble threateningly, as if warning her of what it would do if she again tried to eat. Avelyn had no intention of doing so, but neither did she want her husband coming to bed and seeing that she hadn't eaten. Picking up the meat, she moved back to the tent flap, made sure no one was looking, then slipped out around behind the tent and tossed the food into the woods.

Back inside the tent, Avelyn picked up Paen's discarded tunic. Runilda normally would have picked up any clothes lying about, but Avelyn supposed she wouldn't know what to do with the scrap of cloth. It was Paen's, and good for little but a rag anymore, though she doubted her husband would agree with that since it was all he had to wear. He was out there now without even it to cover him. Not that it would have been much use in keeping him warm, she thought, examining the holes in the item.

Turning the cloth over in her hands, she glanced toward her chest against one wall of the tent. There was cloth in there that her mother had sent with her, cloth to make new dresses to replace the two that had been destroyed on her wedding day. Surely she could make her new husband new

135

clothes? He certainly needed them, and it would be something she could do to please him.

Avelyn dropped the tunic on the end of the fur bed and moved to the chest. Setting the candle carefully on the floor beside it, she opened the chest and peered in, then frowned. There were three different colors of cloth—a red that was deeper and lovelier than the red gown she'd lost in the fire, an ivory cloth, and a baby blue very similar to the cloth they'd used in her wedding gown. Avelyn dropped the red and baby blue, but set the ivory aside and picked up a black gown similar to the one she was wearing.

Avelyn peered from the dress to the ivory cloth, an image rising in her mind of her husband in black braes and a white tunic. Once the image took hold, she couldn't seem to let it go. It would mean tearing out the seams of the black gown, of course, but there was plenty of cloth there for her to make Paen a pair of braes from it. Besides, she already had one black dress. Who needed two?

Decision made, she moved to the bed to begin work on ripping open the seams of the black gown.

Once she had the stitches out, Avelyn spread the cloth of the skirt out on the furs and began to cut it. She had sewn a lot of clothes for both her brother and her father. By her guess, her husband was more her brother's size than her father's, but still bigger. She cut accordingly, then began to sew, happy to finally find something she could do to please her husband.

Avelyn worked until the candle began to gutter

in its wooden holder on the chest. Frowning, she rubbed her sore eyes and glanced toward the candle just before it went out. She should have been left in complete darkness, but wasn't. Gray light was filtering in through the open flap of the tent.

Setting the unfinished braes aside, she got to her feet, groaning low in her throat as her body complained at the movement after sitting so long in one position. Rubbing her aching back, Avelyn moved to the tent flap and peered out, dismayed to find herself peering out at the pale gray predawn. She'd worked through the night.

Avelyn had barely acknowledged that when she realized that her husband had never come to bed. Peering out toward the center of camp, she glanced over the dark shapes of the sleeping men and knew that her husband was one of them. He had slept out on the hard earth rather than join her in their tent.

Swallowing the lump that had suddenly lodged itself in her throat, she turned and eyed the furs in the corner of the tent. She knew that if she lay down now, not only would she cry herself to sleep, she would just feel worse when she woke up. Everyone else would be stirring soon, and the bit of sleep she would manage wouldn't be enough. In fact, she suspected it would just make her feel worse.

Sighing, she moved to the chest instead. Avelyn shifted the dead candle aside and fetched a strip of linen and her brown dress from the chest, then slipped out of the tent. She moved silently out of camp, finding and following the path to the river with ease. Paen's mad rampage through it the night before had left a trail.

At the water's edge, Avelyn paused and inhaled deeply as she peered around. The air was fresh with early morning smells, and the woods were just beginning to stir. It was a quiet and peaceful time. Smiling faintly, she slid out of her gown and made her way into the water.

The river water was cold, and Avelyn was quick about her bathing. She was quicker still about drying and dressing herself in the brown dress. She picked up the black dress she'd slept in and started to make her way back to camp when she spied a quail at the edge of the clearing. Avelyn paused.

Imagining her husband's surprised pleasure when she presented him with fresh eggs cooked in the embers of the night's fire, she dropped her black dress and moved after the bird, following it as it waddled along the trail. She hadn't gone far when she spied the nest just off the trail. Her lips curved at the sight of the eggs nestled there. Avelyn shooed the bird away, then dropped to her knees to get closer, uncaring that she was tangling her hair horribly in the branches and muddying her gown. She could repair that later. She wanted those eggs for her husband.

Paen rolled onto his back, grimacing at the stiffness in his bones. He'd never enjoyed sleeping out in the open on the hard ground, but last night it had seemed the lesser of two evils. His gaze slid to the tent where he'd been expected to sleep, and he scowled. After spending the evening unable to stop recalling her naked body cuddled against his, the idea of joining his pretty young wife in their nest of furs had been appealing. Too appealing. Paen had easily been able to imagine her warm, soft, naked body cuddling into his in the darkness, her bottom pressing into his shaft, her breasts resting against the arm he would wrap around her. Just the idea of it had stirred him, and the knowledge that he wouldn't be able to do a damned thing about that stirring had kept him away.

Paen pushed away the fur he'd wrapped around himself and shivered at the cool morning air. It reminded him that he was still bare-chested. Even with its holes and the stench of smoke that clung to it, his ruined tunic had afforded some protection from the elements. But he hadn't wished to risk slipping into the tent to fetch the tunic, not with the memory of Avelyn's naked breast still dancing in his head.

Good Lord! Paen had never considered himself a terribly lusty fellow. He had the usual urges and had, in the past, dealt with them as they'd arisen, but he'd never been one to wallow in carnal pursuits. But with his wife's image burned on his brain as it was, he was tempted to wallow. He'd like to run his hands and lips over every part of her soft, rounded body and—

Killing his thoughts there, Paen gave up any idea of fetching his tunic until he'd had a nice cold dip in the river. A nice *long* cold dip. Really long.

Sighing, Paen stumbled sleepily across camp to

the trail leading to the river. An energizing dip was just the thing, he assured himself, and rubbed sleepily at his face, trying to wake himself up as he moved along the trail.

Paen wasn't good in the morning. He usually needed a good head-soaking to thoroughly wake up.

Stifling a yawn with one hand, Paen tried to plan his morning. He needed to drain the dragon and take a dip in the river, then start waking the others up to get under way. He hoped to reach Hargrove today to greet his new squire. The boy was Hargrove's son. The man had approached him about taking the boy on when he'd heard that Paen's last lad had been lost, but not until he knew that Paen was giving up the battle trail.

Paen's eyes alit on a berry bush, and his feet slowed as he approached it. The berries were full and ripe and juicy-looking, and he immediately felt his mouth water in anticipation of eating them. Paen was more of a meat, cheese and bread man, but his refusal to allow anyone to help him eat meant it had been too long since he had eaten properly. Fasting wasn't so bad. He had done it before, and it wasn't really affecting him after only one day. Fortunately, he was able to hold a goblet between his two bandaged hands so was still able to drink, but he was hungry enough that in that moment, the berries looked as good to him as whole legs of lamb roasted and hung from the branches.

Pausing beside the bush of berries, Paen glanced back the way he'd come. No one was following him down the trail. Licking his lips, he turned his attention back to the fruit, then slid to his knees before the bush and leaned forward to catch one ripe berry between his lips. Paen tugged it from the bush, almost moaning as the fruit burst in his mouth, spraying its sweetness over his tongue and the top of his mouth. It was a taste of heaven, the finest nectar, and he was leaning forward to catch another before he had even swallowed that one. Paen knelt there for quite a while, gobbling up the berries one after the other like a bee sucking the nectar from a flower . . . until he heard a crackling in the bushes to his right.

Pausing, he peered along the trail in that direction, his eyes narrowing. There was nothing to see, but Paen could still hear something moving about in the brambles, something large. Some sort of animal? He briefly forgot about the berries as he spied a bird through the branches. Its stocky body and brown and buff coloring made it recognizable as a quail before it slid back into the brambles and out of sight.

Still on his knees, Paen started to follow with some idea of catching the animal for a meal later in the day, or perhaps following it to its nest to see if there were any eggs there. It might be nice to wake his wife with a hot meal to break her fast with.

He moved slowly and quietly on his knees, following the sound of breaking branches now. When he spied a flash of brown through the branches ahead, he judged himself close enough to catch the

141

bird and lunged forward, bandaged hands out-stretched in the hopes that he could capture it be-tween the cloth stubs. As it turned out, however, his target was much bigger than he expected. This became clear as he fell through the branches that had been barring his view. By then it was too late—he was already landing on someone's back and der-riere covered in a long brown wool skirt.

Paen grunted at the impact as the body col-lapsed beneath his weight, the sound almost drowning out the surprised squeal of the woman he'd landed on. He rolled off of her at once, and she thrashed away from him before rolling onto her side to gape at him.

"Husband?" She stared at him with amazement.

"Wife." Paen stared at Avelyn in bemusement, trying to reason what she was doing there. Then he noted her damp hair and his eyes narrowed. "You were swimming."

Avelyn blinked, then nodded slowly. "Aye. I bathed in the river."

"After nearly drowning yesterday, you thought you should go swimming this morning *by your-self*?" Paen glared, furious that she had risked her-self that way when he had nearly lost her the day before. Where was her sense? How had he ended up married to a woman so beautiful, but so dense? It was bad enough that she was weak and frail and untutored, but how disheartening it was to find she was completely senseless as well.

"I—"

"Avelyn," he interrupted sharply. "You could have drowned again, and this time I would not have been there to save you." He struggled to his feet in the bushes, then reached down, waited until she caught his wrist, then tugged her to her feet.

"I did not drown—"

"Nay, and I am grateful for that," he interrupted again. "But since God did not see fit to bless you with common sense to match your beauty, in future you will never go anywhere or do anything without asking my permission first," he ordered grimly, then frowned even harder when he noted the state of the front of her dress. The skirt was mud-covered, but the upper torso of the gown was covered with a slimy mixture that was yellowish in spots and clear in others. Her face and neck also carried the shiny goop. "What the devil is that all over your face and down the front of your dress?

"Quail eggs," she admitted on a sigh. "I spotted a quail as I was about to return from the river and thought you might like a treat. I was collecting the eggs when you leapt on me."

Some of Paen's anger faded at her explanation. Whether it was because she'd had the same thought as he and had hoped to present him with the same tasty gift, or because he was responsible for the mess now coating her front, he couldn't say, but most of his anger slid out of him on a long sigh and he swallowed the rest of it as he noted the disheartened expression on her face.

"Eggs would have been nice. I thought of them

143

myself when I saw the quail, 'tis how I ended launching myself upon you. Now come," he said gruffly, offering his hand before he recalled the stubs they presently were.

Avelyn simply placed her hand on his arm and ignored his hand.

Grateful that she did not make a big deal of his temporary handicap, Paen led her out onto the trail and down to the river's edge. He waited patiently as she waded into the water, then scooped up handfuls of silt and small pebbles and used it to scour the egg off her face, neck and the front of her gown. Paen had rather hoped that she might strip and bathe again, but supposed the dress would be harder to clean if the eggs were left to dry before washing.

His disappointment soon gave way to interest, though, when Paen noted the way the damp gown clung to her curves. He found himself moving closer to the river's edge as he watched her bend and scoop the water up, and then noted the way it cascaded down the brown cloth that enveloped her like a second skin. Paen found himself wishing she was in the red dress she'd worn to their wedding celebration. That gown had been a silky cloth, the color brighter and more flattering to her than the dull brown. He wasn't complaining, however. Brown or red, the cloth was clinging lovingly and giving him thoughts of joining her in the water and stripping the cloth away, or running his hands everywhere it now clung.

Despite the thickness of the wool, Paen was sure he could see the outline of her nipples where the water had made them erect. He wanted to peel the damp cloth away and replace it with his mouth. He wanted to catch the nubs between his lips and flick his tongue over—

"God's toes!"

"My lord husband?"

Avelyn turned to him in surprise at the curse, and Paen immediately stumbled forward to join her in the water.

"Husband! What—?"

"I got some egg on myself as well," Paen lied abruptly. The truth was, his wayward thoughts had encouraged a certain part of his anatomy to awaken and stretch with interest. Paen had glanced down in mid-thought to find himself sporting an erection . . . and unable to do anything about it.

He could hardly admit that to her, so Paen had plunged into the water up to his waist to hide his sorry state and lied about the reason for it. The good news was, the cold water had taken care of the erection almost at once; the bad news was, he was urgently reminded that he'd originally headed down here to relieve himself and he was no more capable of managing the task of undoing his pants than he had been before, and he'd be damned if he'd ask his wife's help in the matter.

"Come, we're clean enough," he said shortly, then turned and stomped out of the water. He turned his back and waited impatiently as she changed from

145

the now soaked gown into the black one he'd noted lying on the ground when they'd entered.

The moment Avelyn was finished dressing, Paen hurried her back to camp. He left her at their tent and moved off to find his father to help him see to his own ablutions. It was always an embarrassing chore, and he was glad when it was quickly finished. Paen could not wait until he could remove his damned bandages, but his mother had suggested it would be at least two weeks before he was healed enough to go without them. Paen already knew those two weeks would be the most miserable of his life.

Sighing over that sad fact, he led his father back into camp, frowning when he saw the half-collapsed tent and the two men moving into the woods behind it. Paen called out to them and walked over to see what was going on.

"One of the tent pegs was stuck pretty tight into the ground. It flew out of Hob's hand and over his shoulder when he did manage to pull it out," Paen was told. "Neither of us saw where it went, so we are having to look for it."

Paen shifted with irritation at the holdup. "Get back to taking down the tent. I shall look for the peg."

When the man's gaze dropped dubiously to Paen's bandaged hands, he felt his mouth tighten. "I will call when I see it and one of you can come get it. Just get the tent down. You can help me look when you are finished."

Shrugging, the two men returned to breaking down the tent, and Paen turned to step into the woods. He had no idea how far the peg could have flown, or in which direction, and he wouldn't be able to pick up the damned thing, but he did have eyes and they, at least, were working.

Paen had been scouring the forest floor for several minutes when he nearly stumbled over a dead fox. He peered down at the poor animal with pity, then noted the gnawed rabbit leg inches from its mouth and knelt to examine the scene more closely. The rabbit leg was only lightly gnawed, leaving it obvious that the meat had been roasted. Since he doubted that foxes had taken to roasting their rabbits, Paen could only assume that the poor sick creature had stumbled across someone's leavings and managed a couple of bites before expiring, or that someone was deliberately setting out poisoned meat to kill the creatures.

A shout from somewhere to his left made him raise his head. One of the men announced they'd found the tent peg. Apparently, the men had finished taking down the tent and had joined him in the woods. Now that the tent was down and the peg found, they could leave. Another day's journey meant another day closer to Hargrove and his new squire.

Forgetting about the fox, Paen straightened and had taken several steps when he set his foot down in something squishy and nearly lost his footing. Glancing down, he saw that someone had been sick in the woods. Grimacing, he wiped his boot through the grass for several steps to remove the muck as he hurried back to camp.

Paen prayed every step of the way that his morning so far was not an omen of things to come. He was really hoping that today would go better than the day before—actually, better than the last two days had gone, Paen thought. Things hadn't proceeded well since he'd arrived at Straughton. He supposed the wedding had gone well enough until his bride had fainted, but everything since then had been nothing but one calamity after the other. Paen was starting to think he was cursed.

Chapter Nine

Avelyn talked nonstop throughout the last hour of the day's ride. As she had the day before, she'd taken her place before her husband on his mount and taken the reins so he could continue "teaching her how to ride a horse." Paen hadn't thought she needed any more instruction, but Avelyn had insisted she was anxious about handling her own horse and he'd relented and agreed to continue the lessons for another day.

Unfortunately, about half an hour into the journey, her all-night sewing session, combined with the rhythmic sway of the horse, had conspired to lull her to sleep. Paen had apparently taken the reins from her slack hands, somehow managed to shift her to nestle against his chest without waking her, and let her sleep.

She'd woken well into the afternoon, dismayed to realize she'd slept for so long. Determined to remain awake for the rest of the day, Avelyn had begun to chatter, saying anything that popped into her head. She had managed to stay awake . . . but then it was only an hour later that Paen had decided to stop the horses for the night.

While Avelyn was upset that her husband would no doubt see her nap as another sign of her weakness, she herself saw it as a failure of monumental proportions. Her job as wife was to protect and nurture her husband. She'd failed by letting him take the reins while she slept. Avelyn could only hope it hadn't further damaged his hands. She vowed to set the sewing aside early and sleep that night so that she would be bright-eyed and ready to handle his horse tomorrow.

Avelyn feared it would be a difficult task. After sleeping all day, she was now wide awake and impatient to do something. Unfortunately, her husband had other ideas.

Avelyn watched unhappily as the others bustled about, setting up camp. She'd wanted to help, but Paen had ordered her to sit and would brook no argument. She hadn't minded at first while Lady Gerville sat with her, but once the tents were up, her new mother-in-law had disappeared inside her own tent to help arrange the interior. When Avelyn had tried to do the same, Paen had repeated his order for her to sit and had sent Runilda in to take care of the matter.

As if drawn by her thoughts, her husband suddenly appeared before her. Avelyn managed to smile in greeting.

"Your maid is done setting up the tent," he announced. "I want you to go rest until the meal is cooked."

"But—"

"Now," Paen insisted.

Avelyn hesitated a moment, then gave in with a sigh and stood. Having slept through whatever meal the rest of them had managed in the saddle at noon, she was starved. She also needed to relieve herself, but her husband didn't appear in the mood to hear either comment. Deciding she could wait on both counts, Avelyn made her way to the tent.

"I have made the bed if you would like to rest, milady," Runilda greeted as she entered the tent.

"I slept all day, Ru. I am not tired," Avelyn said dryly.

"Aye. I know you slept through the day. Lord Paen was very concerned about you. Are you not feeling well, milady?"

"I am fine, I just stayed up all night sewing. I did not mean to," she added when Runilda looked surprised. "I intended to put it aside when my husband retired, but he never came to bed, and the next thing I knew it was dawn."

"Well . . ." The girl seemed at a loss, then offered, "I am sure he will be pleased when he sees the new clothes."

"Aye." Avelyn cheered slightly at the thought. Surely he would appreciate having proper clothing? And presenting them to him would allow her the chance to explain away her exhaustion and perhaps persuade him she wasn't as fragile as he thought. The idea made her decide to get to work on the clothes again right away and she moved to the chest to dig the project out.

"You slept through the day and missed the cheese and bread Lady Gerville had passed out at noontime as we rode. I'm sure there is some left. Shall I fetch you something to eat?"

"Aye, please, Runilda. I would appreciate that," Avelyn murmured, closing the chest and moving to the bed with the braes she'd started the night before. She should have them done in an hour or so, she thought, then could at least start on the tunic ere sleeping. By her estimate, she could have both done in another night or two.

Avelyn was working diligently away when Runilda returned. The maid had managed to find cheese, bread and an apple. She set them all beside Avelyn and asked something about the goods in the cart, then asked if she could go help Sely with something or other. Only half hearing her, Avelyn nodded and waved her off, then continued to work, pausing every few minutes to take a bite from the food the girl had brought her. She was still working when Diamanda came some hours later, bearing a goblet of stew.

"Stew?" Avelyn asked with surprise as she accepted the goblet.

"Aunt Helen used the big black pot your mother sent with you from Straughton." She looked uncertain. "She did ask Runilda to ask you if it would be all right."

"Oh, aye," Avelyn murmured, recalling the maid

chattering away at her when she'd brought the food earlier.

"Aunt Helen thought it would make it easier for Paen to eat if he could drink it out of the goblet."

Avelyn nodded slowly, wishing she'd come up with the idea herself. It hadn't occurred to her to wonder how Paen was managing to eat. She was a most thoughtless wife.

"Runilda was supposed to ask if she might borrow the goblets as well," Diamanda said when Avelyn was silent so long. She immediately nodded.

"Of course, that is fine." Her mother had sent six goblets with her. All had been specially made and bore her and Paen's initials. There were a lot more than six people in their party, though. "What is everyone else eating out of?"

"The men are eating roast rabbit again. Aunt Helen only made enough stew for the family because there would not be enough goblets for everyone," Diamanda explained. "Anyway, Paen suggested I bring you some so that you would not need trouble yourself to come out of the tent and could continue to rest. You were terribly tired today."

"I did not sleep much last night," Avelyn said vaguely in response to the question on the younger girl's face.

"Will you be all right for traveling tomorrow?" Diamanda queried. "I only ask because Paen is fretting that you are sickening and—"

"I shall be fine. I *am* fine. I just did not sleep much, so was weary today. I will sleep tonight."

Diamanda didn't look as if she believed her, but nodded politely, then turned a curious gaze on the black cloth in her lap. "What are you sewing?"

Avelyn glanced down and smiled. "I thought to make some braes and a tunic for Paen. His are in such a disreputable state from the fire. 'Tis why I was so weary today. My stomach was a tad upset and I could not sleep, so I started on these. The next thing I knew, it was morning," she explained and held the braes up for her to see. "Do you think he will like them?"

"Oh." Diamanda's eyes widened and she reached out to touch the cloth. "He will love them."

Avelyn smiled with relief and let them settle back in her lap. "I hope to have them ready in another night or two."

"Well, do not make yourself blind working on them. You should have another candle in here."

Avelyn glanced toward the candle on the chest. She had a vague recollection of Runilda entering at some point and setting the lit candle there, but wasn't sure how long ago it had been.

"The one will be fine," Avelyn said, smiling at the girl's concern.

"Well, at least set it a bit closer so that you do not strain your eyes." Diamanda moved to collect the candle as she spoke and set it on the ground next to the furs. "There—that is better. Well . . ." She straightened and beamed a smile at Avelyn. "I should go eat my stew. I shall come back when I have finished and collect your goblet to clean with mine," she announced, then added firmly, "And I shall expect you to have eaten every last drop."

Avelyn watched the girl slip out of the tent, a small smile playing about her lips. Despite her occasional verbal blunders, Diamanda seemed to be a charming young woman, and she appreciated her efforts to befriend her. Avelyn's gaze dropped to the stew and she gave it a sniff. It did smell delicious, but she wasn't really hungry after the fare Runilda had brought her. She didn't wish to offend her mother-in-law, or hurt Diamanda's feelings by not at least appearing to have eaten it when the girl returned for the goblet.

Avelyn's gaze slid to the tent flap. It hadn't closed all the way, and she could see the people gathered around the fire in the center of the campsite. Setting her sewing aside, she picked up the goblet and stood. Paen had never approached her about tending to personal matters, and while she knew he had insisted that she ask his permission before going anywhere on her own, surely he didn't include tending to matters such as finding a handy bush. It would certainly be embarrassing to approach him by the fire to request an escort into the woods.

Avelyn recalled the day before and how uncomfortable it had been having him stand only feet away—within hearing distance—as she'd watered the bushes. No, she decided, he couldn't have meant to include this task in his orders. Besides, what he didn't know wouldn't hurt him, and she could surely manage without coming to any harm.

Mind made up, Avelyn took the goblet of stew with her and slid out of the tent, then quickly around behind it. It was dark here away from the campfire, and she hadn't a clue where the path to the river would be since her husband hadn't seen fit to take her there, but she moved into the woods, pushing her way through the clawing branches until she felt she was a good enough distance from the tent. Then she turned the goblet over and gave it a good shake to make sure all the stew was out, then set the goblet down while she tended to her needs.

Avelyn caught the hem of her skirt on both sides and lifted it up over her hips as she dropped to squat in the bushes, then gave a startled little squeal of pain and straightened abruptly, one hand going to rub her bottom. Stinging nettles—leave it to her to squat in a patch of them.

Grimacing, she moved several feet from where she'd been, felt cautiously around with her hand to be sure there were no nettles here, then repeated the procedure. This time she managed the task without incident.

Relieved to have the matter tended to, she started back toward the tent, then paused. She'd forgotten the goblet. Staring into the darkness around her, Avelyn considered returning for it in the morning, but feared she wouldn't know where exactly to look. On top of that, Diamanda was going to return for it to clean. How could she explain losing the goblet? The girl would know she hadn't eaten the stew, and her feelings would be hurt.

Heaving a resigned breath, Avelyn moved to

where she thought she'd first stopped, and knelt to feel around for it. Of course, she found the stew first. Muttering under her breath, she wiped her hand on the grass, then continued searching, and this time found the stinging nettles.

It just was not her night, Avelyn thought with exasperation, rubbing the tips of the injured fingers with her other hand, then tried one more time. Fortunately, she found the goblet without further incident and stood up with relief.

There, that wasn't so bad, she told herself silently as she made her way back to the tent, but even she didn't believe it. Avelyn paused behind the tent and peeked around first to be sure no one was looking, then hurried quickly around to the flap and slipped inside with a sigh of relief.

She set the goblet on the ground by the furs, picked up her sewing and winced at the irritated sting in her fingers. She switched the sewing to her other hand. The moment she put weight on her bottom, she was reminded that her fingers weren't the only thing that had come in contact with the nettles.

Gasping, Avelyn shifted to her knees, then dropped the sewing altogether and lifted the back of her skirt in an effort to see how much damage the nettles had done. Of course, no matter how she strained and twisted, she couldn't see much. However, when she ran her uninjured hand over the area, she could feel welts.

Avelyn let her skirt drop back into place with a disheartened sigh. It did seem her husband might be right about her wandering off on her own. Her behind stung from squatting in the nettles, the fingers of her right hand too, and she'd apparently knelt in the stew. She plucked off the bit of meat stuck to the knee of her gown.

Avelyn dropped the meat in the goblet, set the sewing out of the way and lay down on her side. It would take an hour or so at least before the welts went away. Sewing was out of the question for now.

She supposed it was for the best. She'd determined to sleep tonight anyway. She would just get more than she'd hoped for, Avelyn told herself. Still, she was depressed by her own ineptitude.

"Well?" Paen asked the moment Diamanda returned from the tent.

"She is asleep," the girl said apologetically. "I was not sure, shall I wake her, or—?"

"No," Paen said on a sigh. He'd asked Diamanda to invite Avelyn out to join them if she was feeling better, but it seemed that wasn't going to happen. He shook his head and pushed a log further into the fire with the toe of his boot.

"Did she eat anything?" he heard his mother ask and glanced up as Diamanda held up the goblet she'd fetched while there.

"Aye, all but one little piece of meat."

"Well, I am sure she is just a little weary from the journey," his mother said.

Paen grunted. "She slept through the journey today, and she is sleeping again now," he pointed out grimly. "I think she is ailing."

"I am sure she is fine, Paen," his mother insisted, but he wasn't fooled. He could see the concern on her face. Still, he let the matter drop; at least outwardly. Paen couldn't help but think that he had the most fragile of wives and he would have to take special care with her to be sure he got her home safely. Once there, away from the rigors of travel, perhaps she would do better.

They should reach Hargrove's late on the morrow, where he could collect his new squire. It was only a two-day journey back after that. It was really only a two-day journey from Straughton to his family's home, but the need to collect his squire had taken them out of their way. He'd suggested that his mother and father continue on home with most of the men, leaving only a small escort for him and Avelyn, but his mother wouldn't hear of it. She wanted to be close by to change his bandages and assure herself that he didn't further hurt himself.

His gaze slid to the tent, and he decided he would keep Avelyn on his horse with him for the remainder of the journey. That way, she could rest and conserve whatever strength she did have.

Birdsong made Avelyn straighten from her sewing and glance toward the tent flap to see that dawn was breaking. She'd worked through the night again.

Her nap after the encounter with the stinging nettles had been a short one, but it had been long enough that her backside had recovered. She'd found that after sleeping all day, she wasn't tired. Avelyn had settled into sewing, telling herself that she would only work for a little while, then would sleep. Of course, she hadn't. The sewing had gone so well, she'd worked through the night again.

She knew she would regret it later today, but at the moment, Avelyn was terribly pleased with herself. She'd finished the braes and had made a good start on the tunic. Another night and she might even have it done.

Imagining her husband's pleasure when she presented them to him, Avelyn straightened her back from the hunched position she'd been working in, then got slowly and painfully to her feet. She should have moved around some to prevent the stiffness from setting in, but she hadn't thought about it at the time. Now she was paying the price for sitting in one position for hours.

She folded the unfinished tunic neatly and put it in her chest with the braes, telling herself she didn't mind that her husband had again neglected to join her in the tent. Avelyn wasn't a very convincing liar, even to herself.

Married life seemed to be a lot lonelier than she'd imagined it would be. Or perhaps it was just her marriage.

Sighing, she moved to the tent flap to peer hopefully out. Now that she was up and about, Avelyn was aware of a rather urgent need to relieve herself again. Unfortunately, none of the lumps of male flesh around the fire were moving or showing any sign of waking up yet.

Glancing toward the surrounding woods, Avelyn thought she spotted a path on the opposite side of camp. It probably led to the river, she realized, then glanced again at the bodies asleep around the fire's ashes.

She'd encountered a bit of difficulty on her errand last night, but that had been in darkness and Avelyn was sure she could manage fine now that there was more light. But her husband *had* ordered her not to wander off again without his permission.

Avelyn started to consider the repercussions of disobeying her new husband, but her body was making its needs painfully clear. If she didn't go out and attend to the matter, she would be attending to it in the tent, like it or not.

Muttering under her breath, she stepped out of the tent and moved stealthily around camp till she found a path.

She walked the path for several moments until it opened into another small clearing. She gazed around then, a bit befuddled. There was no river in sight. Still, she could see the beginnings of another path directly across from her. Shrugging, she crossed the clearing and started down the new path, but it seemed to grow smaller as she went along until it dwindled out altogether.

After a moment's hesitation, Avelyn gave in to need and relieved herself, then turned back the way she'd come.

At the small clearing she'd just crossed, Avelyn paused. There were the beginnings of two paths across from her and Avelyn wasn't sure which she'd used. The one on the right? The paths were rather close together, and it could have been the one on the left. Deciding to go with her first instinct, she started up the path on the right, assuring herself that if it was the wrong one, she'd simply turn back a few minutes later, and take the other one. However, when Avelyn did turn back, she seemed to walk an awfully long time before finding a clearing, and then it seemed smaller than the clearing she'd started out from.

Deciding she was imagining things, Avelyn took a new path and headed out again . . . and ten minutes later admitted to herself that she was lost. Worse yet, considering that the sun was now fully up in the sky, there was no way she could slip back into the tent without her husband noticing.

Avelyn felt ready to sit right down and have a good cry. It was almost as if the fates were telling her that this marriage was doomed. However, it was her considered opinion that the fates were a stupid bunch if they didn't know enough to give her these warnings *before* she'd married rather than after.

Forcing away unwanted tears, Avelyn took a deep breath, peered around the clearing and then chose a path at random and started out once more.

She'd walked perhaps a hundred feet when she nearly knocked someone over. Her relief at finding somebody lasted about as long as it took for her to realize who she'd nearly knocked over and what he'd been doing at the time. The man presently cursing at the interruption was Lord Gerville. Her father-in-law had obviously come out to tend to the same matter as she, and had more than just the situation in hand at the moment.

"Oh!" Avelyn whirled away from him. She even started back along the path, desperate to give him privacy. However, she hadn't gone far when she realized he was her only hope of returning to camp before the day was out. Avelyn paused.

She did wonder if she shouldn't explain why she wasn't continuing forward to give him more privacy, but before she could decide what to say, he finished his business and stomped up next to her.

"Sorry if I gave you a start, girl," he said gruffly. "I thought I was the only one awake or I would have gone further from camp to tend to matters."

Since she'd been walking for a good half hour, Avelyn couldn't imagine how much farther from camp he could have gone. However, she didn't say as much, but merely offered him a smile and hoped the shadows cast by the trees were hiding just how red and embarrassed she was.

"Is my husband not yet up?" she asked hopefully as she fell into step with him.

"He was still asleep when I left camp, but . . ." He paused as they both became aware of the sound of someone crashing quickly through the woods. Shaking his head, Lord Gerville finished, "But I would guess that is him coming now."

"Avelyn!" Paen stumbled out on the path directly ahead of them and came to an abrupt halt.

"There you are! I feared you had got yourself lost in the woods. Did I not tell you not to wander off by yourself?"

"I—" Avelyn began, but snapped her mouth closed as he used one stump to urge her back in the direction he'd come. They'd barely taken a dozen steps when they broke out of the trees and into the clearing.

"Why, I wasn't far from camp at all," she said with amazement as the sounds of talk and activity washed over her.

"You *were* lost," Paen accused, and Avelyn grimaced. She really needed to think before she spoke.

"Perhaps a little, yes," she admitted. "But then I found your father, and everything was fine. Besides, I did not go to the riverside, I merely wished to attend to . . . er . . . other things," she finished vaguely, then added, "Rather urgent other things which you did not take me to attend to yestereve when we stopped for the night."

"You did not ask me to take you to attend to these personal needs," Paen said shortly, sounding annoyed at her tone of voice. "And I know you did not go to the riverside. We are not camped *near* a river today."

"We aren't?" Avelyn asked with surprise. "Then how shall we clean up today?"

"We won't," he answered bluntly. "But hopefully, we shall arrive at Hargrove by evening and may clean up there."

"Oh." She frowned over that. She truly didn't

care for the gritty, dusty feel that traveling caused and had looked foward to bathing in the river. On the other hand, she supposed after yesterday's debacle it might be safer to bathe at Hargrove.

Sighing, Avelyn turned away and started toward her tent, only to be drawn up short by her husband's stump on her shoulder.

"Wife?"

"Aye?" she asked warily, turning back to face him.

"If you need to drain the . . . er . . . use the garderobe," Paen corrected himself quickly, "in future you need only ask me. I cannot read your mind on such matters."

"Oh." She blinked as his words sank in. He couldn't read her mind. Of course he couldn't, yet she'd expected him to somehow know that she needed to relieve herself. While she'd been thinking he must realize she would have need to attend to the matter, he had probably been thinking she would mention it if she did. Sighing, she nodded, "Aye, husband."

Paen nodded, apparently satisfied, then turned and hesitated in front of his father. "I am going for a walk in the woods."

Avelyn was just frowning over the slightly strained voice he used to make the announcement, when his father used the same tone to say, "I shall join you, son."

She watched them walk away, then shook her head with bewilderment and turned to make her way to the tent to start packing. Her husband would wish to leave as soon as everyone had broken their fast. Besides, it would help her to stay awake. Avelyn was already starting to feel tired. The day ahead was going to be a long one, but she thought if she kept up a line of chatter with her husband, the ride would be less boring and she could perhaps stay awake.

Chapter Ten

"My lady."

Avelyn glanced up and smiled at the slender, dark-haired boy rushing across camp toward her. David Hargrove, Paen's new squire, was ten years old, but tall for his age. He was also very slim and had the face of an angel. The lad would break hearts when he was older.

As he rushed toward her, David stumbled over a rock and crashed to the ground. Avelyn had to force herself not to leap to her feet and run to see if he was all right. Paen was watching from the other side of camp, shaking his head at the child's clumsiness, and she knew he wouldn't approve of her hurrying to the boy. She'd learned that the day before when they'd arrived at Hargrove to collect the lad and he'd tumbled down the stairs to land in a heap at their feet. Avelyn had started forward to help the boy then, but Paen had raised one arm before her to hold her back, then shook his head when she peered at him.

As he had then, David quickly scrambled back to his feet and continued on as if nothing had happened. His grin was back in place by the time he stopped before her.

"His Lordship says you can go to prepare the tent for the night, my lady. The men have it up, and the chests and furs are inside."

"Thank you, David," Avelyn murmured, unable to resist returning his grin.

Nodding, he turned to hurry back to Paen's side, then paused suddenly and whirled back as Avelyn got to her feet. "Oh, and he said he would take you down to the river to wash up once he is finished overseeing . . . overseeing . . . er . . . when he is done whatever he is doing," the boy finished, obviously having forgotten what exactly his lord had said.

"Thank you, David," Avelyn repeated.

The boy nodded and turned away, managing to make it all the way back to Paen's side without falling again.

Shaking her head, Avelyn continued on to the tent. The lad was enthusiastic and cheerful, and clumsy as could be, but Avelyn suspected the clumsiness was simply due to nervousness. Once he settled in, she was sure much of his awkwardness would vanish.

There wasn't really much to do inside the tent. The men had piled the furs in the corner as usual, and Runilda was putting linens and another fur on as Avelyn entered. That was pretty much all there was to arranging the tent, other than to set the candle on the chest in preparation of lighting it when the last of the sunlight disappeared.

Thanking Runilda for her efforts, Avelyn nodded when her maid asked if she might go help Sely. The maids were becoming friends. Once alone, Avelyn moved to the chest to retrieve the tunic and braes she was making for Paen. Avelyn wasn't sure how long Paen would be, but she was so close to finishing the tunic, she couldn't resist getting in even a few moments' work on it. First she wanted to recheck the seams on the braes and be sure they were perfect.

Avelyn would have finished the tunic the night before except that Paen had surprised her by joining her in bed at Hargrove. Actually, if she were to be honest with herself, she probably wouldn't have gotten it finished last night. She'd been struggling to stay awake and sew when her husband had entered the room. Staying up all night, then forcing herself to remain awake all day in the saddle had left her feeling limp and exhausted by the time they'd arrived at Hargrove to collect David.

They'd arrived at Hargrove just after the evening meal, were welcomed warmly by Lord and Lady Hargrove and were served a quick meal while their rooms and baths were prepared for them. Avelyn had been so exhausted by then, she had nearly fallen asleep in her food. Once finished eating, she'd been grateful to escape above stairs to bathe.

Avelyn didn't think she'd ever before enjoyed a

bath that much. She'd soaked in the scented water for much longer than she normally would have, blissfully washing away the grime of two days' travel. Afterward, she'd dried her hair by the fire before settling in the comfortable bed with her sewing. She'd found herself nodding over the work, her eyes continually blinking closed and trying to stay that way. It was almost a relief when Paen had entered the room ten minutes later with his squire on his heels.

The boy had smiled at her, but Paen had merely grunted something of a greeting in her general direction, then walked to the tub where the boy helped him undress.

Avelyn had gaped at his muscular, naked back until he'd settled into the tub. Finally able to think again once most of that nude flesh had been hidden by the sides of the tub, she'd balled up her sewing and tucked it under the bed. She'd lain down and pulled the linens up, planning on pretending to sleep until Paen finished his bath and left the room. Then she would go back to work on his tunic. However, she'd barely closed her eyes when the pretending became reality.

Avelyn had slept deep and hard and woken up to find Paen in bed next to her. He hadn't left the room to sleep below with his men. He'd spent the night not inches away from her . . . and she'd slept through this most auspicious occasion.

Avelyn sighed over her sewing. If he hadn't come to their room to bathe and she hadn't fallen asleep, she would have finished his tunic last night and presented it to him this morning. Instead, she got the first full night's sleep she'd had since the start of this journey, but the tunic was unfinished.

She supposed it didn't matter much. She would finish it in an hour or so and then be able to present it to him. At least he would be able to arrive home looking splendid, as the son of the lord of the manner should look, instead of as if he'd just escaped a fire.

"Avelyn!" Diamanda rushed into the tent, then paused abruptly at the sight of her sewing.

"Aye?" Avelyn asked, but Diamanda was staring at the tunic in her lap with amazement.

"Why, you are nearly done," she said with surprise and came forward to look at it. " 'Tis lovely. You are very good at stitches. I can never seem to keep my seams straight," she admitted wryly, then frowned. "But, again, it is too dark in here for you to be doing such delicate work."

Avelyn glanced around to note with surprise that while she had worked, the sun had continued its downward journey.

"Goodness, you will ruin your eyes like this," Diamanda remonstrated, moving to collect the candle off the chest and carry it over to set on the ground next to the stack of furs. Avelyn was surprised to see that it was lit. Runilda must have once again slipped in and attended to it without her noticing. She was very fortunate in having the girl for her maid. Runilda did not just do what was expected, but saw to those little extras that made her indispensable.

"There, that is better," Diamanda announced with a pleased smile as she straightened. "At least we need not fear you shall go blind on us." She patted Avelyn's shoulder affectionately before leaving.

Avelyn stared after her, realizing that the girl had been so distracted by concern for her eyes that she'd forgotten to ask or tell her whatever she'd come into the tent for. Shaking her head, she turned her attention back to her sewing, her mind pondering what it might have been.

Moments later, an exasperated Paen ducked through the flap, muttering under his breath about silly, feather-brained girls. Avelyn quickly hid the tunic behind her back. She offered an enquiring smile as her husband straightened.

"Diamanda was to tell you I can take you down to the river now, if you like," he announced, then frowned as he spotted the candle on the ground so close to the furs. "Ye'll start a fire setting the candle there, wife."

"I—" Avelyn closed her mouth on the explanation that it hadn't been her, but Diamanda who had put it there. She wasn't the sort to tattle. Besides, she hadn't protested the girl's actions.

"Blow it out, grab whatever you need and come along," Paen said, apparently deciding to let the matter go, then turned and ducked out of the tent.

Letting out a little breath of relief, Avelyn blew the candle out as she got up, then collected a wide swath of linen from the chest and hurried after him.

* * *

"I cannot hear you." Paen started to turn toward her as she bathed in the river.

Avelyn immediately responded, "I do not know what to say."

Paen stopped turning and relaxed a little. This was the first time he'd taken her to bathe in a river since her near-drowning. Once here, he'd at first said he would not turn his back on her, explaining he did not wish another incident like that. However, when her shoulders had slumped and she'd said she would be fine without bathing that night, Paen had relented. It seemed his wife was still shy. But he would not let her shyness deny her the opportunity to bathe after a long day in the saddle. He'd agreed to keep his back turned so long as she continued to talk so that he knew she was well. At first, she'd simply told him what she was doing: "I am not in the water yet; I am still undressing," she'd announced the moment his back was turned. "Shall I just tell you when I am going to go in, or—?"

"Aye," Paen had said abruptly, not wishing a blow-by-blow of her stripping. His imagination was filling his mind with images enough on its own, and it was sheer torture. His wife was clumsy, accident prone, weak and apparently not very hearty, but she was also a sexy little bundle. It was torture enough to have her riding before him during the day—hours in the saddle with her bottom pressed up against him, her outer thighs pressed against his inner, the bottoms of her breasts brushing against the top of the arm he kept around her waist while they rode.

Paen had spent a good deal of the last three days trying to keep from shifting in the saddle to grind against her, or raising his arm to rub over her breasts. With her handling the reins, he'd had little else to do but fantasize. In those fantasies his hands were healed and busy—undoing and tugging the cloth of her gown off her shoulders so that her naked breasts spilled out into his waiting hands, then squeezing and kneading the soft round flesh, gently pinching each nipple. In his mind, he was kissing and nibbling her neck as he fondled her breasts, her soft, excited murmurs and panting breath music to his ears as he let one hand drop down over her gently rounded stomach to slide between her legs, teasing her to such a level of excitement that she worked herself around to face him on the horse, then worked him free of his braes and managed—with his help—to raise, then lower herself on his staff, which she rode even as they rode his horse.

Of course, in reality his mount probably wouldn't take well to such goings-on and would no doubt rear up and dump them both in the dirt. But then, in reality his hands were bandaged stumps and he couldn't do any of it anyway . . . which was something he resented mightily.

The fire had not just injured his hands and taken his clothes, it had robbed him of a wedding night . . . and every night since. Paen was sure he would have given his wife a good "seeing to" every chance he'd gotten were he not injured. Certainly, his lower body showed interest every time he was near her. It no longer seemed to help that he avoided being near her at night, sleeping by the fire with the men rather than in the tent with her naked and so temptingly near, yet as untouchable as a nun thanks to the state of his hands.

If he could, Paen would make her ride her own horse, but it was his place to train her in the areas she was lacking. Although it did seem to him that she was a natural at horse riding, she claimed to not be confident enough in her skills to ride alone. That being the case, he saw it as his duty to keep her on his mount until she felt more sure of herself. Having learned the hard way that she was accident prone, Paen wasn't taking any unnecessary chances.

"What should I talk about?" Avelyn asked, distracting Paen from his thoughts.

"It matters little, just speak," Paen said. "Tell me what it was like growing up at Straughton." Paen wanted to know what she had been trained in. Riding was a skill most ladies would have, and he thought it best to know what he was up against and what he would need to see her trained in.

"Oh, well," Avelyn said, then launched into a rambling speech. Paen soon realized that he should have been more specific and simply asked what she'd been taught, for his wife did tend to like the sound of her own voice. Despite her obvious exhaustion, she had talked nonstop yesterday on the last day of their journey to Hargrove, and now today, the first of their two-day journey home, she continued chattering. Not that he really minded. In that time he had learned a lot about his wife. He was getting a rather thorough picture of who she was, of her family and childhood.

Probably more thorough than she realized, Paen thought. Avelyn did not say a cross word about her cousins. She did not tell him they taunted her and made her feel inferior, or that their arrival at Straughton had been a blight on what until then had been a perfect childhood, with loving parents, an affectionate brother and a secure home. She did not say a word against them, and yet he saw it. He had been quick to recognize the trio as resentful and cruel, and had found little patience for them. He understood their resentment at having their father, home and inheritance stolen from them, but thought little of their taking it out on Avelyn.

Paen supposed it was envy and an instinct to go for the weakest member of a group that made them behave so badly. They could not attack their aunt and uncle the same way, and Warin wouldn't have hesitated to beat them had they tried this business on him. No doubt he would beat them when he caught them tormenting Avelyn, but Paen was equally sure that they never attacked her when others might witness it, and that Avelyn would never tattle on them. Her refusal to carry tales was an honorable choice, but had left her undefended against their verbal attacks on her self-esteem.

By the time Avelyn finished bathing and was safely out of the water dressing herself, Paen had come to the conclusion that what he needed to teach his wife was her own value. He was also quite sure that he had not gotten such an inept bride as he'd thought. Parents as loving and caring as hers appeared to be would not send their daughter out into the world without the skills she'd need to carry on successfully in life.

Paen suspected that Avelyn's clumsiness and apparent ineptitude were really just a result of her low-esteem and awkwardness with him . . . just as David's tendency to trip over his own feet was a result of nervousness and an eagerness to please.

Given time and proper tending, Paen was sure he would have himself the perfect wife.

"I am ready, husband."

Paen glanced down at her and found himself smiling. She was dressed in another unattractive, overlarge and dark gown, and her hair was damp and scraped back harshly from her face. Still, her beauty showed through to him. Her eyes were huge and alight with good humor and kind-heartedness, and her mouth curved in a gentle smile.

His parents had done well, Paen decided. He was pleased with the bride they'd chosen for him. He thought he might even come to develop affection for her someday. For now, it was enough that he liked her. It was good to like a wife. It made it easier to spend a lifetime with her.

Realizing he was standing there grinning like an idiot, Paen did his best to wipe the smile from his face and gestured for her to move ahead of him to the path back to camp. As they walked, he consid-

LYNSAY SANDS

ered ways he might bolster her self esteem. If she were his horse, he'd feed her an apple every once in a while and pat her on the rump. If she were his squire, he'd give her a hearty pat on the back and a "well done." Paen had no idea, though, how to bolster a wife.

"Oh, no! What—?"

Avelyn's startled cry drew him from his musings. He started to ask what had upset her so, but she was already rushing toward their tent. Paen followed, noticing that a crowd had gathered around the smoking tent.

Cursing, he broke into a run, chasing after Avelyn as she pushed her way through the crowd.

"Wife!" He caught her arm to try to stop her as she started to duck into the tent, recalling his bandaged hands only when his linen stump slid uselessly off her arm.

Cursing, he ducked into the tent after her.

" 'Tis all right," his mother said as she turned from surveying the damage. "No one was hurt, and that is the most important thing."

"Aye," his father agreed, moving quickly to his side.

Judging by the mournful cry as Avelyn stared at the charred remains of the furs, Paen guessed she didn't agree.

"What happened?" he asked grimly.

"It looks as if a candle set the furs alight," his father admitted reluctantly.

Paen immediately glared at his wife and growled,

178

"I told you it was too close to the furs. I also told you to blow it out before coming with me."

"I did!" she cried. "I did blow it out."

"Obviously not," he snapped. "No doubt you were in a rush and just gave it a good blow, then came after me without waiting to see that it was out."

Avelyn's shoulders sagged in defeat. "You are right, husband. That must be what happened. This is all my fault."

Paen frowned at her reaction; she sounded heart-broken, and huge tears were rolling down her cheeks. It was damned hard to give her a dressing-down for this latest catastrophe when she appeared so beaten.

Sighing, he shifted on his feet and muttered, "Well, 'tis just a bunch of furs. No one was hurt and nothing important was damaged."

"Nothing important," Avelyn echoed, then, much to his bewilderment, dropped to her knees and burst into great noisy sobs.

Paen was more than relieved when his mother shooed him and his father out of the tent, assuring them she would tend to Avelyn. He hadn't a clue what to do for her. It was obvious she'd grown an attachment to the fur bed—that was the only thing he could think of. Her chest was at the opposite end of the tent and untouched by the fire. It was only the furs that had suffered. Apparently, some-one had noted the fire before it spread far. Even the tent itself was undamaged.

Aye, it must be the furs she was upset about, Paen decided, and determined to get a whole passel of them for her when they reached Gerville castle. He'd have them arranged in front of the fireplace for her so she could lie on them whenever she liked. In fact, he would join her there. The idea was appealing—relaxing before a roaring fire on a chill winter evening, drinking mulled cider.

No, no cider, he decided. Avelyn would probably spill it down her dress. Taking the cider away might affect her self-esteem, though, and make her think he believed her clumsy beyond redemption. Perhaps if he got her naked first and then gave her mulled cider before the roaring fire on the furs? Aye, that would work, he decided, smiling at the image. Avelyn naked, a goblet of mulled cider in her hand. He wouldn't even mind if she did spill it then. He would simply lean forward and lick it off of her. Now, that was an idea. Licking cider off of her full round breasts, letting his tongue curl around her nipples, coaxing them erect, then—

"What the hell are ye smiling about? Yer wife just set your bed on fire," his father snapped.

"Aye, she did." Paen's smile widened, then he caught himself and managed to dampen his expression.

" 'Tis sorry I am, son. Avelyn is a nice enough girl, but she does seem prone to calamity. If I had realized—"

"She is fine. There is no need to apologize. I am well pleased with her to wife."

"What?" Wimarc Gerville stared at him with amazement. "Did she knock you over so ye hit your head while the two of you were down by the river?"

"No, of course not." Paen scowled at the suggestion.

"Well, something has happened," his father said. "You've done little but fret and worry that she is sickly and inept since first seeing her. And now, when she has burned your bed to a pile of ash, you are *'well pleased with her to wife'*?"

Paen frowned at the older man in irritation, but didn't argue the point. Instead, he called his new squire to him and headed for the river to bathe and consider ways he might start work on his wife's self-esteem.

"Avelyn, my dear. Please do not take on so." Lady Gerville knelt beside her and wrapped her arms around her.

Avelyn tried to stop weeping, but couldn't seem to help it. She simply sagged against the woman and sobbed her heart out. She was exhausted from lack of sleep, and really, this was just too much. Everything had gone wrong since the wedding, absolutely everything. This burning of the furs was just the final straw.

Avelyn had counted on the tunic and braes repairing much of her husband's mistaken opinion of her. She couldn't tell him that she could ride, or that she wasn't presently prone to misfortune—for clearly she was—but giving him the tunic and braes would have shown at least one of her skills in a good light. It also would have given her the opportunity to let him know that she wasn't normally so weary and sickly. She could have explained that she was exhausted during the day because she had been working nights on his clothes. On top of all that, she'd worked so hard, and all that work had been ruined in a moment of inattention. Avelyn had thought the candle was out and even had a vague memory of the small curl of smoke coming off it, but apparently she'd been wrong.

"Avelyn, dear," Lady Gerville almost moaned as she rocked her in her arms. "Surely this is not about the furs. They are replaceable."

Avelyn shook her head against the woman's chest. Her tears were finally slowing, but she was in no state to talk.

"What is it, then, child? Is it that you fear Paen will just see this as another example of your clumsiness and ineptitude?"

Avelyn paused, then burst into loud sobs again.

Lady Gerville gave up trying to soothe her for a while and simply rocked her like a child. When her crying finally slowed to sniffles and hiccoughs and Avelyn finally pulled free to hold herself upright, Lady Gerville took her hand and patted it as she waited for her to speak.

"Do you think you can tell me now?" she asked after another moment had passed.

Avelyn nodded wearily, but merely sat staring with dejection at the smoldering remains of the bed.

"Would you like a drink first?" Lady Gerville prompted. "I could call Runilda and have her fetch some mead."

Avelyn shook her head.

Another moment of silence passed; then Lady Gerville opened her mouth to speak again, but Avelyn blurted out, "I have been sewing new braes and a tunic for Paen."

Lady Gerville relaxed and patted her hand. "Aye, dear. I know," she said, then explained, "I was fretting over your being so exhausted all the time and Sely mentioned it to your maid. Runilda told her to tell me not to fret, that you were staying up well into the night, sewing new clothes for Paen." She patted her hand again. "Runilda said tonight that they were nearly done."

"They were," Avelyn admitted, and much to her consternation, fresh tears began to roll down her cheeks.

"Were?" Lady Gerville asked with the beginnings of dread in her voice.

Avelyn nodded. "I was working on them when Paen came to fetch me to go to the river. I set them aside on the furs, blew at the candle, then hurried after him." She shook her head miserably. "I thought the candle was out. I did not really wait to see, but I just assumed—"

"You mean they went up with the furs?" Lady Gerville asked with horror.

Avelyn nodded.

"Oh, you poor child!" Paen's mother drew her into her arms again, but Avelyn seemed to be

183

mostly out of tears. She did manage one gasping sob, but that was it. The well was dry. She'd cried herself out.

They sat in silence for several minutes, but Lady Gerville seemed to be at a loss as to what to say to make the situation better. She just kept murmuring "poor child" over and over, and Avelyn supposed there really wasn't anything that could be said to make her feel better at that point. She was exhausted. Depressed and defeated. All she really wanted to do was sleep.

Just then Sely ducked inside carrying a couple of furs.

"Lord Gerville had me bring these over," she explained, then glanced behind her and stepped out of the way to allow Runilda to enter. Avelyn's maid was followed by four men.

"Lord Gerville sent the men to remove the burned furs," Runilda said. Avelyn knew that while Sely was referring to Paen's father when she said "Lord Gerville," Runilda was referring to Paen himself as Lord Gerville. For some reason, the fact that both were Lord Gerville made an almost hysterical giggle slip from her throat.

Lady Gerville looked her over with concern. "Come, let us get out of the way, dear, so they can work."

Avelyn allowed Lady Gerville to help her to her feet, and moved to the corner of the tent with the older woman as the men began to drag the damaged furs out. Runilda had brought a leaf-filled branch with her and used it to sweep the remaining ashes out of the tent. The moment that was done, she fetched some linens from Avelyn's chest's. Then she and Sely fashioned the furs into something of a bed and made it up with the linens.

"Here we are, then." Lady Gerville urged Avelyn to the little nest of furs and linen. "Why don't you rest for a bit, dear? I shall have Runilda fetch you when the sup is ready."

"I am not hungry," Avelyn said dully as she allowed herself to be tucked into the bed. She did see the concerned glances the women exchanged, but couldn't seem to work up the energy to care about it.

"Just rest for now, dear," Lady Gerville said finally. "You'll feel better after some sleep."

Avelyn dutifully closed her eyes and was asleep at once.

Chapter Eleven

Paen had just come in from overseeing the men's training and had settled himself at the trestle table to enjoy some mead when the sound of a woman's soft step made him tense and glance toward the stairs. He relaxed the instant he realized it was his mother. For a moment, Paen had feared it was his wife. He wasn't in the mood for her sad face just then.

"Oh, Paen." His mother moved a little more quickly when she saw him. "Good—I wanted to talk to you. Where is your father?"

"He's just coming up from the stables now. He shall be here shortly," Paen answered, then arched an eyebrow. "Where is my wife?"

"She is in the solar, sewing."

"Of course she is," he said dryly. His wife seemed ever to be sewing, but he had yet to see any results from it. Paen assumed it was a new gown she was working on. The few she possessed seemed all to be dark, drab and too large for her. He'd been hoping she was producing a new one that would be more colorful and fit properly, but surely it didn't take this long to make one.

She had been sewing in their tent the few times he'd peered in to check on her on their journey, and it was all she'd done in the three days since arriving at Gerville, that or sleeping. Or weeping. Sometimes she even wept in her sleep.

While Avelyn had seemed a happy chatterbug during the journey to collect his squire, all had changed on the last day of the journey to Gerville. Since the night of the fire, she'd been walking misery. Paen missed her cheerful chatter, but more than that, he couldn't stand to see her so weary and unhappy, especially since he didn't have a clue what to do about it. He'd hoped she was just missing her family and would get over it, but rather than recover her good cheer, she seemed to get more melancholy each day.

"You need not sound so put out. She is making new braes and a tunic for you. Again," his mother added testily as the hall doors opened and Wimarc Gerville entered.

"A new braes and tunic? For me?" Paen asked with amazement. "Whatever for? She is the one who needs new clothes, not I."

"Aye," Lord Gerville agreed as he approached the table. "The girl does not have a single gown that fits her, and every one she has seems to be dark and drab." He paused to kiss his wife on the cheek, then settled on the bench next to Paen. "I suppose the blue one that burst at the wedding dinner and the red one that went up in flames were the only colorful gowns she possessed."

Lady Gerville frowned at her husband, then turned to glare at Paen. "Your wife stayed up nights during our journey sewing you new clothes to replace those ruined in the fire. 'Tis why she was always in the tent of a night, and always exhausted during the day. She was making clothes for you."

Paen blinked at the news, but it was his father who commented first. "Well, she is damned slow at sewing if she is not yet finished."

"Wimarc." Lady Gerville frowned at her husband. "She had nearly completed them when they burned up in the tent. She was quite distraught, but started on them again when she got here. I believe she has another set nearly done."

"Hmm." Paen's father scowled at the reminder of the fire. "Is that why she has been so unhappy? Because of a set of clothes?"

"I believe it is part of it, but I think she is also missing her family." Lady Gerville turned a displeased look on Paen. "And you are not helping with that."

"Me?" His eyes widened. "What can I do to help with this? I have done naught to cause her unhappiness."

"You have done naught to prevent it either," she argued. "You pay Avelyn less attention than the dogs. You at least throw them a bone once in a while."

Paen scowled. "Well, I cannot pay her attention, or have you forgotten my hands are injured?"

"I did not mean bedding her," she said with exasperation. "Have you spoken more than a word to her at all?"

"Spoken to her?" he asked with disbelief, and his mother's eyes narrowed.

"Have you been so blind all these years? Or is it that you have been away on Crusade so long that you have forgotten that your father speaks to me all the time?"

"That is not what I meant," Paen said with irritation. "I meant she is the one . . . well, she used to be the one who . . . she was quite—"

"He means he could not get a word in edgewise on the journey here," his father said with amusement. "At least when she was on horseback."

"Aye, well, I suspect that was an effort to keep awake," Lady Gerville said.

"Aye, I noticed the girl likes to sleep a lot," Wimarc said dryly. "She slept on horseback one day when she was supposed to be learning to ride."

"Only one day," Lady Gerville defended her. "And that was only because she'd been up all night sewing." She paused, then sighed. "I promised not to tell you, but I know she is also upset that you think she is so inept, so I am going to share something with you."

Paen and his father exchanged a glance. It was Wimarc who said, "She is not so inept?"

"Nay," Lady Gerville said firmly.

"Wife, I know you like her, but the girl cannot even ride a horse," Wimarc pointed out.

"Aye, she can."

"She—"

"Mother is right," Paen interrupted when his father would have argued the point. "Avelyn may not have been able to ride when we first left Straughton, but she is a natural. She was very good by the time we arrived here. I would have let her mount her own horse on the way back from Hargrove, but she did not feel confident she could manage it on her own, so I let her ride with me."

"You do not understand," Lady Gerville said. "She knew how to ride ere leaving Straughton."

"Do not be ridiculous, Christina," his father said with disbelief. "Why would she lie about something like that and let us think her so incompetent?"

"To save Paen's hands," she said.

"What?" Paen stared at her with dismay.

"You were insisting on handling your own mount. She—like me—feared you would do your hands further injury, so she let you think she could not ride so that you would let her take the reins while you 'trained' her."

His father snorted at the suggestion. "The chit slept through the second day."

"Because she was up all night sewing," Lady Gerville reminded him. "But she sewed each night after that, yet stayed awake despite her exhaustion."

Lord Gerville considered this news. "So, you are saying the girl is trained in proper wifery?"

"Aye. Her mother gave me a list of her skills at the wedding meal. She is fully trained, probably better than most girls her age."

190

"Running a household? Tending injuries and illness? Instructing staff?" he queried.

"Aye, all that and more."

"Then why has she not tended to Paen's injured hands? 'Tis always you checking and bandaging them."

Lady Gerville looked uncomfortable. "Aye. Well, I have apologized to her for that, but . . . he is my son."

"And this is your home to run," Lord Gerville said with gentle understanding.

Paen's mother stiffened. "What do you mean?"

"You said you think her sadness had to do with Paen's thinking her unskilled, as well as missing her family and home."

"Aye."

"But mayhap it is more than that."

"What else could it be?" she asked.

"She has not only left her home and family behind, Christina. She has come to ours. If Avelyn was trained and is as skilled as you claim, it was so that she could be a proper wife, so that when she married she would be prepared to move to her new home and run it," he pointed out. "But this is *our* home, *yours* to run. You have everything well in hand and she has nothing to do. She has no way to make a place for herself. She is like a guest here."

Lady Gerville moved to the bench and dropped to sit on it between her husband and son. "I had not thought of that."

"I know," Lord Gerville said softly. He was

silent for a moment, then said, "I received news on our arrival here that old Legere is dead."

"Aye, I know," Lady Gerville said with some confusion. "You told me at the time."

"He was my chatelain at Rumsfeld," Paen's father pointed out, speaking of his wife's childhood home. The two lands had been merged when they married, but they lived at Gerville.

"Aye." Now she appeared more irritated than confused.

"I have been wondering who to replace Legere with ever since."

Paen stiffened, understanding where his father was heading, even as his mother did. He could see the dawning realization on her face. She did not look pleased.

"Wimarc," she began, but Lord Gerville continued. "Perhaps Paen and Avelyn should go there."

"But—"

" 'Twould give them a chance to get to know each other better without our interference," he pointed out over her protests. "And 'twould give her a home of her own to run, someplace she would not feel like a guest on sufferance."

"Oh." Lady Gerville sighed in defeat.

"Are you all right, dear?"

"Hmm?" Avelyn glanced up at Lady Helen blankly. They were seated at the high table, eating dinner. Avelyn sat between Lady Gerville and Lady Helen. Paen, as usual, was not there. He had been seated at the table speaking to his father when she'd come below stairs, but had left shortly afterward.

Avelyn supposed he had left to get away from her. Paen seemed always to be avoiding her . . . to the point that he would not even sit at table and eat with them. She didn't know where he was sleeping either, but it wasn't with her.

"You sighed, dear," Lady Helen pointed out gently. "Are you unhappy?"

Avelyn forced a smile to her lips. Lady Helen was a kind woman, as was Paen's mother. All of them had been wonderful to her since their arrival at Gerville—kind and considerate and keeping her company all the time so that she hardly noticed that her own husband couldn't be bothered with any of that. Avelyn sighed again, then realized she'd done it and shook her head, impatient with herself. "I am sorry, my lady."

"You need not apologize, Avelyn." Lady Gerville joined the conversation and patted her hand. "It is hardly your fault."

Avelyn grimaced at the word *fault*. "But I should apologize to you for Paen's never joining us at table. That apparently *is* my fault."

"What?" Lady Gerville appeared surprised at the claim.

Avelyn swallowed and admitted, "Your son does not seem pleased with me as his wife. He avoids me at all costs now we are here. He will not even eat at the table because I am here, let alone sleep in his own room."

193

"Oh, Avelyn." Lady Gerville peered at her with dismay. "And you thought this was because of you?"

"What else could it be?" Avelyn asked with a shrug. "I asked Diamanda and she said that he did sleep in his room and dine at table before I was here. She did not think it was my fault that he does neither now either, but could not come up with another explanation."

"Because she does not know . . ." Lady Gerville paused and bit her lip.

Avelyn was about to ask what Diamanda didn't know, but before she could, the older woman shook her head with disgust.

"So many secrets—'Do not tell him this, do not tell her that,'" she said with exasperation. "I should have realized that he wouldn't explain. The boy is just like his father in that regard. Well, let me save you some heartache, child, by telling you what it took me years of marriage to Wimarc to realize. If you do not know or understand something, you must ask. Never fear looking foolish by asking, for the only fool is the one who does not ask and makes assumptions in ignorance."

She paused to take a drink from her goblet, then said, "Now take yourself above stairs. Go to the chamber on the right of your own and enter without knocking. You shall learn a lot without saying a word, but after that you will have to ask your husband why he has not slept with you. I suspect the answer will surprise you."

Avelyn stared at her with bewilderment. She hadn't understood much of what Lady Gerville had said. So many secrets? Who had secrets? She supposed she had made the woman keep one or two herself. Now it seemed that hers weren't the only secrets here.

"Go," Lady Gerville insisted, drawing her from her thoughts.

Avelyn glanced at Lady Helen, but Diamanda's aunt appeared to be as perplexed as she was. She got reluctantly to her feet, stepped over the bench and moved slowly toward the stairs. Part of her was curious at what she might find upstairs, but most of her simply didn't want to know. It was bad enough suspecting her husband could not bear to be near her. To actually have him tell her so would be much worse.

Avelyn grimaced at her own cowardice. Her parents had not raised her to be a coward, but so much had happened in the last week—she felt rather like the camel whose back might break with the next straw set on it.

Not that it was all bad. Things were a little better here at Gerville. In some ways, living here was like being home again. Lady Gerville was much like her mother, running the castle with seeming effortless ease. It left Avelyn with nothing to do but sew, but she didn't mind that so much. With her track record to date, she was relieved not to have tasks and chores to attend to that might further reveal the ineptitude she hadn't realized she suffered.

Avelyn felt safer sewing new clothes for Paen instead. Fortunately, Paen's brother Adam had been the same size and Paen was now wearing a pair of the dead man's braes as well as one of his tunics. Avelyn still felt he should have clothes of his own, so she was pleased to make them for him. At least she knew she was competent at that. And it was very pleasant spending the day chatting with Diamanda, Lady Helen and Lady Gerville while she sewed. Lady Gerville and Helen were very kind, and Diamanda was bright and seemed to have appointed herself the task of trying to cheer Avelyn.

Avelyn's only discontent came from her husband's apparent rejection of her. What else could it be? The man avoided her at all times, and had yet to bed her. It was disheartening after the high hopes she'd had on her wedding night, when he had touched and caressed her with seeming enthusiasm.

Avelyn's musings came to an abrupt end as she found she'd reached the room next to the one she was supposed to share with her husband.

Taking a deep breath, she put her ear to the door, trying to anticipate what to expect, but there was nothing to hear, not even a murmur of voices. Straightening her shoulders, Avelyn raised her hand to knock, then recalled that Lady Gerville had instructed her not to knock.

Lowering her hand, she hesitated a moment more, then opened the door.

David had just slipped a spoonful of stew into his mouth when Paen heard the door open. He turned toward it, expecting to see his father, then nearly choked as he spied his wife standing there.

He stared. The surprise on Avelyn's face told

him she hadn't expected him to be here, or perhaps she'd known he was here but hadn't expected him to be eating.

Paen's gaze slid back to his squire. He'd been most relieved to finally have the boy at his side. The first few days after the fire had been the most frustrating of his life. The injury to his hands had made it difficult to manage the simplest of chores—feeding himself, dressing, bathing. Even relieving himself became something of an exercise in humiliation. He could use the stumps to push his braes down over his hips, but had difficulty getting them back up. His father had helped as much as he could, but it had been humiliating for Paen.

Aye, the day they'd reached Hargrove had been a bright one for Paen. He'd then had the boy to help him with such things, but Paen was too proud to allow everyone else to realize how helpless he was, no matter how temporary that helplessness might be. So, every mealtime since they had collected the lad, he'd had David bring his meal to him away from everyone else. The boy fed him in a clearing by the river the first night of their journey. The second night, they'd arrived at Gerville, and Paen had asked David to bring his meal up here to Adam's old room. Then the lad had helped him strip for his bath, though that was where he drew the line. The lad had offered—rather reluctantly—to help with scrubbing up, but Paen simply couldn't subject either himself or the boy to that embarrassment, so he made do with soaking in the water.

They'd followed the same pattern each night

since. Every morning, David helped him dress, then followed him around, doing his squire's duties until the nooning meal, when they returned to the keep and Paen came up to wait while the boy collected his meal from the kitchen and brought it up to feed him. He did the same for the evening meal. Then at night, the boy helped him prepare for bed before taking to his own pallet in the corner.

"'Tis fine, David. I am done. You can take that back to the kitchens."

The squire hesitated briefly, clearly doubtful that Paen was done with his half-eaten food, but he nodded and moved past Avelyn and out of the room. Paen then turned his attention to his wife, who was hesitating in the door. Finally she drew her shoulders up, stepped into the room and closed the door behind her. Paen waited warily for her to speak, but when she finally did, her words were unexpected.

"So you do not stay away from the table at mealtimes to avoid me?"

Paen felt his mouth drop open in shock, then he quickly closed it and said, "Why would you think that?"

Avelyn let her breath out on a slow sigh. "Because you seem to constantly be avoiding me. You leave a room shortly after I enter it, as you did today when I came below. You have not sat at table with me since arriving here. And while you joined me in our room at Hargrove, you would not share our tent, nor have you slept in your own bed since arriving here at Gerville." She said the last part in a rush, her face flaming.

Paen blinked in confusion. "I left the hall when you entered tonight because I knew it was time for the sup and—as you now know—I have been eating up here."

"Aye, I understand that now," she said quietly, but ducked her head and mumbled, "However, that does not explain your reluctance to share our marriage bed . . . I understand if you do not want me. I know I am not the most attractive—"

Paen snorted, and she glanced up to frown at him.

"There is no need to be rude about it, my lord husband. I am aware that I am overlarge and—"

Another snort slid from Paen's lips and he shook his head. "You are beautiful, wife."

He saw the anger in her eyes and wondered if she really did not know how lovely she was to him. But then, he realized suddenly, of course she didn't. Her cousins had spent years doing what they could to convince her that she wasn't. He just wished he had realized this while he was still at Straughton. He would have done more than threaten them.

"Oh, aye," Avelyn said wryly. "I am so beautiful you have yet to consummate our marriage, and 'tis more than a week after it was done."

Paen gasped in disbelief, then held up his bandaged hands. " 'Tis a bit difficult to bed you just at the moment, wife."

"Hugo said 'twas not your hands that were important, and that if you could ride a horse, you could ride me," Avelyn snapped, then realized what she'd said and blushed at repeating the crude words.

"Hugo," Paen said with disgust. "Why would you believe him?"

"Because he is a man and more versed at such things," Avelyn said quietly, then tilted her head and asked, "Is it not true, then? Was Hugo wrong?"

"Aye, he was wro—" Paen came to a sudden halt as he realized he would be lying. He could consummate the marriage with her, of course. It would be difficult but not impossible. While his hands were useless, his manhood was not and had let him know it several times since the fire. He couldn't sit on a horse behind her without ending up as stiff as a sword, and when he'd had to take her to bathe in the river . . . Dear God, he hadn't even had to see her, just the sounds of her disrobing and splashing in the water were enough to have him erect as a post.

Paen had avoided sleeping next to her at night because the idea of being close enough to smell her and reach out and touch her, but still unable to, had been unpalatable. He'd had no choice the night they'd stayed at Hargrove—Paen would never have humiliated her by asking for his own room—but other than that, he'd slept as far away from her as he could and had intended to do so until he was recovered enough to finally do all the things he'd been fantasizing about.

Apparently, that decision had led his wife to be-

GET UP TO 5 FREE BOOKS!

Sign up for one of our book clubs today, and we'll send you
FREE* BOOKS
just for trying it out...with no obligation to buy, ever!

HISTORICAL ROMANCE BOOK CLUB

Travel from the Scottish Highlands to the American West, the decadent ballrooms of Regency England to Viking ships. Your shipments will include authors such as CONNIE MASON, CASSIE EDWARDS, LYNSAY SANDS, LEIGH GREENWOOD, and many, many more.

LOVE SPELL BOOK CLUB

Bring a little magic into your life with the romances of Love Spell—fun contemporaries, paranormals, time-travels, futuristics, and more. Your shipments will include authors such as KATIE MACALISTER, SUSAN GRANT, NINA BANGS, SANDRA HILL, and more.

As a book club member you also receive the following special benefits:

- **30% OFF** all orders through our website & telecenter! (Plus, you still get 1 book FREE for every 5 books you buy!)
- **Exclusive access** to special discounts!
- **Convenient** home delivery and 10 days to return any books you don't want to keep.

There is no minimum number of books to buy, and you may cancel membership at any time. See back to sign up!

*Please include $2.00 for shipping and handling.

YES! ☐

Sign me up for the **Historical Romance Book Club** and send my THREE FREE BOOKS! If I choose to stay in the club, I will pay only $13.50* each month, a savings of $6.47!

YES! ☐

Sign me up for the **Love Spell Book Club** and send my TWO FREE BOOKS! If I choose to stay in the club, I will pay only $8.50* each month, a savings of $5.48!

NAME: _____

ADDRESS: _____

_____

TELEPHONE: _____

E-MAIL: _____

☐ **I WANT TO PAY BY CREDIT CARD.**

☐ VISA　　☐ MasterCard.　　☐ DISCOVER

ACCOUNT #: _____

EXPIRATION DATE: _____

SIGNATURE: _____

Send this card along with $2.00 shipping & handling for each club you wish to join, to:

Romance Book Clubs
20 Academy Street
Norwalk, CT 06850-4032

Or fax (must include credit card information!) to: 610.995.9274. You can also sign up online at www.dorchesterpub.com.

*Plus $2.00 for shipping. Offer open to residents of the U.S. and Canada only. Canadian residents please call 1.800.481.9191 for pricing information.

If under 18, a parent or guardian must sign. Terms, prices and conditions subject to change. Subscription subject to acceptance. Dorchester Publishing reserves the right to reject any order or cancel any subscription.

lieve he couldn't bear to be near her. He'd merely added to the poor image her cousins had worked so hard to instill in her.

Sighing, he tried to explain. "Without my hands to help, it would be uncomfortable for you, but aye, it would be possible to consummate the marriage. We could not do it in the normal way, of course. You would have to perhaps sit on the window ledge, or bend over something . . ."

Paen's words slowed as his mind was immediately filled with images of the possibilities. Avelyn sitting on the window ledge, him urging her legs apart with his body, then moving between them, his body brushing against hers as he kissed her, then drove himself into her. This picture was quickly followed by an image of her bending over the ledge as he drove into her from behind.

"Are you saying you have neglected to consummate our marriage out of consideration for my discomfort?"

Avelyn's voice drew him from his imaginings and Paen scowled at her. Much to his annoyance, she didn't sound as if she believed him. "Well, aye, of course, and 'tis why I have not been joining you in our bed. Did you really think I preferred the hard-packed earth to the soft warm furs in our tent?"

"Nay, of course not," she said, and her voice too was becoming impatient. "Which is why I assumed you prefer the hard-packed earth to my company."

Paen opened his mouth, then closed it again. He could understand that her cousins had affected her confidence, but he thought his desire for her on their wedding night had been pretty obvious. He'd been as stiff as a sword and eager as a lad his first time out. How could she have missed that?

Paen pursed his lips as he considered one reason she might have missed it. "Were you sotted on our wedding night?"

"No!" Avelyn said, appearing shocked at the question.

"Well, then surely you noticed my"—Paen paused, seeking an alternate term for the crude one that came to mind to describe his erection—"eagerness."

When Avelyn just stared at him, Paen heaved his breath out on an exasperated sigh. "Trust me, wife, if my hands were not injured I would be consummating our marriage every chance I could. But I will not cause you unneeded pain."

Avelyn bit her lower lip and paused a moment before responding. "Well, my mother did warn me of what to expect, and she said that the first time could be quite uncomfortable and even painful. I appreciate your concern, but if you wish to—"

"Avelyn," Paen interrupted. "You do not know what you are asking. The first time is not always pleasant for the woman, but without my hands it could be downright unpleasant."

"I see," Avelyn murmured, then jumped at a knock on the door. Turning, she opened it to find David standing there, looking uncertain.

The boy glanced from her to Paen. "Did you still want your bath, my lord? Or shall I—?"

"I will leave you to your bath," Avelyn murmured and slipped out of the room.

With a sinking heart, Paen watched her go. He was sure he'd seen the sheen of tears in her eyes before she'd turned away, and knew he hadn't managed to convince her of the truth. Nor did he know what to do about it.

Realizing David was still standing in the door, he waved him in. Paen had been overseeing the practice field today and had taken a tumble when one of the men had bumped into him. The field had been muddy after last night's rain, and while David had used a rag to wipe the worst of the mud away at the time, he needed a bath to remove all of it. However, Paen hadn't been willing to trouble the kitchen staff to heat up water for him, so had decided to wait until after the sup.

Paen pondered the problem of what to do about his wife as his bath was prepared. He found himself only half listening to the lad's chatter as the tub was carried in and filled for his bath. He had already noticed the boy had a great deal in common with his wife. Aside from showing a propensity to clumsiness, the lad could carry on whole conversations without anyone else contributing to it.

Oddly enough, Paen found this tendency soothing. With David, the chatter was generally about battles, weapons and horses. Of course, the first night he had served as Paen's squire, David had asked if his hands had been burned during a battle with a dragon. He'd seemed mightily disappointed to learn that it wasn't a dragon that had wounded his master, then had gone on to lecture Paen about the dangerous and dastardly nature of dragons.

He'd explained quite authoritatively that they had the very worst case of bad breath ever, and tended to eat ladies and make them cry.

The tub was full, the room empty. David helped Paen to disrobe before he said anything that actually required a response. "What do you do when you bed a lady?"

Paen gaped at the lad, his mouth open for a moment before he gasped with amazement, "Why would you ask about bedding?"

"Well, I heard Lady Helen telling one of the maids that Lady Avelyn thinks you are displeased with her because you have not yet bedded her," he explained, "Are you not tucking her in of a night?"

"Dear God, the whole castle knows," Paen muttered as he stepped out of his braes and into the tub, then realized that he should have expected as much. It was impossible to keep secrets in a castle. He suggested the boy go below and ask the cook for a sweet treat to enjoy while he waited for Paen to finish soaking.

Once the boy was gone, Paen sank into the water and closed his eyes as he pondered what to do about his wife. It seemed obvious he couldn't leave things as they were, but he didn't know what to do. He was rather sure he wouldn't be able to convince her with simple verbal arguments. Paen had never considered himself very good at such things. He was more comfortable with taking action than merely discussing matters. He hadn't a clue what he could say to convince Avelyn that he really did find her attractive and wished to bed her. Paen suspected he could say so until he was blue in the face and she would not believe him. Probably the only way to convince her was to actually bed her. He was mightily tempted to do so. However, she wouldn't thank him for it afterward, despite what she said.

Avelyn had no clue what she was asking for, and Paen could not prepare her properly without his hands to caress and hold her. Without his hands, he had only his mouth to work with—

Paen sat up abruptly in the tub, sending water splashing every which way as a wave of images and thoughts assaulted his mind. Avelyn naked before him. Him kissing and caressing her with his mouth until she cried out with pleasure. Him rising up and driving himself into her . . .

"Damn, why did I not think of that before?" he muttered, then shouted for his squire.

Chapter Twelve

Avelyn returned to her room to find a tub half full of water and Runilda stoking a fire to life in the fireplace. She was surprised the servants had managed to heat enough water for two baths, and almost wished they hadn't gone to all the trouble. All she really wanted was to go to bed.

Avelyn was discouraged after her talk with Paen, though not as depressed as she'd been before it. She didn't believe his claim that he was refraining from consummating the marriage out of consideration for her. Even he had admitted that it was possible to do so despite the injury to his hands, which, she supposed, meant he wasn't consummating it because he couldn't be bothered. However, it was a relief to know that he wasn't so repulsed by her that he was avoiding the table at sup.

Avelyn rushed through her bath, then wrapped herself in a linen and moved to sit by the fire to dry her hair before the flames. She was still seated there several moments later when the chamber door suddenly opened and Paen entered.

"Husband?" Avelyn turned on her chair and stared at him with surprise, noting that he too wore only a swath of linen, though his was much smaller and wrapped around his waist.

"I have figured it out," Paen announced by way of greeting, and Avelyn stared at the wide smile on his face, unsure what to make of it. Her husband hadn't smiled much since she'd known him; for some reason his wide grin just made her nervous.

"You have figured what out, husband?" she asked with bewilderment.

Paen crossed the room to the window. "Come here, wife."

Avelyn felt her eyes squinching up with suspicion as she recalled his saying something about her sitting on the window ledge. Surely he didn't intend to—

Nay, Avelyn told herself as she got reluctantly to her feet. The man had followed that picture up with ridiculous explanations about how it would hurt. He had gone on about discomfort she'd already known she'd experience, with or without his hands. Her mother had not left her ignorant of the marriage bed. Expecting the marriage to be consummated on the wedding night, she'd explained the ordeal quite thoroughly, and had said that, while painful the first time, it could be quite enjoyable afterward if Avelyn was fortunate enough to have a considerate husband.

Having listened with bated breath to her mother's descriptions of what exactly would take place, Avelyn had found it difficult to imagine any of it being enjoyable. Still, her mother was not prone to lie to her, so she'd given her the benefit of the doubt before the wedding night. And even though they'd never completed the act, Avelyn had experienced more than a little pleasure in her marriage bed under her husband's kisses and caresses . . . at least until the room had gone up in flames.

Avelyn paused beside her husband at the window and waited curiously.

Paen smiled at her brilliantly and then suddenly nudged at his linen with his bandaged hand. The covering dropped to the rushes with a plop.

Avelyn gaped. His manhood was hard as a rock and standing up like a pole sticking out of the ground. She managed to tear her eyes from his huge staff and lift them to his face for half a second, then let them drop down to his manhood again.

She had seen it before, of course, on their wedding night. Only Avelyn didn't recall it being quite so big then . . . or . . . well . . . solid.

Avelyn was suddenly grateful that he'd decided to wait until recovering from his burns before consummating their marriage. She didn't even mind so much if he had a disgust of her. . . . And what was so wrong with a man having a mistress? Why did men not just stab women with their swords? It surely couldn't be any worse than having those great huge things impaling them.

Realizing she was becoming a little hysterical

over something she needn't yet fear, Avelyn again forced her gaze upward and managed what she hoped was a pleasant smile of enquiry.

"Why are you grimacing?" Paen asked, and Avelyn supposed she hadn't managed a very good smile after all.

"I . . ." She sought a viable excuse, but nothing was coming to mind, and after a moment Avelyn gave it up and instead asked, "You said you had figured something out?"

"Oh, aye." Turning, he drew the fur away from the window and forced it to the side, allowing moonlight into the room.

Avelyn turned to peer curiously down into the bailey below, but could see very little. The ledge was a good three feet deep, and she would have had to practically lie on it to get her head near the window itself, so she peered at the glass instead and tried for a suitably interested expression. Glass was very expensive, such a rarity. It really was impressive that the windows actually had glass in them. If she hadn't known she'd married into a wealthy family, this would have told her.

"Well, this is a very fine window, my lord husband. Thank you for showing it to— Awk!" Avelyn squealed in surprise and grabbed at his shoulders as he suddenly turned her to face him, then caught her under the armpits and set her onto the ledge. "What are you—"

Avelyn's question died a quick death, silenced by Paen's lips as he grabbed her by both knees, pushed them apart and stepped between them to press a kiss to her mouth. At first, she was too startled to try to pull away and say anything, but within moments of his mouth covering hers, his tongue had slid out to urge her lips apart and she quite forgot what she would have said as his tongue danced with hers.

By the time Paen ended the kiss, Avelyn had melted against him, her mind incapable of holding a thought.

"I have sorted it all out," he whispered, his mouth moving to her ear as he tried to nudge her hands from where they were clutching the linen to her chest.

"That is nice," Avelyn breathed on a sigh, turning her head for him and pressing the side of her face into his lips like a cat under a caress.

"Since I cannot use my hands to prepare you, I shall use my mouth," he explained. "But first you shall have to let go of the linen."

"Mmm hmm." Avelyn smiled. "Do you think you could kiss me again?"

A slow, purely male smile curved his lips as he noted her expression. "Do you like it when I kiss you?"

Despite having asked the question, he looked as if he already knew the answer. Avelyn didn't care. Taking one hand away from the linens, she reached out to slide it into his hair and urged his head down for another kiss. Paen obliged her, this time starting slow and tender, then deepening it until it became almost a battle to see who could devour the other first. They were both panting when he finally

THE PERFECT WIFE

moved his mouth away and again kissed a trail
across her cheek to her ear.

A shudder ran through Avelyn as his tongue
swept over and around her ear and she turned her
head to make it easier for him, then suddenly
twisted her face back to catch his mouth with her
own. Paen obliged her and kissed her again. The
sensations he stirred in her made her arch mind-
lessly against him, responding to her body's de-
mands. She wanted to be closer to him, all of her
seemed to ache to press against him, and she
shifted her bottom forward on the ledge until she
was plastered against him. The moment she did,
Paen broke the kiss and followed the length of her
throat with his lips, forcing her to lean back so that
he could find and nibble at the sensitive hollow of
her collar bone.

Avelyn moaned and clutched his shoulders to
help keep her balance, only aware that it left her
linen free to drop to her hips when Paen continued
his downward journey unimpeded.

When Paen's lips moved over the slope of her
breast to catch one aching nipple in his mouth,
Avelyn gasped. Her feet pressed flat against the
wall as her bottom lifted right off the ledge, pressing her more intimately against him. She could feel
his hardness rub against her through the linen still
covering her lower body. It felt so good, she found
herself again grinding her lower body against his.

Avelyn thought she heard Paen growl; then he
ground back against her and she let her head fall
back with a groan. Then the cool air touched her

211

still damp nipple and she lifted her head with a shiver, glancing down as he kissed a trail down her stomach that almost seemed to make those muscles buck under her skin. Gasping for breath and feeling off balance as his shoulders lowered out of her reach, Avelyn clutched at the fur that had covered the window. She didn't seem to have enough breath to protest as he knelt and used one bandaged hand to brush aside the linen gathered around her hips.

With her very center now revealed to him, Avelyn opened her mouth on a gasp of protest, then nearly choked as he urged her legs further apart and pressed his mouth to her.

"Dear God!" Avelyn's hips lifted of their own accord, her bottom rising off the ledge again. She was now a bundle of confusion and sensation. Her mother had never mentioned this when instructing her about the wedding night. Nor had she mentioned the burning tension building deep inside her.

Avelyn was positive that she would go crazy if Paen didn't stop whatever magic he was working. She was equally positive that if he did stop she would die. She wanted to close her legs and stop him, and at the same time to push his face tighter against her and grind herself against him. He didn't stop, and—realizing she was tugging thoughtlessly at his hair—she pulled that hand free and grabbed at the fur hanging to the side of the window, pulling on the material and using it to lift her hips up again until her body suddenly exploded with the pleasure he had built in her. Screaming, Avelyn pulled on the furs and threw her head back . . . just in time to see the fur come tumbling down over the them both.

"Wife?"

Avelyn was vaguely aware of Paen struggling to push the fur off of them with his bandaged hands; then he was standing between her legs again. She threw her arms around him, clutching him close and even wrapping her legs around his hips as she pressed her face into his neck, her body wracked with shivers and sobs. She felt as if she'd come apart, as if he were the only solid thing in the world to hold on to.

Avelyn felt his arms wrap carefully around her back as he moved in closer, and she groaned as his hardness pressed against the still sensitive area between her legs. Paen groaned too, then suddenly urged her face up and claimed her lips in a kiss.

Avelyn kissed him back passionately and arched against him. They both moaned as their bodies pushed even closer together. The action made her realize that the pleasure might not yet be over. Then Paen shifted and she felt him nudge against her.

"Hold on," he whispered, then plunged into her. Avelyn cried out, her body instinctively recoiling and rising upward away from the pain she knew to expect.

Paen inhaled deeply, forcing himself to remain completely still. He wanted to move. His body was buried deep in her warm heat, and he desperately wanted to move, but he knew he shouldn't. For Avelyn's sake it was better if he gave her a moment to adjust.

"Why, that hardly hurt at all," Avelyn said with surprise, and Paen pulled back enough to peer down at her face. Her expression was one of amazement.

"I was expecting real pain, but that was barely more than a pinch," she explained and smiled widely, then wriggled experimentally against him. "It does feel odd, though."

Paen ground his teeth together as she wriggled again; then he leaned his forehead against the top of her head and breathed slowly in and out to stop from pounding in and out of her like his body was urging him to do.

"Husband?" she asked suddenly.

"Aye?" he got out between clenched teeth.

"Is that all, then? Are we done?"

A short laugh slipped from his lips and he straightened, drawing himself out of her as he said, "Nay."

"Oh," Avelyn gasped. "That is . . . er . . . nice."

She looked perplexed, and then surprised when he plunged back into her.

"Oh, that is . . . er . . ." She paused as he withdrew again and murmured another "Oh."

Recalling his wife's penchant for chattering on the ride here, and fearing she might feel a need to do the same while riding him, Paen caught her mouth in a kiss as he withdrew again.

Paen's baser instincts were still urging him forward, and Paen was still trying to restrain himself for her sake. Avelyn didn't appear to appreciate that. Her legs were wrapped around his hips and her hands clutched at him. He could only control her with his arms, and then only cautiously, because he was hesitant to bang his injured hands and allow pain to dampen any of this for him.

Paen's good intentions died abruptly when his wife suddenly dug her nails into his behind, very obviously urging him to move faster. He gave in to his desire then, driving himself into her with quick, hard thrusts, encouraged by Avelyn's moans into his mouth and the way she was arching into him. Then suddenly she tore her mouth from his and threw her head back with a scream as she bucked against him. Paen felt her squeeze around him, drawing him deeper into her, then roared with his own release.

It wasn't until he had collected himself enough so he could stop leaning on his wife that Paen glanced over her shoulder at the window. The parchment was open a crack. Someone must have opened it to air the room on their return and forgotten to close it. He wondered if anyone had heard them. Paen's gaze dropped to the bailey, and he stiffened at the sight of the audience below. It looked as if half his father's men were standing staring up at the window, and he found himself grateful that the fire across the room had burned low enough that all they could possibly see were shadowy figures. Then one of the men moved forward, separating himself from the rest and Paen squinted at the familiar form. It wasn't until the man held up his thumb in a gesture of approval that Paen recognized his father.

Groaning, he briefly dropped his forehead to his

wife's shoulder, then was suddenly gripped by concern that she might glance over her shoulder and realize they had been seen. Knowing that Avelyn would be terribly embarrassed to realize their first time had not exactly been a private affair, he tightened his arms around her waist and lifted her off the ledge.

"Husband! You will hurt your hands!" she cried, tightening her arms around his shoulders and knotting her ankles around his back to keep from being dropped.

Paen said nothing, but backed away from the window until the backs of his legs bumped the bed; then he fell back, tumbling them both on top of it. Avelyn squealed as they fell, then laughed breathlessly as he turned them on their sides to face each other. He stared at her, noting that her face was flushed with color, her eyes relaxed and smiling. He was just thinking how beautiful she looked when Avelyn suddenly frowned.

"What is it?" Paen asked.

"We did not . . . the linen . . . it . . ." She paused, flushing with embarrassment, then managed to get out. "The linens are usually hung up as proof of the bride's innocence, and so that all may know the marriage was consummated, but we did not . . ." She let her words trail away and glanced toward the window ledge.

"Ah." He bit his lip. "Well, I would not worry. I do not think anyone will demand proof that the marriage was consummated. I am sure they will accept my word for it."

"But—" Avelyn tried to protest, but Paen silenced her with a kiss, then slid his arms out from under her and shifted to lie properly on the bed. Once comfortably on his back, he held his arms open to her.

"Come—pull the linens up and sleep."

Avelyn hesitated, then crawled up to lie beside him and pull the linens and furs over them both. After another hesitation, she lay her head on his chest. Paen closed his arm around her as her hand crept up to rest tentatively on him.

He was just starting to dose off when she lifted her head and began to speak, but Paen used his forearm to press her head back to his chest and simply said, "Sleep."

He closed his eyes and pretended to sleep himself. After several moments, he sensed her relax against him. When a soft snore emitted from her, he smiled to himself, finding it utterly charming. His wife snored like a sailor, he thought with something like affection, and pressed a kiss to the top of her head. Relaxing into the bed, Paen peered up at the drapes overhead and smiled. He'd managed the consummation and—even without the use of his hands—succeeded in giving her pleasure. *Damn, I was good*, he thought.

Avelyn woke to a tingling sensation in her right breast. Smiling, she murmured sleepily and stretched on her back, her body arching upward into the sensation. When she opened her eyes, she found herself staring down at the top of her husband's head.

Morning sunlight glinted off his dark hair as he laved and suckled at her breast.

Moaning, Avelyn slid her hands into his hair, scraping her nails lightly across his scalp before letting them drop down to run across his back. He raised his head to peer at her. Realizing she was awake, Paen shifted up her body, half lying on her as he kissed her good morning.

Avelyn took half a moment to worry that her breath might be unpleasant, then decided that if he didn't mind, she didn't mind. It was a delicious way to wake up, made more so when he slid one knee between her legs and pressed it against her. Avelyn moaned and arched into the caress, her body tingling with eagerness.

"Should we move to the window ledge?" she gasped when he shifted over her, resting his elbows on either side of her head to prevent putting weight on his hands.

Paen stilled, then for some reason gave a little laugh as he shook his head. "Nay. I think we shall bypass the window this morning."

"But—" Avelyn paused and glanced toward the door when a knock disturbed them.

"Who is it?" Paen growled, still on top of her.

" 'Tis David, my lord," the boy called through the door. "Your father sent me up to see if you are yet up. He said you were to ride out with him to Rumsfeld today to have a look around."

Paen rolled off of Avelyn with a sigh. "Aye. I am up."

"Do you want me to help you dress, my lord?" David asked through the door.

Paen sat up and reached for the bed linens, then paused at the sight of his bandaged hands.

Sitting up quickly, Avelyn snatched at the linens and furs and pulled them up to cover them both, but Paen slid out from under them and stood.

"Did you bring my clothes, boy?" he called as he started across the room, and Avelyn bit her lip at the sight of his erect staff.

"Aye, my lord," came the prompt answer.

"Come in, then."

Avelyn managed to tear her gaze from her husband and tugged the linens a little tighter to her chin as the door opened. She watched David enter, Paen's clothing, boots and mail piled in his arms. The mail told her that Rumsfeld was far enough away that they had to guard against bandits or attacks. It took a moment before Avelyn recalled where she had heard the name before; then she glanced to her husband, making sure to keep her gaze above his waist as she asked, "Is Rumsfeld not your mother's birthplace?"

"Aye. How did you know?" Paen glanced back at her with surprise as David kicked the door closed with one foot, then carried his burden to the chair by the fire.

"Your mother mentioned it the day after we arrived here," she murmured. "She said the chatelain had died while you were away."

"Aye. Legere. He was old."

"Is that why you are going there? Because the

219

old chatelain is dead?" Avelyn asked curiously. "I suppose your father has to arrange for a new chatelain."

Paen paused beside the chair where David had set his clothes and turned to peer at her, his expression chagrined.

"I forgot to tell you," he realized.

"Tell me what?" Avelyn asked as David held Paen's braes open for him to step into.

Paen waited until his pants were on and done up before answering. "Father asked if I would be chatelain there."

"What?" Avelyn asked with surprise as David climbed onto the stool and Paen bent at the waist so the boy could work his tunic over his head. Once it was in place, Paen turned to face her with a smile, obviously expecting her to be pleased.

"Aye. He needs someone there he can trust, and he thinks it will give me more experience."

When Avelyn stared at him blankly, he explained, "I have been away on Crusade for much of the last years. I am an expert at battle, but could use some practice at being lord of the manor." He knelt to help David get his heavy mail on, then got to his feet and added, "He also thought you might be happier if you had a home of your own to take care of."

Avelyn stared at him as he asked his squire where his belt and sword were. David had left it in the room Paen usually slept in. Apologizing, the boy hurried out of the chamber to collect it as Paen moved to the bed. Leaning over, he gave her a quick, passionate kiss, then straightened and left the room, leaving Avelyn staring after him.

Paen was taking over as chatelain at Rumsfeld. They would be moving there. She would have her own household to run.

Avelyn felt the horror creep over her. A week ago, she would have thought it was a fine thing and would have looked forward to being mistress of her own home. Her mother had taken great care to teach her all she should know for the task. However, that had been before Avelyn had somehow fallen under a cloud of calamity. Now, the idea horrified her. She would reduce Rumsfeld to rubble within a week with her clumsiness, she supposed miserably.

"Rumsfeld is where Lady Christina grew up—'tis her family home. When her parents died some years ago, it passed to her and Lord Gerville."

"Lady Christina was an only child," Lady Helen put in and her niece Diamanda nodded.

For her part, Avelyn remained silent, simply listening as the trio walked upstairs, headed for the solar.

They had just left the hall after breaking their fast. Paen and his father had already left for Rumsfeld by the time Avelyn had taken care of her morning ablutions and gone below. It had just been the four women and several hundred servants and soldiers at the tables this morning.

Of course, the first thing out of Lady Gerville's

mouth had been about the move to Rumsfeld. It seemed everyone had already known about it, including Diamanda and Lady Helen. Avelyn had been the last to know.

She'd learned at table that it had been decided they should wait another week to go. It was hoped the extra time would give Paen's hands a chance to finish healing. Avelyn thus had another week to repack her chests in preparation of moving. Not that there was much to repack. Other than her clothes, nothing had come out of the chests since the journey. None of it had been needed here.

Lady Gerville had spoken with forced cheer about the move, and it seemed to Avelyn that Paen's mother was no more happy about it than she herself was. Even Diamanda and Lady Helen had seemed subdued. Avelyn had been grateful to escape the solar to finish off her new efforts at a tunic and braes for her husband. She'd started the project the day after their arrival here at Gerville. After wandering the castle aimlessly for most of the morning, she'd decided she might as well start on another outfit for Paen. While he still wore a pair of braes and a tunic that had belonged to his brother, they didn't fit as well as they might.

"Rumsfeld is quite lovely," Diamanda continued as they reached the solar. "I am sure you shall like it."

"You have been there?" Avelyn asked curiously as Lady Helen pushed open the door.

"Aye. My family traveled by it on our way here

when I first came to train with Lady Chris—!" Diamanda stopped abruptly and glanced around when she bumped into her aunt. Lady Helen had suddenly stopped in the door to the solar, blocking either woman from entering the room.

"Aunt Helen? What is it?" Diamanda shifted past the older woman and peered into the room, then gave a soft "oh" as Lady Helen suddenly turned and tried to usher Avelyn away from the room. "Why do we not go for a nice walk in the bailey?"

"What? But 'tis raining out," Avelyn reminded her, then frowned at her pitying expression and moved past her, determined to see whatever was in the room.

"My dear, I do not think—" Lady Helen touched Avelyn's shoulder to stop her, then fell silent and let her hand fall away with a sigh as Avelyn slipped past Diamanda and into the room.

At first, Avelyn didn't see anything unusual or amiss. The room was empty except for Boudica and Juno. Lady Christina's pet greyhounds were curled up asleep on top of an old strip of cloth their mistress had laid out for their comfort.

Avelyn started to turn back toward the other two women, then paused and peered back at the bit of cloth sticking out from under the hounds. It was the very same forest green as the fabric Lady Christina had given her to sew Paen's new outfit—the remains of the cloth the lady had made his wedding outfit from.

"Avy?" Lady Helen asked with concern.

Avelyn crossed the room as carefully as if she were walking a narrow tree trunk laid over a river, placing one foot in front of the other, her gaze locked on the cloth.

When she reached the dogs, she knelt just as carefully and plucked at the cloth, waking the dogs as she slowly pulled it out from beneath them. Boudica and Juno scrambled to their feet and stood watching, tails wagging as Avelyn held up the tunic she'd nearly finished for Paen. It was clawed and chewed up. Ruined.

"Ohhh." It was a pained moan from Lady Helen. "And after all your work. Oh, Avelyn."

"I shall go fetch Lady Gerville," Diamanda said and hurried from the room.

Avelyn heard the girl hurry off, but simply sat there staring at the ruined remains of Paen's top. She could hardly believe it. She *couldn't* believe it. Her stunned mind was floating useless in her head, unable to grasp this latest catastrophe.

A whine sounded, then Boudica's wet tongue brushed up her cheek. Avelyn blinked her eyes back into focus and peered at the animal even as Juno moved closer to give her a wet swipe on her cheek as well. An apology? Comfort?

Boudica gave another whine, followed by another lick as if begging her not to hurt them. Avelyn smiled faintly at the thought. As if she could hurt the silly creatures. A long sigh slid from her, taking all the tension from her body with it. She dropped the cloth to pet them both reassuringly.

" 'Tis all right," she told the animals, finding herself soothed by the feel of their soft fur as she petted them.

"But all your hard work," Lady Helen said.

" 'Twas just a tunic," Avelyn murmured.

Lady Gerville had suggested the fates might be acting against her. Avelyn was beginning to believe it. If that were the case, she had two choices—to give up and stop trying to do anything, or to make the best of the situation and keep on plugging until the fates tired of toying with her.

Avelyn was not the sort to give up.

"Avelyn?"

She lifted her head as Lady Gerville moved slowly into the room to stand beside Lady Helen. She was a little out of breath, so had obviously hurried up here, but now she was moving slowly, almost cautiously, uncertainty on her face. Avelyn supposed Diamanda had told her what had happened and the woman feared her reaction to what the dogs had done.

"I—" Paen's mother began,

" 'Tis all right," Avelyn interrupted her. She ruffled the fur of both Juno and Boudica one last time, then picked up the scrap of cloth that used to be a lovely tunic and got to her feet. "I fear we shall need more cloth, though. I hope the fabric merchant is expected to come around soon."

"I shall send a man out to hunt him up," Lady Gerville said, eyeing her with concern.

Avelyn supposed that because of the way she'd fallen apart after the fire had destroyed her first efforts, Lady Gerville was unsure what to expect this time. But that had been an unusual reaction from Avelyn, a result of exhaustion, she suspected. She hadn't slept much in the days before that disaster. Besides, it had been one of many catastrophes over a short span of time. This was the first untoward event in the three days since arriving here. She wasn't going to fall apart.

Patting the lady's arm as she walked past her, Avelyn said, "I think I shall go see if there is enough ivory cloth left to make a tunic."

Avelyn slipped from the room and walked to her own, the cloth clutched in her hand. She could use the destroyed garment to measure the ivory cloth, and slung it over her shoulder as she knelt at her chest, only to pause and sniff the air. She smelled . . . Avelyn sniffed again, turning her head toward the tunic hanging over her shoulder. Pork. She lifted the garment to press it to her face to be sure. The tunic smelled of pork.

Avelyn sat back and stared at the garment. They'd had pork for dinner the night before, but she had no idea how the scent could have got on the tunic. Avelyn hadn't sewn after the meal last night. She'd gone to talk to Paen instead, and then . . . well, she certainly hadn't even thought of sewing after Paen had come to the room.

She fingered the material. With the tunic smelling as it did, it was no wonder the dogs had gone after it. But how had it ended up smelling of pork? It had to have been done by someone else, but who? Just touching it with grimy fingers wouldn't have done it. The cloth was saturated with the scent, as if the meat had been rubbed across it.

It was the second outfit Avelyn had been making for Paen that had been ruined. The first in the fire and now this. She shook her head at the sudden thought that struck her. Surely someone wasn't sabotaging her efforts? Avelyn couldn't believe it. But she truly had thought she'd blown that candle out in the tent. And now the pork smell. On the other hand, she *had* been incredibly accident prone of late, and it was possible she hadn't blown the candle out after all.

She was being silly, Avelyn decided. Perhaps the smell of pork had gotten on the tunic accidentally . . . though she couldn't see how that could happen. Still, it just *couldn't* have been done deliberately. Everyone was so nice to her.

Avelyn folded the tunic and put it in the chest on top of the ivory cloth, thinking that perhaps it was a good thing that she and Paen were going to Rumsfeld. She didn't think she'd start another tunic until she reached her new home. Just to be safe.

Chapter Thirteen

"Diamanda, I may have a faulty memory, but I am sure you said Rumsfeld was quite lovely," Avelyn said weakly as they rode close enough to see the crumbling walls.

"Aye." The younger woman shook her head helplessly, her own gaze locked on the castle ahead. "It *was* when I saw it."

"How old were you?"

"Six," she admitted.

"I see." Avelyn let her breath out on a sigh, then tried for an expression she hoped was serene as her husband slowed his horse to fall back next to them.

It was a week since the morning Avelyn had discovered Lady Gerville's dogs sleeping on the ruined tunic. A perfectly peaceful, calamity-free week. Avelyn had come to the conclusion that her brief concern that someone might be trying to sabotage her efforts had just been too much imagination. Nothing had happened since then.

Actually, nothing at all had happened during the

last week. It had been a string of boring days and boring evenings. Paen had ridden out with his father to Rumsfeld first thing every morning. The castle was a half-day travel away, and by the time the two men had returned each night, it was quite late. Avelyn was often asleep when Paen returned. If not, she was as soon as he collapsed into bed exhausted and began to snore.

Paen had not bedded Avelyn again since the night they had consummated the wedding—much to her disappointment—and she was once again fighting off the fear that it was purely out of a lack of desire to do so. She tried to tell herself that he was just tired, but it was as if her three cousins had made a place for themselves in her head, for Avelyn could hear their voices claiming that he had only approached her the first time out of duty and now could not bear to be bothered with her plump body again. When those voices arose, she pushed them away and told herself to wait until they were at Rumsfeld to see what would happen. So Avelyn had waited.

In the meantime, she had learned from Lady Gerville that there had been some trouble with reavers at Rumsfeld over the years. Scottish raiders had crossed the nearby border to steal animals and harass the people of the area. It seemed that on one or two occasions, they had attacked the castle itself. This last point, Lady Gerville claimed, was the thing that upset Lord Gerville the most, for his chatelain, Legere, had never informed him of these problems. Instead, he'd chosen to deal with them on his own, much to the detriment of the castle and its people. Apparently, there was a great deal to do, and Paen and his father had been rushing to get all in readiness for Avelyn and Paen to move there.

Avelyn peered at the holes in the outer wall of Rumsfeld with concern. The holes were clearly the result of attacks. Most of them were small, and there was evidence that several much larger holes had been repaired. In some areas, whole sections of the wall had obviously been recently rebuilt. She had no doubt that repairing the walls was one of the chores her husband and his father had been seeing to this last week. Neither man would have been willing to bring their wives to an unsafe castle.

"Rumsfeld is not the home it once was," Paen said once his mount was alongside her.

Avelyn nodded at her husband's words, but managed not to comment.

"It was Mother's childhood home."

Avelyn glanced to where Lady Gerville rode next to her husband. Paen's mother had decided to accompany them to Rumsfeld, so of course Diamanda and Lady Helen had joined the party as well. Realizing that her husband was waiting for some sort of response, Avelyn nodded.

"She will be upset when she sees what time and trouble have done to it."

When Avelyn nodded again, Paen grunted with satisfaction and urged his horse back up beside his father's. She stared after him, rather bewildered as to what she was supposed to understand from their brief conversation. She'd thought at first that he meant to warn or soothe her. Perhaps he wished her to help his mother over any upset the woman might experience when they arrived.

Avelyn would be more than pleased to cheer and comfort her new mother-in-law if the situation arose. The woman had been kindness itself to her. However, if it was what Paen wanted, she wished he'd simply said so. Honestly, men could be the most unforthcoming of creatures.

Shaking her head, she remained silent for the remainder of the journey, paying more attention to Lady Gerville than the bailey itself as they rode through it to the steps of the keep. Paen's mother bore up well at first, though her back did grow straighter with each step the horses took, her neck stretching and head rising higher and higher until Avelyn thought it might snap. Still, those were the only outward signs of her upset.

They dismounted at the steps of the keep. Paen and his father took the horses by the reins and began to lead them toward what she supposed must be the stables, but the building was so full of holes, it was a wonder that it was still standing.

No one commented on the fact that no one was there to take the animals, but Avelyn saw Lady Gerville's fingers tighten where she had them clasped in front of her. After a pause, the lady straightened her shoulders and led the women up the stairs to the keep.

It was when they stepped through the open large double doors and saw the state of the interior that Lady Gerville finally lost some of her composure.

Her eyes widened, her shoulders drooped, and a soft "oh" of dismay and pain slipped from her mouth, which remained open after the sound died.

Avelyn immediately took her arm lest she grow faint. Her touch spurred Lady Gerville to speak. "This is . . . this is—"

"Easily fixed with a little effort," Avelyn finished firmly, garnering a disbelieving look from Diamanda.

Fortunately, Lady Helen was more helpful, murmuring an agreement as they moved toward the trestle table in the center of the hall.

"Oh, Avelyn," Lady Gerville sighed, then turned large eyes on her. "Truly I had not realized . . . You cannot stay here. This is—"

"It will be fine," Avelyn assured her, doing her best to ignore her own dismay at the state of the place. The floor was covered with a scanty carpet of rushes so old there were plants and—worse—molds growing in them. The walls were blackened and soot-stained as if they had never been whitewashed, though Avelyn was sure they must have been while Lady Gerville had lived here. The stairs to the upper floor were in a terrible state of disrepair, with steps missing in places. There were also great large holes—some the size of beds—in the wooden floors of the rooms overhead.

"My poor home," Lady Gerville murmured as she sank onto the table bench under Avelyn's urging, and tumbled to the floor when it collapsed beneath her.

"Are you all right?" Avelyn asked with alarm as she and Lady Helen helped her back to her feet.

"Yes, thank you," Lady Gerville murmured as the women all proceeded to brush at the dust and dirt her fall had collected.

"My skirt is fine, it will wash," Lady Gerville said with a sign when it became obvious their efforts were useless. She then turned to stare forlornly around the great hall, only to pause and blink. "Is that a pig?"

Avelyn followed her gaze, her own eyes widening as she stared at the large sow rooting in the filthy rushes in a corner. As they watched, the beast pawed at the rushes several times, then dropped onto its side with a huff, apparently ready to sleep out of the midday heat.

"I believe it is," Avelyn said faintly, at a loss as to how to react. She knew many people kept their animals inside the keep at night to keep them safe and warm, but her mother hadn't been one of those people, and—aside from her dogs—neither was Lady Gerville. However, Avelyn hadn't a clue what to do about the beast.

"Your mother is bearing up better than I had hoped. I tried to talk her out of coming today, you know," Wimarc Gerville commented as he and Paen finished with the horses and started back toward the keep.

"Did you?" Paen asked.

"Aye. I did not wish her to see her childhood

home like this, but she's a stubborn woman, your mother. Nothing would talk her out of coming to see the two of you settled in." He grimaced. "Now I worry she will try to insist on staying until it is set to rights, or that the two of you should not stay until it is better prepared."

Paen nearly groaned at the idea. The last week of traveling back and forth had been exhausting, but while the walls of Rumsfeld had to be repaired to make it safe to bring Avelyn over, he hadn't been willing to stay here by himself. The lure of his marriage bed had called him home each night, and he had returned only to find himself too exhausted to enjoy it.

He peered down at his hands and squeezed them shut. His mother had removed the last of the bandages that morning, and while the skin felt tight when he closed his hands into fists, he was well pleased with their shape. They were a tad sensitive and were not fully healed, but would do. He couldn't wait to touch Avelyn with them, and planned to do so that very night. Having only journeyed one way this time, Paen was sure the exhaustion that had been plaguing him this last week would not be a problem and he would finally be able to enjoy his sweet, gentle wife again.

"What the devil!"

His father's startled exclamation made Paen glance toward the keep. Both men stopped walking as they took in the struggle taking place at the top of the keep stairs. Paen's sweet, gentle wife, her maid and his usually dignified mother were yelling and shrieking and pushing a rather large sow out of the castle. The three women were positioned at the back of the large, obviously pregnant animal, bent over, hands on the generous hindquarters as they shoved and pushed and tried to force her through the front door of the keep.

Diamanda and her aunt were also there. With no room left at the back of the beast, the aunt stood a safe distance away with a dubious expression. Diamanda was jumping about, clapping her hands and yelling "shoo!" at the top of her lungs as if she thought the louder she yelled, the more likely the animal would hear and understand her.

Heaving his breath out, Paen started forward again. "I guess we had best see to this ere they get themselves bit. Do they not know that pigs have teeth?"

"The question is, does the pig know your mother does?" Wimarc Gerville asked with amusement as he followed.

The two men reached the women before the pig got too annoyed. Paen calmly used an apple to lead the beast down the stairs, while his father ushered the excited women inside. The five of them were standing by the trestle table when Paen returned, his father shaking his head unhappily as Lady Gerville insisted, "They simply cannot stay here, Wimarc."

" 'Twill be fine, my lady," Avelyn said, but Lady Helen shook her head and added her support to Lady Gerville.

"Your wife is right, my lord. Avelyn is a gently bred lady, a noblewoman. You cannot expect the poor child to stay in this rubble."

"We are staying," Paen said firmly as he walked up to them.

His mother turned a displeased scowl his way, but—despite his helplessness the last two weeks—Paen was not a child. He refused to back down. "We will have this place cleaned up and in proper order in no time now that Avelyn is here to direct the servants. She can tend to the inside, while I see to the outside of our home. By the time you return for a visit, it will be in good shape."

"I agree with the boy, Christina," Lord Gerville said. "This is to be their home now, and the repairs will go much more quickly if they are here full-time rather than wasting so many hours riding back and forth to Gerville every day."

"Fine," Lady Gerville said abruptly. "Then I shall stay as well, to help."

"Christina," Lord Gerville chided. "Do you stay, you will simply take over the task as you would at home. 'Tis the girl's home. Let her tend it as she sees fit."

"But . . ." Lady Gerville peered around at the ruin. "There is so much to get done before they will be near comfortable. Help would make it all go so much more quickly."

"I could stay to help," Diamanda offered.

"That is a fine idea," Paen said, then shrugged when everyone turned to stare at him. "She can help out, and be company for Avelyn as well. If

Lady Helen will allow it," he added. Diamanda's aunt pursed her lips, then nodded.

"Certainly we can stay. It will be useful for Diamanda. After helping here, she will be more than capable of handling any emergency a noblewoman might encounter," Lady Helen said dryly.

"But—" Lady Gerville began, even as Avelyn protested, "Oh, that really isn't necessary." They were both overridden by Paen's father.

"That sounds a perfect solution. We shall send your things from Gerville when we return, and return ourselves in a week to collect you ladies and bring you back. However, if you change your mind at any time and wish to return to Gerville before that, you are welcome and Paen will supply an escort." He waited for both women to nod, then clapped his hands. "Good, good. Well, we may as well head out home then and leave you to gather your servants for the task ahead. We've a long journey back."

"But, Wimarc, we just got here," Lady Gerville protested.

"I told you I did not plan to stay long and you should not trouble yourself to come," he pointed out. "I only wished to be sure the last section of wall was finished this morning as ordered. It had to be done ere Avelyn and Paen could stay here."

"Aye, but—"

"I had Sely pack a picnic for us to enjoy on the return trip," Lord Gerville went on. "Let us go so the children can start setting things to rights here. They shall want much done ere nightfall so that they can sleep comfortably."

Paen held his breath, sure his mother would protest further, but she gave in with a sigh.

"Good!" He patted her arm. "I shall leave you to find out what the ladies wish sent from Gerville, and to say your good-byes, while I have a word with Paen."

Paen walked outside with his father, nodding as the older man gave suggestions and advice on what to see to next. Apparently, while Lord Gerville thought his lady wife should not give advice to Avelyn on running the household, he was not of the same opinion when it came to his son. Paen didn't mind, though.

They were just winding up their talk when the women finally made their way out of the castle. Paen had no idea what the women had been discussing inside. He was sure that Lady Helen and Diamanda had given his mother a long list of things they wished sent on, and he doubted very much if his mother had managed to avoid giving some instruction to Avelyn. It was second nature to her after training Diamanda for so long. However, he didn't know what was responsible for the red-eyed, sniffling state of the women.

"Women," his father sighed his exasperation as the women approached. "You would think we were going to be three days' travel apart rather than half a day's journey."

"Aye," Paen agreed.

"Come along, wife. They will not be far away," Lord Gerville said when the women paused at the bottom of the stairs to embrace each other in a tearful tableau.

Reluctantly stepping away, Lady Gerville moved to give Paen a hug, holding him so tightly he feared she would crack a rib ere she let him go. "Take care of her, son. She's a very sweet girl."

Paen nodded, though he wasn't sure whom she was referring to. His first instinct was that she meant Avelyn, but he did not to think of his wife as a girl. Diamanda was a girl. Paen's wife was all woman.

"Christina," Wimarc said in long-suffering tones.

"Men," his mother muttered, but finally released Paen and moved to mount her horse.

"We shall visit in a week's time and see how things are going," Lord Gerville announced as he too mounted. "Send a messenger if you have any trouble."

Paen nodded, then watched his parents ride out of the bailey, with their men and Lady Gerville's maid following. The moment they were out of the bailey and heading for the hill, Paen turned to glance at the women at the base of the steps. They were staring after the small traveling party as if watching their very last friend ride away.

Shaking his head, Pain cleared his throat to draw their attention. "I shall leave the servants and keep to you while I see about matters out here. Come find me if you need me."

"Aye, husband," Avelyn murmured and even managed a smile.

Paen grunted his satisfaction and turned to cross the bailey to where several men were repairing the smaller holes in the wall. Rumsfeld had been in terrible shape when Paen and his father had come to inspect things a week earlier.

Legere had run the castle since Paen's grandfather's death, shortly after his parents had married. While his parents had made visits to the castle when he was a boy, Paen couldn't recall them returning there in the last ten years at least. It had been a mistake his father bitterly regretted when he'd seen the dilapidated state of the place last week. Legere had been no young man when he'd first taken up the role of chatelain, but he had been very old by the time of his death, obviously too old to take care of the castle properly, and too stubborn to admit it.

Paen's father was apparently the only person in the area who hadn't known the man was no longer up to the task of running Rumsfeld. Certainly, the Scots who had stolen all the cattle and repeatedly attacked the castle had been aware of it. They'd carried away everything of value that wasn't nailed down, including parts of the wall itself.

All that had been left when Paen and his father first arrived to inspect the castle was a broken wall, a shell of a keep with rotten wood everywhere, a band of tatty servants, fifty poorly dressed soldiers and a couple of pigs and chickens.

The first problem Paen had encountered was the soldiers. The men had been surly and resentful that their lord had neglected them so by leaving them to an incompetent chatelain and never troubling himself to check on them.

It had taken Paen the better part of two days to assure the men that things would now change for the better. It was only then that he'd managed to get much work out of them, but they'd worked hard since, and things were coming along nicely. The extra men his father had brought from Gerville helped too, and if things continued as they were, he expected to have Rumsfeld back to its original state by autumn. At least the outside. He needed to finish repairing the walls and build new stables, a blacksmith's hut, a cobbler's and other critical structures. He also needed to find good people to fill the positions. The skilled men had fled long ago, taking their skills where they would be better appreciated.

Paen was hoping that Avelyn would have the inside of the keep in shape long before that. Her job should be easy compared to his, he thought as he reached the men working on the wall and joined them in the endeavor. It was mostly a matter of cleaning, and he doubted the servants would be as resentful and hard to deal with as the soldiers had been.

He was rather proud of her reaction to the keep's sorry state. His father had been positive she would be upset, but Paen had guessed otherwise. In his experience, nothing made a woman happier than setting things to rights, and there was plenty for her to set to rights here.

Aye, he thought, Avelyn would have the keep

shipshape in no time. No doubt, right that moment she had an army of servants cleaning like mad.

"Husband?"

Paen turned from the wall to watch his wife approach. He found himself licking his lips as her hips swayed and her breasts jiggled as she walked. He had high hopes for being able to bed her tonight. Without the return journey to wear him out, Paen expected not to drop into exhausted sleep the moment he lay down.

"Husband? Did you hear me?" Avelyn asked, and Paen frowned as he realized that she'd been speaking and he'd been too busy anticipating the evening ahead to hear her.

"No," he admitted. "What did you say?"

"I said I have lost the servants."

Paen stared. And stared. Then, sure he'd heard her wrong, he asked, "Excuse me?"

"Well, I have not really lost them. I simply cannot find them," Avelyn said. "They are neither in the hall nor the kitchen, and I have no idea where else to look."

"Have you tried above stairs?" Paen asked.

Avelyn stared at her husband blankly. "They could not possibly be upstairs, husband. The steps are broken."

"Only three or four of them," he pointed out. "Otherwise they are sound enough. Father and I used them the first day we came here. The servants are probably upstairs preparing the rooms for the night."

"Oh." Avelyn shifted from one foot to the other,

then sighed and murmured dubiously, "I shall check above stairs."

Leaving him to his work, Avelyn returned to the keep. She quickly came upon Runilda, who was digging through the items on the back of the cart. The maid was in search of cleaning equipment, something they had not seen much of in the castle when they'd gone to find the servants. Avelyn left her to her chore and walked up the stairs and into the hall.

"Where is Lady Helen?" she asked Diamanda. The girl stood staring at the remains of the bench that had collapsed beneath Lady Gerville.

"She went to see if there is an herb garden behind the kitchens. She said she expects that if there is it will have grown wild, but hopes it may be salvageable."

Avelyn nodded. She hadn't even considered that issue yet, but a garden and the herbs and medicinal plants it provided could be as indispensable as a well. The thought made her say, "I wonder where the well is. There should be one. Even if the original were contaminated, Paen and his father would have had a new one dug."

"Aye, and we shall need water to clean with." Diamanda glanced toward the door. "Shall I go ask him?"

"Would you mind? I needs must check upstairs for the servants."

Diamanda's eyes widened incredulously. "Why? It is not safe, and they cannot possibly be up there."

"Aye, well, I do not think so either, but Paen

suggested they may be up there preparing the rooms."

Diamanda snorted at the idea.

Avelyn smiled slightly. "Please go check with Paen on where the well is and I shall look for the servants."

Diamanda hesitated. "Well, be careful. Those stairs do not look at all safe."

"Nor does the floor up there," she acknowledged. "I shall be careful."

She waited until Diamanda had headed for the door, then started cautiously up the stairs, gripping the rail when there was one. She retained a clear image of the bench collapsing beneath Lady Gerville, and with her own recent record of accidents and calamities, was not all that confident she was going to master the stairs without at least scraping a knee.

Avelyn grimaced at the thought and wondered why she was even bothering with this task. In truth, she thought it a fool's errand. However, Paen seemed to think the servants would be found up there, busily preparing the upper rooms, and so she would check. It was hard to believe they would be busily working away in the bed chambers when they obviously had not lifted a finger to make any preparations in the great hall . . . or the kitchens, for that matter.

If the great hall was bad, the kitchens were worse. There the floors and counters and tables were just as neglected as the hall; but also coated with layers of grease and smoke. Avelyn's slippers had stuck to the floor and she'd been afraid to touch anything.

Avelyn had nearly made it to the top of the stairs when the step she was on creaked ominously. She leapt back, nearly falling through the missing stair she'd just stepped over. She landed on one knee on the edge of the broken step, the other leg dangling into space through the hole and both hands on the railing.

"Sound enough," she muttered her husband's words to herself as she held on to the rail with a death grip and pulled her leg back up through the hole. She didn't have to look at her leg to know she'd scraped it nicely. The burning pain in her shin told her as much. Gritting her teeth against the pain, she got shakily back to her feet.

Avelyn leaned against the wall briefly and considered turning back, but there were only a couple of stairs left after the missing step. Slowly letting her breath out, she forced herself to straighten and continued up, this time being sure to keep her foot as close to the wall as possible as she bypassed the missing step. She was sure the wood closest to the wall would be the least likely to give out on her.

Much to her relief, there was no creak this time and she continued safely up the last few steps. On the landing, she released a relieved breath, then paused to lift her skirt and look at her legs.

Aye, she'd done a fine job on her shin, she

thought with disgust as she let the skirt drop back into place. She could only hope the trip back down would be less eventful.

Now that she was above stairs, Avelyn realized that she should have brought a torch with her. While the open doors allowed light into the great hall, the hallways were much darker. Avelyn eased forward, feeling her way carefully with her foot. From below she had been able to see the great holes in the wooden floor and had no desire to step into one.

Avelyn checked each of the three rooms on the second floor. The first room was the biggest, and she supposed it was the one Legere had used. If so, either he hadn't owned much, or his possessions had been stolen after he died. The room held nothing but a rickety old bed. The next two rooms, however, had nothing at all. They weren't even furnished and both had at least two holes in the floor. The last room had the biggest hole, though it wasn't quite as big as she'd thought. Avelyn doubted a bed would fit through it.

She stopped a few feet from the hole and leaned forward to peer through it. The great hall below looked no better from the higher vantage point. The rushes really were in a shameful state. The entire castle was.

Shaking her head, she started to back away from the hole, then paused when a creak sounded behind her. She had half turned when what felt like a plank of wood slammed into the side of her face. Avelyn stumbled under the blow, falling sideways.

That was probably what saved her. She reached instinctively for the floor as she fell, but while her right hand slapped it with a stinging impact, her left hand found only open air. Then her head slammed into a broken bit of wood and darkness rushed to claim her as she felt herself falling through the hole she'd been looking through.

Chapter Fourteen

The first thing Avelyn noticed on waking was that her head was pounding. She didn't think she'd ever experienced such pain and squeezed her eyes tightly shut in reaction, but that only seemed to make it worse.

"Avy?"

Recognizing Diamanda's voice, Aveyln forced her eyes open and peered up at the girl with confusion. She stared at the pretty blonde's anxious face, then let her gaze drift past her to the cloth overhead and all around them.

"The traveling tent." Her voice was a husky whisper and she licked her lips, then swallowed before trying again. "Why?"

"Paen had the men set it up so that we would have someplace to put you," Diamanda explained. "You hit your head pretty badly when you fell."

"Fell," Avelyn echoed with confusion; then her heart jumped as she recalled standing in the upper room, being hit, falling forward and her left hand finding no purchase as it went through the hole in the floor. She also now remembered her head slamming into what had felt like broken wood. The edge of the hole, she thought. Then she'd realized she was falling through the hole.

"Someone hit me," Avelyn said. "I fell through the hole."

"Hit you?" Diamanda shook her head. "Paen said you must have hit your head on the side of the hole. Your face was scraped, and there was blood on the planks upstairs."

"No, someone hit me," Avelyn insisted weakly, then glanced to her other side as Lady Helen patted her hand and leaned forward.

"It must have been a dream, dear. You were alone above stairs." She gave her a reproving look. "You never should have gone up there in the first place. You are fortunate you did not fall down the stairs and break your neck. As it is, if it weren't for your skirt catching on the edge of a broken plank, you would have certainly fallen to your death when you stumbled through the hole."

"My skirt?" Avelyn asked.

"Aye, my lady." Runilda stepped closer to the bed, peering at her over Lady Helen's shoulder. "I was coming into the hall with buckets and a broom when you fell through the hole." The maid pressed a hand to her chest as if the very memory made her heart flutter. "You fell several feet, but your skirt caught on something and you jerked to a stop and

249

just dangled there, hanging by your skirt like a doll made of rags." Runilda bit her lip and shook her head. "I just stood there screaming."

"I heard her screaming and came running," Diamanda said.

"As did I." Lady Helen shuddered delicately. "I never want to hear a scream like that again. I thought my heart would stop with fear."

"Aye." Diamanda nodded agreement. "It was chilling. I thought Runilda had hurt herself, then I saw you hanging there." She gave a little shiver at the memory. "I sent Runilda for Paen and hurried upstairs to see if I could help you."

"Which was where I caught up with Diamanda." Lady Helen squeezed Avelyn's hand gently. "The silly child was trying to figure out how to unhook you so she could pull you back up, but I cautioned her to wait for Paen. She wasn't nearly strong enough to pull you back up."

"The cloth was straining," Diamanda said irritably in response to her aunt's condescending tone. "I was afraid the cloth would tear and she would fall to her death."

"That was a concern," Lady Helen admitted on a sigh, "But had you unhooked her as you wanted to do, you might both have gone over."

Diamanda snorted with irritation at the possibility "I'm stronger than you think."

"Child, she is much heavier than you," Lady Helen said patiently. "You never could have held her weight."

"So Paen got me down? Or up, as the case may be?" Avelyn queried to end the argument.

"Aye." Diamanda turned to smile, her eyes brightening. "He is so strong. He lifted you with one hand. He just knelt at the side of the hole, reached down, caught your skirt and lifted you right up. Then he carried you below and started bellowing orders to the men."

"The men?" Avelyn peered at her with confusion.

"Aye. Well, when Runilda went running down to fetch Paen, the men hurried back with him," Diamanda informed her. "They all just froze in the hall staring up at you for a minute, even Paen. They were all horror-struck, of course; then Paen sent the men to fetch the tent cloth and they held it out tight beneath you in the hall, in case you fell before he could pull you up."

"Of course, by the time they had the material stretched out beneath you, Paen had already reached you and was pulling you up" Helen said. "Once he'd carried you downstairs, he ordered the men to set up the tent out in front of the keep so that he would have someplace to lay you while you recovered."

"Aye, my lady. Your husband was so concerned, he held you the whole time while the men set up the tent," Runilda told her with a smile. Avelyn was just feeling her heart thrill at her husband's public show of affection when Diamanda spoke up.

"Well, of course he did. There was nowhere to set her down until the tent was up and we'd arranged the furs inside," the girl said practically.

"We should let Avelyn rest," Lady Helen said with a frown at Diamanda as the small smile that had started on Avelyn's face died a quick death. "We should go see how the men are getting on."

"The men?" Avelyn asked as Diamanda's aunt stood.

"Aye," Diamanda answered. "Paen set some of them to fixing the stairs and the floor on the upper level. The rest are removing the old rushes from the great hall so that it may be scrubbed."

"I see," Avelyn whispered.

"Do not fear," the younger girl said as she got to her feet. "You need not see the men today. Rest and recover—we will oversee them."

"Why would I not wish to see the men?" Avelyn asked with bewilderment.

"Well . . ." The petite blonde looked nonplused for a moment, then said, "I just thought you may be too embarrassed after everything."

"Everything?" Avelyn asked, feeling dread well in her. "What everything?"

"I thought you might be embarrassed that they had all seen . . ." She paused as if just realizing that Avelyn didn't know.

"Come, let her rest; there is no need for her to know." When Lady Helen tugged at Diamanda's arm, the girl followed her quickly out of the tent.

Avelyn turned her gaze to Runilda. "There is no need for me to know what? What did all the men see?"

The maid sighed unhappily, but knew her mistress well. Avelyn would require an answer.

"You were mostly upright, hanging by the back of your skirt, my lady," Runilda explained with discomfort and gestured behind herself.

Avelyn stared at her with dawning horror. "Was all revealed?"

"Nay," the maid hurried to reassure her. "The skirt caught under your arms at the sides and draped over . . . er . . . well it was above your knees in front. Well above," she added.

"And the back?" Avelyn asked. Runilda's expression was answer enough. It seemed—like the day Paen had thought she'd drowned—the men had once again gotten a good look at her backside. "My husband must think me such a pickle."

"Oh, nay, my lady." Runilda knelt at her side and squeezed her hand. "Truly, he went white when he saw you were in peril, and he would not put you down once he had you in his arms. He held you for ever so long, just staring at you with concern. I think he is growing to care for you."

Avelyn found that hard to believe. She was not exactly the perfect wife. In fact, she would guess that to Paen she was something of a nightmare. Too tired to once again make a mental listing of all the injuries and accidents she'd caused or been involved with since her wedding day, Avelyn simply asked, "Where is my husband?"

"After he assured himself you would recover, he set the men to work, then rode out for the village. I believe he is going to see about servants."

Avelyn grimaced at this news. Paen was supposed to tend to the outside of the keep while she tended to the inside. Once again her clumsiness had simply laid more of a burden on Paen. Her husband may not have been injured this time, as he had when his hands had gotten burned in the fire she'd started, but the chores he was tending to were supposed to be her responsibility.

Well, she would not allow that. It was too late to stop him from going to the village in search of servants, but she could at least oversee the men while he was gone. Avelyn started to rise, pausing half upright on the furs when pain rushed through her and nausea followed.

"Please, my lady." Runilda was immediately pushing at her shoulders, trying to urge her back down. "Rest. You were sorely injured."

Avelyn gritted her teeth and brushed the maid's hands aside as she forced herself upright. "I wish to get up, Runilda. My head will ache whether I am lying or standing."

Giving an exasperated sigh, Runilda stopped trying to force her back down and instead put a hand under her arm to help her to her feet.

With Runilda's aid, Avelyn managed to stand. She leaned heavily on the maid and made it out of the tent before the first wave of nausea hit her. Standing very still, she took deep breaths and assured herself that the longer she was up, the better she would feel. Avelyn wasn't sure she believed it, but it mattered little. Her husband had continued to do everything he had to do with injured hands. She would manage to order some men about with a sore head.

As Runilda helped her into the great hall, the first place Avelyn looked was toward the floors overhead. She spotted the hole she thought she'd fallen through and stared at it silently, recalling the last moments before the fall. Despite what Diamanda and Lady Helen had said, Avelyn was sure she'd been hit. Her mind was a tad confused, but . . . She could still feel the stunning blow; the pain had been sharp and hard and had knocked her off balance. She remembered falling, and realizing there was nothing beneath her left hand; then she'd suffered another sharp pain as her head hit the far broken edge of the hole.

Aye, Avelyn was sure someone had hit her. But who? One of the missing servants? The rooms had seemed empty, but . . .

Nay, she had not yet even met the people here. They would have no reason to harm her.

The ruined tunic came to mind. Avelyn recalled the scent of pork on the cloth and her brief fears that someone was sabotaging her efforts, but she quickly brushed the thought away. The two events could not be connected. Ruining her sewing efforts was an entirely different prospect than attacking her.

"Avy! Whatever are you doing up?" Diamanda rushed toward her with concern and Avelyn let her thoughts go. There was work to do.

The moon was high and full by the time Paen rode back into the bailey. He'd had a long night. His trip to the village had proved fruitless. If anyone there was a servant from the castle, they were not admitting it, and not one person had been willing to work at Rumsfeld. Had they been serfs, Paen could have ordered them to the castle, but he'd been informed that the serfs had fled Rumsfeld long before Legere had died. The inhabitants of the village claimed to all be freemen, peasants free to do as they liked so long as they helped tend the castle fields. Without any idea what else to do, Paen had left the village and headed for Gerville. Servants were needed to clean up and run the castle, and he had to get them somewhere.

He'd made the long journey to his parents' home, explained the situation to his father over a meal, then got back on his horse and headed home, his ears ringing with his father's promise to take care of the matter. They should have servants at Rumsfeld by early afternoon of the next day. Now he was returning to Rumsfeld, arriving later than ever he had returned to Gerville during this past week.

Paen rode straight to the broken-down stables. He bedded down his mount, being sure to give him extra feed after the long journey, then walked wearily to the keep. The bailey was completely silent as he crossed it. If it weren't for the men standing guard on the wall to watch for attack, he would have thought the castle had been abandoned. In all his years, Paen had never seen a bailey this silent and empty of activity. It was rather disturbing.

Even more bothersome was the fact that the tent was no longer set up out front as it had been when he'd left. The realization gave Paen a moment's worry before he calmed himself with the thought that Avelyn must have woken up and had it taken away. She was probably resting and recovering from her injuries inside.

She'd better be, he thought, and felt his heart squeeze as he recalled the vision of her dangling high above the hall. Paen was sure the sight had scared a good ten years off his life. It made him feel sick just to think of it. Even more upsetting had been the state of her face when he'd pulled her up. Avelyn had obviously hit her head in the fall, and blood had dripped from a cut on her forehead, spreading down her cheek in rivulets that resembled the long, thin talons of a very large bird. At first, he'd feared she was dead, and had been more than relieved when he'd gotten her up through the hole and saw her chest rise and fall as he held her in his arms. Paen had then found himself reluctant to set her down even when the tent was ready and a bed of furs had been thrown quickly together.

Avelyn was either the most fortunate or unfortunate of women. In the short time he'd known her, she'd survived fire, drowning and now a deadly fall. Though she hadn't really been in danger during the fire, he supposed, still . . .

Paen shook his head. His mother had claimed that the fates seemed at odds with Avelyn since their marriage. It had been her first comment when she'd heard about the latest calamity to befall her new daughter-in-law. Then she'd explained about the dogs attacking Avelyn's latest efforts at clothes for him. Paen was beginning to suspect it was something more than that, though he had nothing to base those suspicions on other than a sense that there were just too many unusual incidents.

Some things weren't adding up. His mother loved her dogs, but she also demanded obedience and good behavior from them and trained them accordingly. In all the time she'd had them, Boudica and Juno had never before attacked anything. Yet, from his mother's description, the animals had ripped the tunic to shreds. And then there was the fire in the tent. He could still recall Avelyn's earnest face as she'd assured him that she'd blown out the candle. Her certainty had waned only when he'd suggested she'd been in a hurry and had not paid enough attention to be sure the candle was out.

This latest incident was what really made him wonder. His father had asked how it had happened, and Paen simply hadn't been able to explain it. He and his father both had been in the room when they'd first inspected the castle. Even if she hadn't seen the holes from the floor below, Avelyn would have noted them at once on entering the room. She couldn't have missed seeing the hole. It was simply impossible.

Nay, Paen felt sure no one could be this unlucky. Something was amiss, and he intended to question his wife carefully about this latest accident. He would also keep a closer eye on her. And would finally start on his campaign to show Avelyn her own value. It was something he'd too long neglected.

The keep's double doors were wide open in welcome and Paen stepped inside. He paused to look around his great hall. Every last one of the men was sprawled on the great-hall floor, snoring up a storm. They were sleeping the deep sleep of the exhausted, and it took little more than a glance around to see why. They had worked hard in his absence. The hall floor was now covered with a thick carpet of fresh rushes. He couldn't see the stairs in the dim light from the fireplace, but suspected they were probably mended and safe again.

Paen was sure there were other changes as well, but it was late and he was willing to wait until morning to inspect them. For now, he simply wanted to know where his wife was. He wouldn't be able to relax until he'd seen that she really had recovered. His gaze was drawn to the tent in the center of the hall. Tired as he was, he'd scarcely noticed it at first. This, then, was where the tent had gotten to. It had been moved from outside to the middle of the great hall. He had no doubt it was his wife's idea—and he fully expected to find her inside.

Had he the energy, Paen would have laughed at the sight of the tent surrounded by sleeping men. Shaking his head at her ingenuity in providing herself and him with a private haven in the midst of their people, Paen began to weave his way through the bodies of his sleeping men.

It was a testament to their exhaustion that not one of the men stirred as he crossed the floor. Paen supposed that spending the morning hauling rock for the outer wall, then the afternoon and probably early evening cleaning and repairing the castle, had knocked out the majority of them.

He managed to reach the tent without tripping over anyone, then slipped silently inside. In here it was pitch-black. He realized there would be no way to check his wife's injuries. He slowly moved across the tent toward the back right corner, where he imagined the furs would be laid out as they had been on the journey to Gerville. Paen immediately stumbled over something on the floor.

Put off balance, he muttered a curse and half hopped and half stumbled to the corner. The moment his foot hit the furs, Paen lost the last of his balance and tumbled to the floor, grunting as he landed. The women had been awfully sparing with the furs, it seemed, but he supposed he should just be grateful he had not landed on and crushed his wife. It had been a close call, he realized when she rolled over in her sleep and curled against him as he lay there.

"My lord?"

Paen froze when those words came to him from out of the darkness.

"Runilda?" he asked, sure it was his wife's maid's voice addressing him from the floor near where he'd tripped.

"Aye, my lord. Why are you not above stairs with Lady Avelyn?"

Paen froze, his eyes shooting downward as he

tried to make out the figure lying next to him in the dark.

"Paen?" Diamanda's sleepy voice drifted up to him and he felt her hand move against his legs as if she couldn't believe he was there.

And then, astonishingly, Lady Helen was heard to mutter, "Good heavens—what is going on?" from another corner.

Cursing, Paen launched himself to his feet and stumbled back across the tent, so flustered by his mistake that he didn't even think to mutter an apology before escaping out into the safety of the great hall.

He hurried across the hall, leaping over bodies and moving too quickly through the darkness. He nearly knocked his wife over before he saw her.

"Husband?" Avelyn caught at his arms to keep her feet as he reached to steady her.

"Aye. What are you doing up?"

"I heard you ride in. When you did not come above stairs, I realized you did not know where our bed is. So I came to find you."

"Oh." He sighed as she felt for his hand in the dark, then followed when she turned to lead him up the stairs. Paen remained silent as they moved through the pitch-black hall, depending on her to know the way. Much to his relief, when they reached the room he was able to see again by the soft glow of a fire in the fireplace.

The light revealed the bandage around her head, and Paen frowned at the sight of it. "How is your head?"

261

"It's fine, thank you," Avelyn murmured, then changed the subject. "Runilda told me you had gone to the village."

"Aye." He glanced around the room, noting that she'd not only had the room cleaned and new rushes put down, but had had their chests moved in from the wagon. She'd also had the old bed removed. Paen knew Legere's bed had been in bad shape, but had expected to make do until a new one could be made. However, Avelyn had made a nest of furs for them to sleep on.

"I thought you were in the tent," he blurted out.

Her eyebrows rose. "Nay. We ran out of time before we could prepare a second room for Diamanda and Lady Helen, so I had the tent set up to allow them some privacy from the men. Runilda is in with them." She smiled faintly. "I guess 'tis good I came to find you ere you stumbled in there and woke everyone up."

Paen grimaced. "I did stumble in there and woke everyone up. It was not until Runilda asked why I was not up here with you that I realized my mistake."

Avelyn gave a soft laugh, then shrugged. "They are probably already asleep again, my lord. Everyone was exhausted after the day's work." She paused and asked, "Were you able to convince any villagers to work in the castle? That is why you went to the village, is it not?"

"Aye, that is why, but I had no luck. No one there was willing to work for us. The village is poor and in no better shape than the castle. Between Legere and the reavers, they have been beaten down time and again. They are angry, and resent that Father neglected to look out for their welfare as he should have done," he admitted on a sigh. " 'Tis why I took so long. I rode to Gerville. Father promised to visit the village at Gerville first thing in the morning and arrange for new servants for here. He will send them at once, and they should start arriving by noon."

"Oh." She nodded. "Well, good. The men got a lot done today, but there is still much to do. The servants will be welcome." Avelyn shifted on her feet, then glanced around the room. "Are you hungry or thirsty?"

"Nay. I ate at Gerville."

She nodded, then turned to walk toward the bed of furs. "It is late and you look exhausted. I should stop asking you questions and let you get some sleep."

Paen followed her to the bed, a small sigh slipping from his lips. He *was* tired, and she'd had a terrible fall today. Neither of them was in any shape for him to bed her, but that didn't stop him from wishing he could.

Tomorrow, he promised himself as he disrobed and climbed into the nest of furs next to her. He would definitely make love to his wife tomorrow.

Chapter Fifteen

Paen was gone and bright sunlight was pouring into the room when Avelyn woke up. Blinking sleepily, she peered toward the window. While she'd slept, someone had removed the furs Runilda had hung over the opening the night before. Either Paen had done it before leaving the room, or Runilda had already been up in the room at least once that morning.

As if drawn by her thoughts, the door opened and Runilda entered carrying a basin of water.

"You are awake." The maid smiled as she crossed the room. "How do you feel?"

"Better," Avelyn admitted after a pause to take inventory. Much to her relief, the pain that had been hammering at her head through the afternoon and evening before was now gone. The fact was enough to make her smile as she sat up in bed. "Much better, thank you, Runilda. Where is my husband?"

"He has been working on the wall with the men

since first light," the maid announced as she carried the washbasin to the chest.

As Avelyn went to wash she pondered what she would do that day. The chests they had brought with them were the only furniture they had in the keep and had doubled as seats and tables the day before. Avelyn decided that was a situation that should be rectified.

The inside of the keep was her responsibility, and she had every intention of taking care of it. She thought she might make a trip to the village that morning before the servants started to arrive from Gerville. Paen had said the village had suffered as badly from the reavers as Rumsfeld had, and Avelyn hoped to relieve some of the poverty and repair some of the hard feelings by having all their goods made in the village.

Furniture wasn't the only thing she would need to purchase, she thought as her stomach grumbled. At the moment, they had no cook at Rumsfeld, and while they did have the foods they'd brought with them, those wouldn't last long. However, she suspected they wouldn't be easily replaced either. The only animal she'd seen so far was the pig that had decided to bed down in the great hall when they arrived. She feared it might be the only livestock they had.

"I shall go let the men know they can start work on the floors in the other rooms now," Runilda said as she laid a clean gown on the chest. "Lord Paen ordered them not to start hammering until you were awake," Runilda explained when Avelyn glanced at her with surprise.

"How long have they been waiting?" Avelyn asked with a frown.

"Half the morning," Runilda said with amusement, then added, "But they kept busy while they waited. Lady Helen had them cleaning and carting in the kitchens."

"Half the morning?" Avelyn echoed with horror. She hadn't realized she'd slept so late. "Why did you not wake me?"

"Lord Paen said to let you sleep as late as you needed, that it would help you heal."

Avelyn let a little sigh slip from her lips. It had been thoughtful of him, but there was much she wished to get done today and the morning was half over.

"I shall just let the men know they can start work, then I'll return to help you dress," Runilda assured her, then slipped from the room.

Avelyn turned her attention to her ablutions, using the rose-scented water and a small strip of linen to wash herself. She heard Runilda open the door again minutes later, but continued to wash, lifting one foot to rest on the chest as she ran the cloth over her leg. When hands closed over her shoulders, she jumped in surprise, then whirled to find herself facing Paen.

"Oh, husband, you startled me," she said breathlessly, then realized she was standing there naked before him. She raised her little linen between them, trying to cover herself with the bit of

cloth. It was a futile effort, worse than useless, really, and Paen gave it the attention it deserved.
None. Ignoring the damp cloth, he caught her by
the upper arms and drew her forward. He then
lowered his head and covered her mouth with his.

At first, Avelyn stood still, too flustered to respond, but Paen soon made her forget her embarrassment. When his tongue slipped out to tease her
lips, she automatically let them drift open and
breathed a small sigh into his mouth as his tongue
slid in. A familiar heat immediately began to pool
inside her. Avelyn soon forgot her linen and let it
drop so she could slip her hands around his neck.
Paen was fully clothed, and the cloth of his tunic
and braes felt rough against her tender flesh, as he
cupped her behind and urged her against him. The
cloth of his tunic rubbed across the sensitive tips of
her breasts, sending a shiver along her back.

When Paen broke the kiss and his lips trailed to
her neck, Avelyn let her head fall back, her fingers
knotting in his hair. She had thought his mouth
would continue down to her breasts as it had when
they'd finally consummated their marriage, but instead, he pulled his lips away. She gave a little start
as he cupped one breast and squeezed gently. Then
he caught the nipple between thumb and forefin-
ger, teasing it until it was hard and aching. Only
then did he finally drop his mouth to lave it.

"Oh," Avelyn breathed as he caught her nipple
between his teeth and nipped lightly. She gasped and
rose up on tiptoes as the hand that had been holding
her breast suddenly swept down between her legs.

He cupped her there briefly, pressing firmly upward; then his fingers slid between the folds and Avelyn found herself clutching desperately at his shoulders as his fingers danced over her most tender flesh.

"Husband?" Avelyn gasped uncertainly as she felt her body begin to tighten with familiar excitement.

Raising his head, Paen claimed her mouth again, his kiss more aggressive this time, his tongue thrusting into her almost forcefully. As it did, she felt his finger slip inside her, and Avelyn cried out into his mouth, her hips bucking instinctively into the caress, and doing so again as his finger slid out and then back in more deeply. She could feel her nails digging into his skin, but couldn't seem to help herself as she rode the pleasure he was giving her.

Had Hugo really said a man's hands were not needed for the bedding? Perhaps they weren't—certainly her husband had proven that the first time they'd consummated the wedding—but, dear God, they could add so much pleasure. Paen drove her off the edge with just his touch until she cried out and sagged against him.

She was nothing but a senseless, trembling mass when Paen scooped her up into his arms and carried her to the furs. Avelyn did not even mind that she was naked, fully exposed as he laid her out on the bed. Her eyes were drowsy and she felt almost drugged as she watched him strip off his tunic and shed his braes. This time Avelyn felt no fear at the size of him, but could enjoy the beauty of his physique as he straightened, then knelt on the furs by her feet.

Watching her face, Paen caught her by one ankle and lifted it to rest on his shoulder, then caught the other and raised it as well. Avelyn blinked, unsure what he was doing, then he slid his hands under her hips and pulled her forward across the furs until his manhood pressed against her. She stared at him with confusion. This was something else her mother hadn't mentioned. Then he slid into her, and Avelyn's back bowed, a surprised moan slipping from her lips as he filled her.

With Paen out of her reach, she found herself clutching at the bed linens on either side of her head as he withdrew and then drove into her again. He reached between them to caress the sensitive center of her as he thrust again. Avelyn cried out, her head twisting on the linen-covered furs as her sensitive body immediately responded. Her heels dug into his shoulders, her legs flexing as one foot slid off his shoulder. Rather than catch it and pull it back up, Paen moved her other ankle off and leaned over her, holding his weight off of her with his arms as he continued to drive into her until they both cried out with pleasure.

Avelyn was as limp as a wet linen as Paen shifted off of her. He settled himself beside her, then drew her into his arms, moving her head to where he wanted it on his chest. She smiled faintly at the action, finding it adorable, for some reason. Avelyn was suddenly too tired to bother to try to sort it out. She simply let her eyes drift closed and allowed her husband's heartbeat to lull her into sleep.

* * *

It was nearly noon the next time Avelyn woke up, and her husband had again already left the bed. She didn't mind, though; it allowed her privacy to wash and dress. Avelyn couldn't even seem to mind that once again she'd slept the morning away. She smiled as she descended the stairs . . . until she spotted the activity by the fireplace in the great hall.

Avelyn paused on the stairs, gripped the new rail the men had put on the night before and stared in disbelief. The sow had returned. Runilda and Diamanda were trying to get the beast on her feet and out of the keep, but the sow appeared to have a stubborn streak. She was ignoring all their efforts to rouse her.

Shaking her head, Avelyn hurried down the stairs and crossed the hall to join Lady Helen, who was standing to the side, wringing her hands as Diamanda poked at the pig, trying to get it to its feet.

"Oh, do be careful, Diamanda," her aunt said with concern. "Can you not fetch one of the men to scare it out of here?"

"Paen used an apple to lure it out yesterday," Avelyn said as she paused beside Lady Helen.

"Oh, Avelyn, dear. How are you feeling? Has the rest helped your head? I know you were in terrible pain yesterday." Lady Helen forgot her worry for a moment to offer Avelyn a smile.

"I am much better, thank you," Avelyn murmured.

"I did try an apple, but she doesn't appear to be interested," Diamanda announced. Pulling an apple from her skirt, she held it before the pig, but the trick wasn't working this time.

"Oh, well, perhaps . . ." Avelyn paused. She had started to walk around the animal, but had only taken a couple of steps before she saw what the trouble was. "Oh, dear."

"What is it?" Diamanda asked, moving curiously toward her.

"I am afraid we are not moving her for a while."

"What? Why?" the petite blonde asked, then reached Avelyn's side, peered at the animal and breathed, "Oh."

"What? What is it?" Lady Helen did not come closer, and Avelyn was starting to realize the woman was afraid of the sow.

"She is birthing!" Runilda said with delighted surprise as she moved to join Diamanda and Avelyn.

"Oh, no!" Lady Helen cried with horror. "She must not do that inside, not here. Dear God."

"My lady!"

Avelyn turned toward the door as Paen's squire rushed into the hall, nearly stumbling over his feet in his hurry. Managing to reach her side without falling, David gasped, "Lord Paen sent me to tell you that Lord Gerville and his wife are riding through the gates."

Avelyn's eyebrows rose at this news. Paen had said last night that his father was sending servants, but had made no mention of his parents returning with them. She supposed she should have expected as much.

Avelyn went outside to greet them, and moments later, Paen's mother was making a fuss over her head wound and telling her not to worry; she intended to stay for a couple of days and would tend to everything until Avelyn felt better. The words brought a resigned sigh from Lord Gerville before he left to find his son.

"Now, you should go lie down and rest." Lady Gerville ushered Avelyn up the steps into the keep. "I will set the servants to unloading things and setting—Oh!" She stopped abruptly and stared around the great hall. "You have made a good start of it despite your injury." Her gaze slid across the fresh rushes spread over the clean floor, then to the newly repaired stairs. "Why, it looks ever so much better already."

"Paen ordered his men to fix the stairs and the floor above after Avelyn's fall," Diamanda informed her.

"Aye," Lady Helen agreed. "And he ordered the men to clean while he headed out in search of servants. We directed them until Avelyn felt well enough to move about."

"I see." Lady Gerville's gaze slid again to Avelyn's forehead with a frown. "You should go rest, dear. Head wounds are such tricky things, and—" She stopped again as her gaze slid around the hall and landed on the sow in the back corner. "Oh, dear, I see she is back."

"I am afraid so. She seems to see the open doors as an invitation to enter." Avelyn followed as Paen's mother moved toward the animal. "The doors are in need of repair and will not close. I had meant to order a couple of men to repair them today, but I was not quick enough. Unfortunately, she is in labor, so I fear we shall not get her moved for a bit," she added as Lady Gerville started toward the back end of the sow.

"Oh, my, so she is," Lady Gerville agreed, then heaved a sigh. "Well, we shall have to let her be for now, I suppose." She turned her attention back toward Avelyn. "Now, why do you not go rest? We have several servants with us, and more are riding with the carts and should be arriving soon. I am afraid I was too impatient to ride as slow as the wagons travel."

Avelyn resisted the lady's urgings toward the stairs. Really, she had already slept most of the day away and had things she wanted to get done. "I have just awoken," she admitted as Lady Gerville began to frown at her resistance. "And it is such a lovely, rare sunny day, I thought I might just take a small stroll . . . to clear my head."

"Oh." Lady Gerville smiled. "That may be just the thing for you, dear. Why do you not take Diamanda with you in case you have any problems? As I say, head wounds can be tricky."

Avelyn hesitated, reluctant to agree to the girl's presence. She liked Diamanda well enough, but had been hoping to sneak down to the village and—

"That would be nice. I'd be happy to come with you," Diamanda said brightly, obviously eager to avoid all the cleaning that was about to happen. The great-hall walls still needed whitewashing, there were still the two smaller rooms above stairs to be tended to, and the kitchens as well, not to mention the herb garden. Avelyn couldn't blame the girl for her relief in avoiding those chores.

Supposing there was no help for it, Avelyn nodded and agreed, "That would be nice."

"Off you go, then, and take Runilda with you to keep you out of trouble. Lady Helen and I shall see to things here; you have a nice walk," Lady Gerville shooed them out of the keep.

Runilda and Diamanda fell into step on either side of her as Avelyn headed across the bailey.

"Where are we walking to?" the petite blonde asked when she led them past the men standing guard at the gates.

Avelyn bit her lip and tried to decide what to tell her.

"Avy?" Diamanda asked, her steps slowing as Avelyn led them toward the path through the woods.

Sighing, she paused and glanced back the way they'd come, relieved to note that they were out of earshot of the guards. "I thought to go to the village."

"What?" Diamanda looked horrified. "But, we cannot—"

"It is not that far," Avelyn soothed. "We passed it on the ride here yesterday, and it is not far at all."

"But Paen said this morning while we were breaking fast that the villagers are angry about Lord Gerville's neglecting them and resent our presence here. We should not—"

"I hope to make a start at repairing the rift," Avelyn admitted.

Diamanda hesitated. "How?"

"Well, we have not got a lick of furniture in the keep, Diamanda."

"Aye, I did notice," the girl said dryly. "There is no place to sit or eat or—"

"Just so." Avelyn nodded. "I thought perhaps we could tend to that and mend some ill feelings at the same time if we hired villagers to build them."

When the blonde looked uncertain, Avelyn added, "I thought we might also purchase some foodstuffs, baked goods if there is a baker, and ale from the alewife. We cannot produce any of these things yet ourselves."

"Ale and bread?" Diamanda said, moving her hand to her stomach. " 'Tis noon."

"Aye, and you have not yet broken your fast, my lady," Runilda pointed out.

"Just so." Avelyn smiled at them. "I brought coins with me. We can sample the foods and buy some for the keep, as well as possibly see about furniture and other things. If the village is as poor as Paen claims, they may be happy for the trade."

"Or they may not *have* anything to trade," Diamanda argued.

"We can but find out one way or the other," Avelyn said with a sigh, then raised her eyebrows. "Are you willing to come with me?"

Diamanda glanced back toward the keep, then nodded slowly. "Aye. I fear it will be a failure, but we may as well go see."

Nodding, Avelyn struck out on the path again. It was a warm, sunny day, and she would have enjoyed the walk if she were not so worried about the coming visit to the village. Paen had said the villagers resented them, so she could not hope for a warm welcome, but she was hoping her coins would help.

"Mayhap we should have ridden on horseback."

Diamanda's voice drew Avelyn from her thoughts, and she glanced around. While the village had seemed only moments away on horseback, it was a bit further on foot. Still, not a great distance, but Avelyn got the idea that Diamanda had led something of a pampered existence at Gerville, with servants constantly at her beck and call.

"It cannot be much further, Diamanda. I am sure 'tis just around this bend."

Diamanda grunted with disbelief, then breathed a small "oh" of surprise as they came out of the bend and found themselves walking into the village.

It was small and not very prosperous, but Avelyn had expected as much. She simply hadn't expected such miserable conditions. The village and its people had truly suffered under Legere's leadership. She suspected her project was going to be more difficult than she'd expected.

"They do not look very welcoming." Diamanda moved a step closer to Avelyn as they neared a group of women gossiping outside a row of tiny, dilapidated huts on the edge of the village. The women turned to gawk at them, their expressions cold and suspicious. "We are not going to talk to them, are we?"

Hearing the fear in the younger girl's voice, Avelyn gave in to her own cowardice and shook her head. "Nay. We shall go to the village center. Perhaps we can find someone there who appears more helpful."

Diamanda made a sound that could have been agreement or not, then asked, "Are you sure this is a good idea?"

"Aye," Avelyn answered firmly, but she was beginning to wonder. It had seemed a fine idea when she'd come up with it, but as they passed one villager after another and were met with silent resentment each time, she began to doubt her plan would work. By the time they reached the village center, she was even beginning to doubt their chances of escaping the village without being attacked, at least verbally.

Chapter Sixteen

"We have a following," Diamanda murmured, glancing nervously over her shoulder.

Avelyn did not look back. She'd been aware of the growing crowd following them as they walked. It was part of the reason her confidence in the endeavor was becoming shaken.

Afraid to stop walking lest it spur their followers on to actually doing or saying something, Avelyn glanced around a bit anxiously. Whereas they had passed nothing but small cruck houses on the outskirts of the village, here in the center were several larger wattle-and-daub buildings that served as both home and business. The biggest bore a sign so faded the only word legible was *Inn*.

Relief pouring through her, Avelyn turned her steps toward it and tried to maintain an unhurried pace.

The women released a relieved breath as they stepped inside the dim building and the door closed behind them. That relief lasted as long as it took for their eyes to adjust to the low light. They stood in a mid-sized room lit only by a couple of torches. There were two large trestle tables, one on either side of the room. There was also a door directly across from them, presumably leading to the kitchens. There were six men in the room, five customers spread out over the two tables and a man Avelyn assumed was the innkeeper. He stood in front of the door across from them, arms crossed and stance belligerent. Every last one of the men was eyeing them with suspicion and intense dislike.

Avelyn sighed. It was obvious that everyone knew they were from the castle. She supposed the fact that they were on foot would be telling, not to mention their clothing . . . or at least, Diamanda's expensive gown. Her own dress fit in rather nicely with the villagers' garb, she noted with a grimace. Though the cloth was a fine expensive weave, it was dark and drab and ill-fitting, as were most of the garments the villagers wore.

Straightening her shoulders, Avelyn ignored the silent glances around them and led Diamanda and Runilda to an empty space at the table on the right. While the other two sat, Avelyn did not. She suspected they were unlikely to get service if they waited, so she didn't bother. Instead, she asked Diamanda and Runilda if they wished food and drink. Despite complaining of hunger on their walk there, Diamanda shook her head. Apparently, she had lost her appetite. Even Runilda said nay.

Avelyn nodded and walked to the innkeeper, pasting a pleasant smile on her face.

She saw a flicker of surprise in his eyes as she approached, but that was all. He did not even ask what she wanted. Aye, these people really resented their presence, she thought on an inward sigh, then simply widened her smile. "I will have three . . ." she paused to glance around at the other customers and noticed most of them were eating some sort of meat pasty. Knowing it must be the best food they served, she pointed to the nearest man and finished, "three of what he is having, as well as three meads and an ale, please."

Avelyn beamed another smile at him as if completely oblivious to the animosity in the air, then turned and walked back to join Diamanda and Runilda, afraid that if she gave him the chance, the man would refuse to serve them. She held her breath as she waited for the man's reaction. He was still hesitating where she'd left him as Avelyn squeezed herself in the small space between Diamanda and Runilda, but after a moment, he huffed with irritation and turned to walk into the kitchen.

Avelyn let her breath out slowly, grateful at least that he hadn't thrown them out.

The three women were silent as they waited for their repast. It didn't take long. Within moments, the innkeeper was back, slamming the drinks down before them.

"Why did you order four drinks?" Diamanda asked as the man moved back into the kitchen.

"I wish to try both the mead and the ale," Avelyn answered, but didn't explain further. Instead, she tried the mead, sipping it cautiously, then relaxing when it did not turn out to be soured or otherwise unpalatable. She'd almost feared the man might do something to their food or drinks to discourage their enjoying it. Of course, the food hadn't come yet, she reminded herself as she set the mead down and tried the ale.

Avelyn paused as the liquid filled her mouth. Although the mead was average, the ale was fine. Quite fine.

"Who makes your ale?" Avelyn asked when the innkeeper returned with their pasties.

"I do. What of it?"

Avelyn peered around the innkeeper to see a woman standing in the kitchen door, staring at them coldly. His wife, she suspected. The woman had probably come to peek through the door at them, then stepped out on hearing Avelyn's question.

"My compliments," Avelyn said solemnly. "It is very fine ale, some of the best I have ever tasted."

The woman's expression became stiffer as if suspecting Avelyn was up to something until she added, "The mead is good enough, but not as fine as the ale."

Such honesty seemed to convince the woman that Avelyn wasn't buttering her up for something, and she relaxed enough that she was at least no longer scowling as she nodded and said, "The mead today is not my best effort. It is usually better."

Avelyn nodded, believing her. "May I ask your name?"

She hesitated, then said in a short, clipped tone, "Avis."

"Thank you, Avis. I am Avelyn." She smiled faintly, then asked, "Can you make both the mead and the ale in quantity?"

The woman blinked, then said warily, "I could."

"Then I would ask that you do so and send as much as you can make to the castle."

Avis hesitated, probably debating whether she could afford to tell her to go to the devil. But her eyes widened as Avelyn stated how much she was willing to pay per keg for each beverage.

There was silence as Avelyn waited for some response, but she seemed to have shocked the woman to the point of being unable to speak. Avelyn supposed that, as poor as the village was, no one was able to pay much for goods. What she offered must have sounded exorbitant, but it was a fair price, and she told her so lest the innkeeper's wife think she was trying to buy her way out of their resentment. The price Avelyn offered was no more than her mother paid on the rare occasions when she purchased such things. Straughton had its own alewife, so rarely needed to purchase extra unless an event such as a wedding cropped up.

"Will you do that?" Avelyn asked finally when the silence had drawn out so long it was becoming uncomfortable.

"O'course she will," the innkeeper said, even as his wife finally nodded. The man was almost smiling now, she noted.

"Thank you," Avelyn murmured, but noticed the woman was hesitating by the door, shifting on her feet as if she wanted to get right to work but had a question to ask.

"Will you want it regular?" Avis finally asked. "Or are you having a celebration or—"

"We will need it regularly," Avelyn assured her. "We have no alewife as yet."

Eyes wide and slightly dazed, Avis nodded several times, then turned and hurried back into the kitchen. The innkeeper hurried after her, and Avelyn picked up her pastie and took a tentative bite.

"This is quite good too," she murmured encouragingly to Diamanda and Runilda after chewing and swallowing the first bite.

Both women reluctantly began to eat, obviously uncomfortable under the stares of the men around them. While the attitude of the innkeeper and his wife may have thawed toward them, the other men were still eyeing them with open dislike. It made the meal uncomfortable, but Avelyn would not allow them to scare her. Still, she was grateful when they had finished and could leave without looking as if they had been frightened off.

They stepped out of the inn to find that the crowd outside had grown in size. Avelyn sensed Diamanda and Runilda moving closer to her, but merely led them toward what looked to be a baker's premises. She didn't experience any relief at all on entering the shop, since the crowd followed them inside. As many of them who could packed themselves into the small front room of the baker's, while the rest crowded around the open door.

On first entering, there was no sign of the baker, and Avelyn was just wondering what to do when there was a disturbance by the door and she heard someone snarling, "Get out of the bloody way, you fools,'tis my shop."

She watched the round little man enter, noted the anger on his face and knew she was in for a time of it. She wasn't surprised when he finally struggled into the room, tugged his clothing into place, glared at her and snarled, "I'm not Avis, so don't be thinking you can buy yer way into me good graces like I hear ye did her. Now be off with ye!"

Avelyn stood very still as a murmur of approval went through the crowd, then nodded calmly. "Very well, sir."

Diamanda and Runilda started to move toward the door, only to pause when they realized Avelyn wasn't moving. They turned reluctantly back as she added to the baker, "However, I feel I should tell you I couldn't care less about your good graces. All I bought from Avis is ale and mead, enough for two hundred soldiers and servants, and all I wanted from you is enough baked goods to feed as many people." She was most satisfied by the realization that dawned on the man's face.

"Two hundred people?" he asked faintly.

"Aye. I realize 'tis a large quantity, but I thought mayhap you could get the women in the village who are the best cooks to make some in their homes. It would have helped you and allowed them to earn some coin too," Avelyn pointed out, knowing the baker could not possibly handle such a large order on his own.

"I must confess, I do not understand your attitude, sir," Avelyn continued. "Especially since I am neither Legere, nor Lord Wimarc, but the new lady of the castle who is in need of goods and would rather purchase them from the people of her village—who are in need of the trade—than send the coins out to another town or village. However, as you are fool enough to turn down good coin for your pride . . ."

Shrugging, she moved to join Runilda and Diamanda by the door as if preparing to leave. She hadn't taken two steps when the man spoke. "Wait."

Avelyn nearly sagged with relief, but, aware of all the eyes watching her, she tried to hide her feelings and simply turned back to the man to negotiate terms with him. In moments, the baker was smiling, his pockets jingling when next she turned away.

Avelyn led Runilda and Diamanda to the door, noting the way the crowd went silent and parted as she approached. She paused in the doorway and peered over the sea of faces. She could not see the other tradesmen's shops with all the people there and so had no idea where to go next. After a hesitation, she asked, "Are there any carpenters here?"

Several hands went up. One man didn't bother to raise his hand, but made his way to the front of the crowd. "I am a master carpenter."

"Did you make the trestle tables in the inn?" Avelyn asked after a reflective pause. They had been good, sturdy tables, yet looked easily collapsible and had shown fine attention to detail in the carving of the legs.

"Aye." He appeared surprised.

Avelyn nodded. "You will need help for what I want."

"I have it if I need it," he said calmly, not looking as if he believed her.

Avelyn shrugged inwardly, then announced, "I need new trestle tables. Enough for two hundred men and servants to sit at. Benches of course, and four chairs for the high table. Four more chairs for the fireside and—nay, make that six chairs for the fireside," she corrected herself. As Lord and Lady Gerville would probably visit often and she had no idea how long Diamanda and Lady Helen would stay, six seemed smarter. "I shall also need three large beds." Avelyn hesitated again, wondering about how much she should spend just now. Could she afford to get chairs for each bedchamber as well? It would be nice to have a chair to sit on while she dried her hair by the fire. Two chairs in their room would allow her and Paen to sit by the fire of a cold winter night.

Avelyn decided to get the chairs. She had her own coins. Her parents had always spoiled her and had included coins among the chests of goods they'd sent with her. "Six more chairs for the bedchambers and several small tables."

When she finished, there were several moments

of complete silence; then the carpenter cleared his throat and admitted painfully, "Even with the help of every capable man here I cannot provide this much furniture as fast as a larger—"

"I realize that, sir," Avelyn assured him, impressed with his honesty. Another carpenter would have been calculating the coins this would bring him and unwisely assuring her he'd have it for her in a trice. Speaking clearly so that a good deal of the crowd could hear, Avelyn said, "While I would like the furniture as quickly as you can manage, I am willing to wait. I would prefer to keep the profit from this venture here in our village."

He nodded slowly. "What would you like first, my lady?"

"The tables, then the beds, then the chairs, then the smaller tables," Avelyn answered, then glanced around at the crowd, becoming aware that the feeling in the air had changed. She had not won them all over, but the crowd was swaying.

Raising her head, she called out, "Is there a grocer here who can supply me with herbs?"

"Oh, Avy! You were wonderful!" Diamanda enthused as they left the village in late afternoon.

"I was, was I not?" Avelyn grinned, buoyed up by her success. It had certainly not started out well, and for a while she had feared she'd made a huge mistake, but it had worked out well in the end. She was very satisfied.

"I was ever so impressed," Diamanda admitted. "I do not know where you found the courage to stand up to the baker when he was so mean to us, but you yelled right back and even called him a fool." Her eyes were huge and round. "I never would have had the courage to talk to him so."

Avelyn blinked. "Yelling?"

"Aye." Diamanda threw an arm around her shoulders and hugged her exuberantly.

"Nay," Avelyn shook her head. She hadn't thought she'd yelled, and glanced at her maid to ask. "Surely I did not yell?"

"Like a fishwife," Runilda assured her proudly.

Avelyn stared at her in horror, and both women burst out laughing.

"You were brilliant!" Diamanda assured her. "I want to be just like you when I am married."

Avelyn felt her lips twist wryly. After a lifetime of feeling inadequate and wishing she were someone else, it was rather strange to hear that anyone would wish to be like her. Still, she had impressed even herself today. Perhaps she wouldn't prove to be a calamitous failure as a wife after all, she thought hopefully.

Buoyed up by her success and encouraged by Diamanda's obvious admiration, Avelyn felt good as they walked back to the castle. It wasn't until she entered the great hall that she began to deflate.

"There you are, girls!" Lady Gerville walked up to greet them, a bright smile of pleasure on her face as she waved toward the changes in the great hall. "What do you think? It is much nicer now, is it not?"

"You . . ." Avelyn stared at the trestle tables and benches now filling the center of the hall. Her gaze then slid to the small collection of chairs by the fire, and she shook her head helplessly as her happiness began to flow out of her like water out of a pail. "You brought furniture."

"Aye. It was on the wagons with the servants. I did not mention it because I hoped to surprise you." Her smile faded somewhat at Avelyn's expression. "Are you not pleased? I thought you would be more comfortable with . . . well, there was not a stick of furniture here."

"Oh, yes," Avelyn said quickly as she realized how rude she was being. "This is lovely. Much more comfortable."

"But we just came back from the village where we arranged for furniture and all sorts of things," Diamanda blurted out.

"The village, you say?"

Avelyn turned to peer over her shoulder at Wimarc Gerville and Paen as they entered. Both men were frowning.

"You went to the village?" Paen growled. "You could have run into trouble. I told you they were not pleased with us there."

"My lady handled it beautifully. Her mother would have been proud," Runilda said firmly.

"Aye," Diamanda added. "When the baker was rude to us, she was rude right back and even yelled at him like a fishwife."

Avelyn closed her eyes with an inner groan as

Diamanda and Runilda regaled them with their adventures in the village. The silence that followed was long, and she finally sighed and opened her eyes to find everyone staring at her. "Of course I shall cancel the furnishings and—"

"You will not," Wimarc Gerville said sharply. "You have done more today to repair our relations with the villagers than any amount of my talking could have done. We will keep the furnishings here until the new carpenter has replacements done, then take them back to Gerville. The castle is mighty bare without them anyway."

"And the breads and so on that you ordered from the baker, as well as the herbs from the grocer, shall be welcome," Lady Gerville said firmly. "The baker's goods shall lessen the burden on the cook while she settles in and arranges things, and certainly the herb garden is not up to scratch." She smiled brilliantly. "You have done well, my dear."

Avelyn could feel her spirits lift. She had done well, after all. Her gaze slid shyly to her husband, and she thought she saw admiration and pride on his face. Surely he would compliment her too? After all the calamities and accidents she'd caused, surely he would be impressed and offer her a kind word for this? Instead he offered her an apple. He had been carrying it when he entered the keep with his father, and now he peered down at it, hesitated, then held it out.

Avelyn accepted the apple with confusion, then gave a startled gasp as he patted her rump.

"Good," he said firmly, patted her rump again

and walked off with his father toward the trestle tables.

Avelyn stared after him with amazement; as did the other women. They were all staring after him as if he'd sprouted horns. After a moment, Lady Gerville turned back to Avelyn and said, "Er . . . dear, why do you not go introduce yourself to your new cook and see if she does not have refreshments you girls might enjoy after your walk. I needs must speak to my son."

Avelyn watched her walk to the trestle tables, then headed toward the kitchens with Diamanda and Runilda on her heels. They had crossed half the hall before the rustling of rushes drew her gaze to the corner and she recalled the sow. The mother pig was still there, and Paen's squire, David, was standing nearby looking on with wide eyes.

Curious as to what had caught his fascination, Avelyn changed direction, heading for the boy. Runilda and Diamanda followed.

"Oh, look," Diamanda cooed as they reached the boy to find that it was the sow's litter that had his attention. The pig was a new mother several times over.

"She has had her babies," David announced unnecessarily.

"Aye," Diamanda grinned. "Are they not adorable?"

Avelyn smiled faintly at the girl's words. The baby piglets were climbing shakily all over each other in a battle to get to the sow's teats. They were indeed adorable with their huge eyes and floppy ears. She watched their antics for a bit, troubled when she noted one tiny pig struggling to get a turn at suckling.

"He must be the runt of the litter," Diamanda commented.

"Aye," Avelyn murmured. The poor little creature was a fighter, but he was weaker than the others and, no matter how many times he tried, he could not force his way in to get to his mother's milk. Avelyn frowned. "He is a fighter."

"Aye," Diamanda said sadly, as if knowing that the poor piglet's courage would make little difference if he could not get to the milk.

Avelyn was worried too. "Do you think Lady Gerville brought anything we might feed him?"

Diamanda perked up at the suggestion. "We could go see."

Nodding, Avelyn knelt to scoop up the piglet. Cuddling him against her chest, she smiled as the warm little body squirmed against her. She caressed him soothingly and cooed, "It's all right, little one. I know you are hungry. We shall find you something to eat." She scratched his ear gently, then said, "I think we shall call you Samson because we intend for you to grow up big and strong."

"Just do not cut off his hair," Diamanda teased, reaching up to pet the piglet, then suddenly grimacing as she glanced over Avelyn's shoulder. "Oh-oh. Aunt Helen is coming. She will make a fuss if she knows we are handling and plan to feed one of the piglets."

"Then we had best take him to the kitchens,"

Avelyn said and started that way, being careful to keep the piglet hidden by her body as she moved. Runilda, Daimanda and now David were following her. They were almost to the door when Avelyn asked, "Why does Lady Helen dislike pigs so much?"

"She does not dislike them, she is terrified of them," Diamanda explained. "She was bitten by one when she was a little girl and has been terrified of them ever since. She will lecture you if she catches you taking him to the kitchen."

Avelyn felt a moment's worry over this, then suddenly realized that Rumsfeld was *her* home. She was mistress here, and no one had a right to lecture her for doing as she pleased . . . except perhaps for Paen . . . and Lord and Lady Gerville, she amended with a grimace. Still, while she would never be rude, if Lady Helen made too much of a fuss about what she chose to do, Avelyn decided she would just have to politely make her own position clear.

"What was that?"

Paen glanced up from the ale he was enjoying with his father and blinked at his mother as she faced him across the trestle table. She had her hands on her hips and a very annoyed expression on her face. "What was what?"

"The apple, the pat on the rump, and the 'good,'" Lady Gerville said impatiently.

Paen blinked. "I was praising my wife."

"That was *praise*?" she asked with disbelief.

He shrugged. "It is how I praise Midnight."

"Midnight is a horse!" she snapped irritably as his father burst out laughing, spitting out ale.

Paen shifted uncomfortably. He'd thought he might need other ways to increase his wife's self-esteem, but truly it was a tricky business and he hadn't come up with anything as yet. He'd never had a wife before, and when he needed to praise his horse or his squire, it was with a "good" or "well done" for the boy, and an apple and a pat on the rump for the horse. He explained this now and watched his mother's irritation abate.

"So you have realized those cousins of hers have damaged Avelyn's view of herself," his mother said with relief.

"Aye, but I do not know how to repair it other than to praise her when she does well," Paen said.

"Well." Lady Gerville relaxed her stance. "You could start by talking to the girl."

Paen rolled his eyes with exasperation. "Talk. Women always seem to think talking will fix things. A sharp sword often solves the problem much more quickly and efficiently."

"Well, you can hardly cut the poor image out of Avelyn. And as your wife is a woman like myself, mayhap you should try my suggestion," Lady Gerville said dryly. "It is sharp, unkind words spoken to her over the years that have caused this poor self-image in Avelyn, so I suggest that kind and complimentary words may also—with time—undo them. You might like to spend some time with her as well. Go for walks with her and play chess of a night, things like that," she suggested. "Now I shall just go have a word with cook about the goods being brought up from the village. It will make things much easier while everything is still in such an uproar. It was very clever of Avelyn to go to the village as she did."

Paen watched his mother walk away, then gave a disgruntled sigh. "With time. I do not want it to take years and years to undo the damage those cousins of hers caused. I want her to know *now* that she is smart and pretty and capable."

"Hmm." His father nodded his understanding, then brightened. "Well, I shall help. If the two of us compliment her, it may speed it up."

Lord Gerville suddenly stood. "In fact, I will go compliment her right now, and again tell her how well she did with her efforts this afternoon in the village."

Paen watched thoughtfully as his father headed for the kitchens in search of Avelyn. The man's words had put a thought in his head. If the two of them complimenting her helped her see that her cousins were wrong and she had value, then many people complimenting her might speed it up even more . . . and if the whole garrison of soldiers and servants here did . . .

Paen stood abruptly. He had to speak to his men.

Chapter Seventeen

"Can I hold Samson? I promise I will not drop him."

Avelyn glanced down at David and smiled at his earnest expression. She was becoming quite attached to the boy after several days of having him trail after her.

It was a week since Avelyn's first foray into the village, and now they were returning from a second trip. She'd acquired David as her constant companion the day after that first journey. The lad had nearly gotten himself crushed by a boulder with his clumsiness while trailing Paen around the wall where the men were working. Her husband had asked her that evening if she would keep the boy with her until he'd finished the wall and moved on to a less dangerous task. Avelyn had agreed at once, happy to be of service to her husband in any small way. The lad had been following her ever since.

Pondering the last week, Avelyn decided that—all in all—it had been a good one. Paen's mother and father had ended up only staying a couple of days. Lady Gerville had acknowledged that Avelyn wasn't injured so badly that she couldn't run her own castle . . . and run it well. The last part had nearly brought tears to Avelyn's eyes as she recognized it for the compliment it was. Lady Gerville had confidence in her abilities, even if Avelyn herself didn't. But that was changing with each success she had. Avelyn could feel herself becoming more confident with every passing day.

The last week had seen the repairs to the castle speed along. The entire castle had been cleaned, the keep doors repaired and the sow and her litter moved. All except for the piglet Samson. Determined to save the feisty runt of the litter, Avelyn had kept him inside when the other pigs were shown the door, and she'd done all she could to improve his chances of survival. In effect, Samson had taken up permanent residence in the castle, or more precisely, he'd taken up permanent residence with Avelyn, for if she was not carrying him around, he was trailing after her under his own steam, his little pink behind wiggling happily as he followed her from place to place. The piglet seemed to think Avelyn was his mother, much to Paen's mingled amusement and exasperation.

This week had also been the week when her husband had seemed to suddenly notice her presence. Not that he'd been completely oblivious before, but this week Paen had taken the trouble to spend time with her—playing chess of an evening, going out with her for walks. He still did not say much. Avelyn was coming to realize that her husband was a man of few words. He tended to grunt more than speak, but on a few occasions he'd had whole conversations with her. She always found these discussions interesting windows into his thoughts. Avelyn was happy to learn that her husband was a good, fair and honest man.

"Please?" David begged, reminding Avelyn of his request to hold Samson. She hesitated, then gave in and handed Samson to the boy.

"Be careful, David. He is getting heavy," she warned. Samson had doubled in weight this last week thanks to some advice from Avis, the innkeeper's wife. The woman had ridden to the castle with the first delivery of ale and mead and had arrived as Avelyn was trying to find some way to feed the piglet. Avis had taken an interest and told her what her own father had done when they'd had a similar problem with a foal. Her father had made a sort of bladder out of oiled cloth. He'd sewn the end in the shape of a teat, filled it with goat's milk and used it to feed the foal, which had apparently done rather well on the substitute for a mother's breast milk.

Avis offered to help with the project, and Avelyn had accepted gratefully. She liked the innkeeper's wife, and they were becoming friends. So when Avelyn had headed into the village today to order more goods and check on the carpenters' progress with the furnishings, she'd decided to take Samson with her to show Avis how well her suggestion was working. Samson had become plump, healthy and happy.

Now they were returning, and Avelyn was eager to tell Diamanda about their trip. The younger girl had been pleasant enough before, but ever since their trip to the village, the two of them were becoming fast friends, spending a good deal of time together and laughing and chatting as they went about their chores. In fact, Diamanda had wanted to come with her to the village today, but the girl's aunt had refused to allow it. Lady Helen insisted Diamanda remain home to practice her seams, as she was still unable to get them straight.

Avelyn suspected the girl would be as bored as mud by now, and wondered if she was watching from a window and could see them approaching the gates to the bailey.

"He is squirmy."

Avelyn smiled faintly and glanced down at David's claim, just in time to see Samson wiggle his way out of the boy's hold. Dropping to the ground with a plop, the piglet raced off along the wall, and David promptly gave chase with a squeal that just seemed to urge Samson to faster speeds. Avelyn set off after the pair, worried that the lad would trip over his own feet.

Sure enough, David took a tumble after a couple of minutes, and Avelyn shook her head as she slowed to a walk to approach him. She knew her husband did not like anyone making a big deal of the child's tumbles, so she paused beside him and raised her eyebrows as Samson turned back and waddled over to snuffle at him.

David giggled as he crawled to his hands and knees, then snuffled back.

Avelyn shook her head at the pair of them, and then bent to scoop Samson into her arms as David climbed to his feet.

"You have some dirt on your braes," she announced, and was waiting patiently as he brushed it away when a grinding sound overhead made her glance up. Avelyn's eyes widened in horror at the sight of a stone block plummeting down toward them from the wall. For a split second, she was sure her heart stopped; then she shouted and lunged forward, pushing David before her as she tried to get them out of the way.

A grunt of pain slid from her lips as her shoulder was struck a glancing blow; then the three of them were falling. Avelyn let go of Samson, hoping to keep from crushing the piglet while trying to avoid falling on David. Then she hit the ground with a crash that sent a jolt through her whole body.

"Are you all right, my lady?"

Younger and more used to tumbles, David was the first to recover and crawled over to peer at her.

Avelyn took a minute to catch her breath. Then she sat up, rubbed the pain from her shoulder and managed a smile as Samson wiggled between them. "Aye. I am fine, thank you, David. Were you hurt?"

"Nay." He offered a hand to help her up, and Avelyn accepted it even though she actually got to her feet under her own steam. The boy wasn't big enough to truly help her, but she wouldn't rebuff his attempt at chivalry.

"Lord Paen will blame me," David said miserably, drawing Avelyn's surprised attention.

"Why would he do that?" she asked as her gaze drifted up the wall to where the cut stone had come from. Avelyn froze as she spotted Diamanda withdrawing from the wall directly above them. The blonde had obviously been leaning over, peering down at them from the spot where the cut stone had been, but had pulled back as Avelyn glanced up. One second slower and Avelyn would have missed seeing her.

"Well, after the boulder nearly hit me while I was with him, he made me stop going with him to the wall every day. He said I would get myself killed, and one dead squire was enough," David said, reminding her of his presence.

Avelyn glanced down to see his eyes widen with alarm.

"You do not think he will make me stop spending time with you and Samson now, do you?"

Avelyn stared at David blankly, finding it difficult to drag her mind from the image of Diamanda peering down at them. What had she been doing up there? Had the stone block really just fallen accidentally?

"He will!" the boy cried unhappily when she remained silent. "Oh, please do not tell him about this, my lady. He will make me stop spending the day with you and Samson. Please do not tell—"

"I will not tell," she assured him quietly, but had reasons of her own to keep this to herself. Avelyn needed to do some thinking. She considered Diamanda her friend, but there were so many questions whirling through her head at the moment . . .

She thought suddenly of the ruined tunic saturated with the scent of pork, and the plank slamming into her head and sending her through the hole in the floor. And now a stone block had nearly crushed her and David . . . and Diamanda had been standing up there, directly where the cut stone had been.

But Diamanda was her friend, she argued with herself. Avelyn truly liked the girl. Of course, that didn't mean the girl truly liked her back, she acknowledged with a sigh. However, her friendship with Diamanda made her feel she owed it to the girl to talk to her before telling Paen about the incident.

Of course, Avelyn wasn't a fool. If Diamanda did mean her harm, she would be an idiot to confront her in private. She decided she would confront Diamanda in full view of others, just far enough away to be out of hearing.

"Thank you, my lady."

Avelyn patted David's shoulder, then bent to scoop up Samson and urged the boy to hurry toward the gate into the bailey. They had taken several steps inside the gate when she thought of the guards on the wall. Surely if Diamanda had pushed the stone block off, the man stationed along that section of wall would have shouted or at least seen her. She turned to look toward where the guard usually stood, only to find it empty. It wasn't until she slid her gaze along the wall that she spotted a man mounting the stairs to the wall. As she watched, he walked back to his post and took up his position.

"Good afternoon, my lady. You look lovely to-day."

Avelyn glanced around, a blush coming to her cheeks as she nodded at the two soldiers approaching.

"Aye, lovely," the second soldier said as they passed.

Avelyn was shaking her head with bewilderment at the sudden penchant everyone seemed to have for complimenting her, when she heard the first soldier say, "*Lovely* was my compliment. Could you not come up with your own?"

"Lord Paen said compliment her, he did not say we had to be creative about it," the second man pointed out with a shrug. "Besides, what should I have said? 'Pretty pig, my lady?' Once you've told a woman she is lovely, there is little else to say to her."

Avelyn turned slowly to watch the men walk away as the first soldier shook his head and said, "If that is what you think, 'tis no wonder you have such trouble with women."

The men obviously had no idea they'd been speaking loud enough to be overheard. Avelyn turned a thoughtful glance to her husband's squire. "David?"

"Aye, my lady?"

"Did Paen tell the soldiers to compliment me?"

"Aye, my lady." David nodded. "He said you needed steam building due to your nasty prick cousins and their years of damned evil insults and we were all to aid in . . . er . . . preparing the damage."

Avelyn bit her lip to hold back a chuckle. She suspected he meant *esteem* building and *repairing* the damage, but he had certainly remembered Paen's curses.

Shaking her head, she urged David to continue across the bailey, but her thoughts were on what she'd just learned. Avelyn had been the recipient of countless compliments of late, and found herself both uncomfortable and embarrassed by it all, to the point that she'd started to avoid the men. Now she understood why she was getting so many compliments: because Paen had told them to. She wanted to cry. Her husband had cared enough to try to repair the damage done by her 'nasty prick cousins.'

The more she learned about her husband, the more she loved him. Avelyn stopped walking as she realized what had just gone through her head. Love? Paen? Certainly she had the dutiful love that a wife was supposed to have for her husband—that was as it should be—but she didn't *love* love him . . . did she?

"There you are."

Avelyn pulled back from her thoughts and smiled at the man in question as Paen appeared before them.

"David, go inside and polish my mail at the trestle table," he ordered. "Do not go anywhere without checking with Lady Helen first."

"Aye, my lord."

Avelyn raised her eyebrows as the boy hurried off.

"Lady Helen agreed to keep an eye on him while we are gone," Paen announced, taking her arm and turning her around to lead her back the way she'd come. She still held Samson in her other arm.

"While we are gone where, husband?" Avelyn asked, glancing curiously at the sack and the folded fur he carried.

"To have our lunch," he said, and her eyes widened.

"Our lunch? Do you mean a picnic? We are having a picnic?" she asked with excited pleasure.

"Aye," Paen grunted, but she couldn't help noticing he appeared embarrassed to admit it. Avelyn supposed that meant this was another of the suggestions his mother had made while she was here. Lady Gerville had told her all about Paen's explaining that the rump patting and the handing over of an apple had been his ways of praising her. His mother had feared that Avelyn might have taken offense at this "praise" and had hoped to prevent or repair it by explaining his actions. Lady Gerville had also told her that she'd given Paen alternate ways to praise her and had suggested he also spend more time with her at pursuits such as chess and walks and so on. Avelyn had appreciated the suggestions this last week as she'd enjoyed her husband's company.

For some reason, she hadn't minded that the

chess games at night and the walks during the day were at Lady Gerville's suggestion. Paen *wanted* to praise her and *did* follow the advice to spend time with her. That was what mattered.

Paen led her out of the bailey and into the woods, following a path he appeared to know. It wasn't long before they came to a clearing with a small brook running through it.

"Oh, this is lovely," Avelyn exclaimed, peering around as he set down the bag and began to lay out the fur. "How did you know this was here?"

"I came out yesterday on horseback and looked for a suitable spot."

"And this spot is so nearby," Avelyn murmured, but her heart was squeezing at the fact that he'd looked for a nice spot for them. Lady Gerville may have suggested the picnic, but Paen had put care and trouble into finding a nice place to have it. It gave her hope that he was perhaps coming to care for her, at least a little.

"Sit," Paen ordered once the fur was spread out.

Avelyn sat, a small smile playing about her lips, then set Samson on the fur. The piglet immediately set out on an exploration of the clearing. She watched him for a bit, but wasn't really concerned that he would go far. He never wandered too far from her unless he was wanting to be chased. Had David not set out after him today, Samson would have stopped and come back on his own.

Paen shook his head with amusement. "I should have had David take the little pest, but I did not notice you had him."

Avelyn's eyebrows rose. "It is hard to believe you did not notice I was carrying him, my lord."

Paen grimaced. "I was distracted."

"By what, my lord husband?" she asked.

"I was considering whether I had forgotten anything," he said.

Avelyn smiled at the admission. Not that Paen noticed, he was busy digging food out of the sack and setting it on the blanket. His face was a picture of concentration as he worked, and she felt her heart swell as she watched him. How she did love this man. Yes, she did. He might say little, but his actions spoke loud and clear. Paen put care into things that mattered to him—his castle, his horse . . . and her. The fact that he had taken great care in finding the perfect spot for their picnic was only one in a list of examples. He had taken on the chore of chatelain at Rumsfeld because he'd thought she was unhappy in not having a home of her own to run. He had ordered his men to praise her to help raise her esteem. He had started playing chess with her and taking her for walks, purely because his mother suggested it would make her happier.

Beneath his gruff exterior, Paen was a good man. A caring man whom she loved, and who she was beginning to hope might care for her a bit.

Paen raised his head and opened his mouth to speak, then froze as he caught the expression on her face. He sat like that for a minute, then closed his mouth, licked his lips and said, "You look all soft and glowing right now."

"Do I, my lord?" Avelyn asked softly.

"Aye. You look lovely."

She smiled and admitted softly, "You make me feel lovely when you look at me like that."

"Like what?" Paen asked, beginning to scowl.

Avelyn grinned at the defensive action and said, "Like I am a delicious dessert you would like to gobble up."

"I would." He began to lean toward her.

"You would what, my lord?" Avelyn asked breathily.

"I would like to gobble you up," he admitted. Then his mouth covered hers. His lips were all that touched her, brushing softly back and forth and feather-light. Avelyn's eyes drifted closed and she sat still for a moment, but then found her lips drifting apart and her body leaning forward of its own accord. She wanted more than his teasing kisses. She wanted a proper kiss, she wanted to touch him, she wanted him to touch her.

But the further Avelyn leaned forward, the further Paen pulled back, forcing the kiss to remain a light brushing of mouths.

Just when Avelyn thought he would drive her mad with his teasing, she felt his tongue slip out to drift across her open lips. The intimate caress made her moan, and her own tongue slid out until the tip of hers touched his. Paen immediately slanted his head and pressed forward so that his tongue could thrust fully into her mouth.

Avelyn gasped and kissed him back. She raised her hands to slip them around his shoulders, but Paen caught them in his own and held on. It seemed he was intent on driving her mad, she thought with a touch of frustration; then he suddenly broke the kiss and sat back.

"Take off your dress," he ordered huskily.

Startled at the request, Avelyn blinked. Her mind struggled briefly, shyness battling with excitement; then she shifted to her knees, only to hesitate.

"Please," Paen added. His gaze was hungry, his expression solemn.

Avelyn took a deep breath and slowly stood. A moment passed as she gathered her courage and then she bent to catch the hem of her gown and draw it up over her head. Avelyn immediately had a terrible urge to hide behind the gown, but she made herself release it to drop to the furs. It was a decision she began to regret when Paen simply sat staring at her, his eyes sliding over every inch of her exposed body. Just as Avelyn reached the point where she decided she could stand it no more and must grab up her gown, Paen shifted to his knees and leaned forward to brush the tip of his thumb across one erect nipple.

Avelyn bit her lip and swallowed at the tingle the action caused. He then leaned closer still until he could take the tight bud delicately between his teeth. Her heart immediately jumped in her chest. It jumped again when she felt his tongue flick over the tip in his mouth. Then he suddenly cupped one hand beneath her breast to hold it and began to suckle eagerly, his tongue repeatedly flicking the end as he did.

Avelyn moaned and slid one hand into his hair,

her fingers holding onto the silky strands. He continued to lave at first one breast, then the other, until Avelyn was trembling in his arms; then he began to ease down on his knees so that he was trailing kisses down across the dancing flesh of her belly.

"Husband?" Avelyn gasped as he continued lower, his kisses shifting to the side and drifting over the sensitive flesh that covered her hip. His teeth grazed and nipped as he went, and Avelyn found herself unable to stand still under the torment. She twisted her hips in his hands, almost writhing against his questing mouth.

When Paen caught her ankles and forced her to shift her stance so that her feet were further apart, Avelyn realized she was breathing in short, shallow pants. It only got worse as his lips burned a trail to the inside of her thigh. Avelyn was now holding her breath, terrified her legs would give out at any moment, leaving her to collapse atop him.

As if aware of her weakness, Paen slid his hands to her hips, his fingers cupping her behind and holding her up as he pressed kisses higher and higher up her thigh.

Avelyn did her best to remain on her feet, but even with his support her legs gave out when he pressed a kiss to the very center of her. She collapsed with a gasped cry, and Paen caught her, easing her to her back on the fur. He then knelt between her legs, nudged her legs further apart and ducked his head to press his mouth to her again.

Avelyn caught at the furs and twisted her head, her mind awhirl with a combination of excitement, desire and the need to touch him. She wanted to please him too, and had wanted to each time he'd bedded her, but Avelyn had no idea how to do so. This time, the need was almost unbearable, but his hands were pinning her thighs down as he used his lips, teeth and tongue to pleasure her. Paen continued to do so until she screamed out and bucked beneath him.

For a moment afterward, Avelyn was too dazed to move; then she became aware that Paen had sat back on his haunches to lift his tunic off over his head.

When he then stood and reached for the waist of his braes, Avelyn shifted to her knees, taking the same position he'd taken before her earlier. Her voice was husky. "I want to please you too."

Paen hesitated, bent to strip out of his braes, then straightened so that she found herself staring at his manhood. Avelyn hesitated. He was hard and erect and right before her face, but she wasn't sure what to do.

When Paen did not instruct her, she decided she might as well try what he had done to her and leaned forward to press a kiss to his hip. She trailed kisses to his thigh and then finally braved pressing a kiss to his staff. Avelyn found herself surprised at how soft and velvety the skin felt over the hard shaft. She pressed another kiss to the shaft, then ran her lips lightly along it to the tip, where she laved him with her tongue. After that, she wasn't sure what else to do.

"Take it in your mouth," Paen growled, sounding pained. She glanced up at his face with a concern that only grew when she saw how his face was now scrunched up in what looked to be agony.

"Am I doing this wrong?" she asked uncertainly.

Paen shook his head, then gasped when she took him in her mouth. His head went back and he stood rock still as she moved her mouth uncertainly over him, then raised her hand and wrapped it around his manhood. Holding him in a similar fashion to how he'd held her breast, she suckled on him until he suddenly pulled away and knelt before her.

Avelyn peered at him uncertainly. "Was I doing it—"

Her question died abruptly when his mouth covered hers. The kiss was so passionate, she thought perhaps she hadn't done it wrong after all; then Paen was bearing her down onto her back on the furs.

Avelyn wrapped her arms around his shoulders and parted for him, expecting him to enter her at once, but he didn't, he just pressed himself against her as his lips claimed hers. Paen kissed her deeply, his tongue thrusting, then turned his lips to one ear, laving that as well and sending shivers through her.

Moaning, Avelyn turned her head and caught his lips with hers, kissing him passionately as she shifted against him, silently pleading with him to fill her. Much to her relief, Paen responded to the request, thrusting into her with a hard, deep stroke that drew a low groan from her throat. He then began to ride her, drawing moan after moan, gasp after gasp, as she writhed and shifted beneath him.

Her nails dug into his back to urge him on as her tongue wrestled with his.

When he tore his mouth from hers, Avelyn pressed her face against his shoulder and alternately sucked and nipped at the flesh there as the tension escalated through her whole body. It felt as if something had been drawn as tight as a bow inside her and she was positive that if it were pulled any tighter it would surely break. And then suddenly it did, and she bucked beneath him, screaming as her body squeezed around him with each pulse of pleasure. Avelyn was hardly aware of it when Paen thrust into her one last time and cried out his own pleasure.

Chapter Eighteen

Avelyn opened her eyes and stared with confusion at the man's chest she lay on . . . until she recalled how their picnic had turned out. They hadn't touched the food, she remembered, and a smile curved her lips. Then she realized she hadn't a clue as to how she'd ended up on Paen's chest. The last thing she recalled was Paen resting half on top of her as they both waited to recover their breath. She must have fallen asleep. And Paen had obviously shifted off of her, then draped her over himself, all without waking her.

"Wife?"

Avelyn raised her head and peered shyly at her husband. As amazing as it seemed, she always felt a little self-conscious after what they did. She had stood there completely naked before him not long ago, but now was suddenly shy.

He smiled sleepily at her expression. "Are you hungry?"

Avelyn blinked, surprised both by the question

and by the fact that she was indeed hungry. Nodding, she slid off to sit on the fur and reached for her gown, eager to cover up now that she was no longer distracted by passion or desire.

Paen sat up beside her and began to dress as well, then moved to the food he'd removed from the sack. Miraculously, they had managed not to crush any of it, which Avelyn was grateful for. She really was terribly hungry.

They ate in silence at first; then Avelyn asked how the wall was coming. She knew Paen had worked the men hard on the wall until he felt it was safe to bring her to Rumsfeld, but he'd taken many of the men off the project once they'd arrived here so they could work on other tasks. Only himself and a handful of men were left to continue working on the remaining small holes and unstable bits of the wall.

Paen told her it was coming along well, which really said nothing at all, she thought. What she really wanted to know was if it was possible that the boulder could have fallen on its own. She really didn't wish to believe Diamanda was trying to harm her.

After another silence, during which Avelyn wondered how to get the information she wanted without giving anything away, she finally simply asked.

"The section of wall to the right of the front gates?"

"Aye?"

"Is it safe?" she asked, then said, "I mean, are there any parts there you still need to work on?"

315

"The inner parapet needs to be replaced in places, but the outer parapet is sound."

"There are no loose stones that might fall out or anything?" Avelyn asked.

Something about her tone made him pause and peer at her. "There should not be," he said slowly. "Why are you asking, wife?"

She dropped her gaze and shrugged, turning her attention to Samson as the piglet returned to the blanket and dropped to sit beside her now that they had stopped moving about and had brought out the food. Avelyn set several slices of apple and a plum on the ground by Samson, but he wasn't interested and merely nosed the fruit before taking himself off to explore some more.

"Why are you asking, wife?"

She lifted her gaze, but hesitated. Avelyn wasn't concerned that he would blame David and refuse to allow him to spend time with her and Samson. She just didn't want to bring up Diamanda until she herself knew if the girl had been involved. Avelyn supposed she could tell him about the stone block falling without mentioning Diamanda.

"Wife, what happened?" he asked. "I had noticed that the sleeve of your gown is torn and your shoulder bruised beneath."

She glanced toward her arm and sighed. Avelyn hadn't noticed either the tear or the bruise after the incident, she'd been too stunned and distracted at the sight of Diamanda. Though she had been aware of a vague twinge of pain if she moved her arm a certain way.

316

"One of the stones fell out of the wall and nearly hit David and me on our way back from the village," she finally admitted.

"Another accident," Paen muttered and sat back, his face pale and his mouth tight.

Avelyn shifted, feeling suddenly guilty. She was sure Paen must think her a plague of accidents.

"When we return, I want you to show me where you were when the stone fell."

Avelyn nodded. The pleasant feel to the outing had suddenly disappeared, and she was sorry to see it go. Paen must have felt it too, for after a few moments of silence, he sighed and began to pack things away.

"Get your pig and we shall head back."

Avelyn rose silently and went to collect Samson from where he was nosing in the bushes. When she turned back, Paen was standing staring at her. He started across the fur, then something went wrong. Avelyn squeezed Samson in surprise as Paen suddenly seemed to stumble; then his foot slid out from beneath him and he crashed forward, hitting his head on a log.

"Husband?" Avelyn rushed forward, anxiety clawing at her stomach. He wasn't moving.

"Paen?" Dropping Samson as she reached her husband's side, Avelyn managed with some effort to turn Paen onto his back. She peered at his pale face. He was out cold, and there was a cut on his forehead where he'd hit it on the log. A large lump was already forming beneath it.

A little frantic now, Avelyn bent her head and

pressed her ear to his chest, relaxing only a little when she heard the steady beat of his heart.

Sighing, she sat back and glanced around the clearing, unsure what to do. Head wounds were a tricky thing, and there was no telling how long her husband would be out. His head would be terribly sore when he woke up . . . but *when* he woke up was the issue. Paen could be out for moments or hours or . . .

Avelyn peered around the clearing and the trees that enclosed it. She had no desire to stay the night there alone with her husband unconscious and unable to defend himself. While he'd had his men riding patrol to make their presence known, and seemed to think that would scare off the reavers, she wasn't willing to risk his life on it.

Unfortunately, Avelyn also wasn't willing to leave him while she went for help. They hadn't walked that far, but a lot could happen in the short time it took her to get to the castle and back with help. That was one lesson Avelyn had learned well since her marriage. It had only taken a moment for her to be knocked into the hole in the floor, and it had taken less than that for the stone to plunge from the wall above her. Anything could happen to Paen while she sought help. No, she would not leave him alone while she went to fetch help . . . which meant, she supposed, that she would have to take him to help.

Avelyn's brother had always accused her of being overoptimistic, but optimist though she was, even she had to admit that it was unlikely that she'd be able to get her husband to the castle—or even far enough out of the woods for the men on the wall to notice them. She could not possibly carry him, and dragging him by his arms or legs through the dirt and grass wasn't likely to do him much good. Then her gaze dropped to the fur he lay on, and Avelyn had an idea.

Calling Samson over, she got to her feet and considered the fur and her husband's position on it and decided it might work. She rolled him into the fur. Picking up the bag of leftovers he'd collected, she set them on the fur beside her husband, pausing when she saw the squashed bits of apple and plum on the fur. Avelyn distinctly recalled setting it out for Samson. She also recalled the piglet's lack of interest. She should have thrown the bits of food into the woods or returned them to the bag, but she'd thoughtlessly left them lying there. Apparently, they were what had sent Paen crashing to the ground.

This was all her fault, Avelyn realized guiltily, then pushed the guilt aside and bent to pick up the ends of the fur. Taking one corner in each hand, she stepped back and tugged experimentally, releasing a sign of relief when the fur slid along the grass carpet with a bit of effort.

Aye, she could do this, Avelyn told herself. She turned her back to the fur, then switched her hold and began to pull. The spot Paen had found for them hadn't seemed far into the woods on the way

319

out. It seemed much further away on the return journey. Avelyn didn't give up, however, and eventually managed to get them out of the woods.

Avelyn paused once past the trees and waved toward the gate, but had no idea if the men could see her. She couldn't make out any figures on the wall. Sighing, she turned to glance at Paen, a faint smile curving her lips when she saw that Samson had decided to hitch a ride on Paen's chest.

Shaking her head at the picture, Avelyn took up the corners of the fur again and continued forward. She hadn't gone much further when several horses rode out of the castle gates, hurrying toward them.

Exhausted by her efforts, Avelyn kept her explanations to a minimum as she and Paen were both taken up on horseback to ride back to the keep. David met them in the bailey. The boy had run halfway to the gates, but turned and began to run back to the keep steps when he saw the party ride in. The squire was smart enough not to ask questions, but simply hurried along at Avelyn's side as she directed the men to take her husband up to their room.

Diamanda and Lady Helen rose from where they sat by the cold hearth in the hall and hurried forward as they entered. Waving their questions away, Avelyn led the men upstairs, opening the chamber door for them to carry him inside.

"My lady!" Runilda rushed across the room as they entered, concern on her face. "What happened?"

"He fell and hit his head, Runilda. Fetch my medicinals," she ordered brusquely, then added, "And my needle and thread. His head has yet to stop bleeding, and I fear he may need stitches."

"How did he fall?" Diamanda asked with a frown, having heard Avelyn's explanation to Runilda as she'd followed the men into the room.

"He set his foot down on a plum, it slipped out from under him and sent him crashing to the ground where he hit his head on a log," she said as the men set Paen on the bed of furs she and Paen were using until the new bed was made. Avelyn could not even look at the girl as she explained. In her mind, she kept seeing Diamanda's blonde head disappearing back over the wall.

"Here you are, my lady." Runilda handed her the small bag that held her medicaments, needle and thread.

"Thank you," Avelyn murmured and moved to kneel on the furs beside her husband.

Paen was still pale, still unconscious and still bleeding from the cut to his forehead. The only change was that the bump on his forehead had almost doubled in size. The man had hit the log hard.

Avelyn managed to find her needle and thread, but only after dumping the contents of her bag onto the furs. When she went to thread the needle, she found that her hands were shaking so hard she couldn't seem to do it.

"My maid is a healer," Lady Helen said gently

321

when Avelyn tried for the third time and failed. "Perhaps I should send for her, child."

Avelyn sagged with defeat and nodded, then remained silent as they waited for the woman to be brought to the room. Avelyn's mind was whirling. She had been berating herself for being a failure as a wife . . . but not now. She wasn't useless. She was proving herself a good wife. Her hands were shaking because she cared so much and feared for Paen's well-being. That wasn't failure. Nor was it failure for one to accept aid when it was needed.

When the door opened and Lady Helen's maid, Joan, entered, Avelyn at first felt relief. Joan was a tall, thin, quiet woman, and one could forget her presence most of the time, but when she walked into the room to tend to Paen, she moved with a quiet confidence that suggested she knew what she was about.

Avelyn was relieved to hand the burden of her husband's care to the woman . . . until Joan straightened from examining him and said, "I shall need my leeches."

"What?" Avelyn gaped at her, appalled. Her mother had trained her in care and medicinals and held no respect for the practice of using leeches to bleed a patient. She said it was a nonsensical thing to do, bleeding a body that was already bleeding.

"Nay." Avelyn rose up on her knees. "There will be no leeches."

"He must be bled," the woman said reassuringly. "We must remove the bad humors. I will return directly."

"No, you will not return, you are not looking after him," Avelyn snapped, then glanced at the men hovering around the furs. "That woman is not to come back in here. Keep her out."

"Avelyn, dear," Lady Helen said soothingly. "Do calm down. Joan knows what she is doing. Her mother was the finest healer I know, and she taught her everything."

Avelyn turned flashing eyes on Diamanda's aunt. "Well, *my* mother is the finest healer I know, and she always despised the use of leeches as a fool's tool. I will tend him myself."

"As you wish," Lady Helen said stiffly, and moved to usher Joan out of the room.

Avelyn felt a moment's regret for snapping at Diamanda's aunt when she had only been trying to help, but it was only a moment's regret. She had more important things to worry about. Taking a deep breath, she picked up the needle and thread again and concentrated on threading the needle. Much to her relief, this time her hands were steady enough that she managed the task. It was as if the release of her fear and anger in her outburst over Joan's leeches had removed whatever nervous energy had set her hands shaking in the first place.

Avelyn quickly cleaned the wound, then bent to stitch it. It was a small cut and needed only three stitches, but she took time and care with the chore, hoping to reduce the scar her husband would carry. Of course, she loved the man and no scar, small or huge, was going to change that. She took care for his sake, though she doubted he would care much either.

Paen remained unconscious throughout, and Avelyn sat back with a little sigh when she finished. She was half relieved that he'd not woken while she'd been poking the needle through his skin, and half wishing he had so that she would at least know he was going to be all right. Avelyn had seen men live through much worse head wounds than Paen had, but she had also seen men die after lesser wounds. It was why those wounds were tricky. One never knew which way the patient would go.

"Will he be all right?" Diamanda asked as Avelyn began to wrap a bandage around his forehead.

"I do not know," she admitted, then glanced at Runilda. "Please fetch me something to mix the medicinals in, Runilda. His head will ache when he wakes, and I would have a tonic here to help him sleep so that he may drink it as quickly as possible."

Nodding, the maid hurried from the room. After a pause, the soldiers who had been hovering began to file out of the room as well, leaving Diamanda and Avelyn alone.

They sat in silence for several minutes, but the silence seemed to make the girl uncomfortable and she cleared her throat. "It was most impressive when you dealt with Joan. She has always made me nervous, and I could never face up to either her or Aunt Helen like you did."

"I was rude to your aunt and shall have to apologize," Avelyn muttered. "But leeches are the sign of an unskilled healer."

"I dislike leeches too," Diamanda murmured.

324

When Avelyn didn't respond, the girl frowned slightly and asked, "Are you angry at me for some reason?"

Avelyn peered at the girl she'd thought of as her friend and could hold her silence no more. "I saw you, Diamanda. I know what you did."

Diamanda's mouth dropped open, and they stared at one another in silence, both stiff and unmoving; then the girl drooped like a flower too long without water.

"I—" She shook her head, then blurted, "I am sorry, Avelyn. I truly am. It was stupid and mean, and my only excuse is that I hardly knew you then and we had not yet become friends. You cannot know how much I regret it now."

Avelyn blinked in confusion. While it was true they had not been as close when she had been knocked through the hole in the floor, they had certainly been friends today, when the girl had sent the stone block crashing down. Or was that what she was confessing?

Avelyn shifted, trying to think of a way to get the girl to talk without having to admit that she wasn't sure what they were presently talking about. "Help me understand. Tell me what you were thinking. Tell me everything from the beginning." She held her breath after that suggestion, hoping it would work. When the silence drew out a painful length of time, Avelyn began to think the girl wouldn't say anything at all. But it seemed she was just collecting her thoughts, for she finally sighed and began to speak.

"I was six when I came to Gerville. I knew I was to marry Adam, but from the very first day I have always loved Paen," she admitted.

Avelyn sat back on her heels, her mind blank.

"When news came to Gerville that Adam had died," she continued, "I was positive it was fate making sure that Paen and I could be married. I did not know about you. No one ever spoke to me about your betrothal, and Paen was so much older than Adam and still unmarried, so I thought he was not betrothed to anyone, or that his betrothed had died. But then Paen returned and they announced we must pack and get ready to travel to Straughton so that Paen could fulfill his marriage contract."

Diamanda grimaced. "I am afraid I hated you at once, without ever having met you. You were stealing my Paen from me," she said sadly, then smiled wryly and added, "I hated you even worse once I met you."

"Why?" Avelyn gasped with surprise.

"Because you were so beautiful and nice and—" She paused abruptly, frowning when Avelyn gave a short burst of laughter.

"Diamanda, I am hardly beautiful."

"Aye, you are," she said solemnly. "You are not thin, but you are beautiful."

Avelyn blinked at this announcement.

"Anyway, then when we were traveling to Hargrove and you showed me the tunic and braes you were making for Paen, I became quite upset. They were lovely, and it was so thoughtful of you to think of it, and I immediately wished I had thought of it, but even if I had, I cannot sew as well as you and it would not work out as well. So when I realized you were nearly done and would present them to Paen, I was in a panic." She took a deep breath, then admitted, "When Paen took you down to the river, I snuck into the tent and set the furs and clothes on fire."

"I *did* blow out the candle," Avelyn said on a sigh, and Diamanda nodded.

Recalling the scent of pork on the second set of clothes she'd started for Paen, Avelyn asked, "And you rubbed pork on the second tunic and let the dogs have at it."

Diamanda grimaced. "That was the plan, but they are too well trained and would not have at it. I had to tear and cut the tunic myself, then left it for them to be blamed." She sighed unhappily. "I am sorry now, Avy. I started to like you despite myself once we were here, and I began to see that you truly cared for Paen and he was coming to care for you. The two of you are perfect together. I know what I did was wrong, and I am sorry about hurting and upsetting you. I hope you will forgive me."

Avelyn stared at her, confusion claiming her again. "But what about the wall, Diamanda?"

"The wall?" Now it was the blonde's turn to stare at her blankly.

"I saw you on the wall," Avelyn announced.

"When? Do you mean today?" She truly seemed confused. "Aye, I went up there to think. I came across Paen while he was arranging the food for the picnic, and he was taking so much care and making such an effort . . . It was just another bit of evidence that he loves you. Did you know he ordered the men to compliment you to try to help repair the damage your cousins' insults had caused? He does love you, Avelyn, and after only a couple of weeks. Whereas he has known me for years and years and cares for me as nothing more than a little sister." She shook her head. "I guess despite everything, it really sank in then and I went up on the battlements to be alone. I was walking along and heard talking and paused to peer over the wall. I did see you and David, but did not realize you had seen me."

Avelyn dropped back on her haunches. She was positive Diamanda was telling the truth. The girl could not fake such innocence and bewilderment. Diamanda had no clue as to the importance of her being up on the walkway, because she had no idea that a boulder had nearly crushed Avelyn and David moments before her arrival. Avelyn was sure of it.

Perhaps the falling stone had been an accident, she thought faintly. But then, who had hit her and knocked her into the hole in the floor?

"You must hate me now," Diamanda said miserably, and Avelyn frowned.

"Nay, of course not." She reached out to take the girl's hand, giving it a squeeze, relieved to know that the girl she considered a friend had not set out to kill her. Of course, she *had* ruined Avelyn's attempts at sewing clothes for Paen, but she could forgive that. She might have been more angry had she known who was behind it at the time, but it all seemed so long ago, and she truly believed Diamanda was sorry.

"If you want me to leave, I shall return to Gerville," Diamanda offered, though it obviously pained her to do so.

Avelyn shook her head. "That is not necessary, Diamanda. We are friends, and friends forgive friends for foolish behavior." She shrugged. "You made a mistake, you have admitted it and apologized. That is good enough for me."

"Truly?" Diamanda peered up hopefully from beneath her lashes.

"Aye."

"You will still be my friend?"

"Most definitely," Avelyn said firmly. "I enjoy our friendship, Diamanda."

"Oh, Avy!" She suddenly launched herself at Avelyn, hugging her tightly. "Truly, you are wonderful! Thank you. I promise, you will not regret it. From now on, I shall be the best friend ever." She shook her head and sat back to take Avelyn's hands. "I cannot believe I thought you lucky to have Paen. In truth, I think we are all lucky that he got to marry you."

Avelyn smiled at the girl's exuberance and found herself touched by her words. Then Diamanda glanced at Paen and frowned. "I shall have to tell Paen, of course."

"I do not think that is necessary," Avelyn assured her.

"Would you keep it secret from him, then?" Diamanda raised one eyebrow and shook her head. "It would never work. One day you would slip and say something that made the whole pitiful tale come out, and then he would be angry it was kept a secret from him. Besides, he has a right to know you are not as accident prone as he thought."

"I am not accident prone at all," Avelyn assured her.

Diamanda shook her head in disbelief. After a hesitation, Avelyn asked, "Do you think you could watch over Paen for me for a bit? I need to go check on something."

"Aye, of course. Go ahead. I would be more comfortable telling him everything alone if he wakes up, and I shall fetch you directly afterward if he does awake."

Avelyn hesitated, considering telling her again that she needn't confess her mischief to Paen, but then decided to let her go ahead and tell him. Diamanda was right that it might slip out someday and cause unnecessary upset. And Avelyn trusted Paen to handle Diamanda with care.

"Fine. I shall not be too long, I just wish to check on something up on the battlements. Send someone to fetch me if Paen wakes up and you finish your chat before I get back."

Up on the parapet, Avelyn ran her fingers lightly over the spot where the stone block that had nearly hit her had rested. She then leaned over to peer down at the boulder below. Avelyn's talk with Diamanda had made her begin to believe that the falling stone truly had just been an accident, but she'd known she wouldn't be fully convinced until she had a look at where the cut stone had come from. She ran her hand across the spot again.

There was nothing here to suggest that anyone had pushed it over the side. There were no chisel marks, or any marks at all that would suggest it had been levered out. On the other hand, it was hard to believe that it had chosen to fall at the exact moment she was walking by. Avelyn frowned as her finger ran over the slight ridge in the center of the outside edge of where the boulder had been.

Bending closer, she ran her hand over the area and saw that there was a slightly upraised portion on the outer edge. The boulder would had had to roll up over it. This boulder, if it had finally just given way, should have rolled the opposite way, onto the walkway where she now stood.

Avelyn straightened slowly. Someone had pushed the boulder down on her. Not an accident. Like her fall through the room. She had been hit and knocked through the hole. Only her skirt catching on the ragged edge of the wood had saved her.

So she was less accident prone than someone would have her believe, and the fates certainly hadn't turned on her. Someone else had.

Avelyn stared down into the bailey, considering the matter. Diamanda had looked so confused when she mentioned the falling rock, she was sure she'd had nothing to do with it. But if not her, who?

Lord and Lady Gerville certainly had no reason to wish her dead. Actually, no one did that she could think of. Diamanda was the only one who might come close to having an excuse to wish her dead. Still, she couldn't believe it was the girl.

A scuffle to her right made her glance to the side, and Avelyn straightened as she peered at Diamanda's aunt.

Chapter Nineteen

Paen opened his eyes and shifted in bed, then sucked in a hissing breath of air as pain shot through his head. It was only then that he recalled slipping on the plum and hitting his head on the log. He was grimacing over his own clumsiness when a sniffling sound drew his gaze to the side to see Diamanda seated on the window ledge, weeping into a bit of cloth.

His first thought on seeing the girl was irritation that she must have woken him with her weeping. Paen was in enough pain that he'd rather sleep than stay awake and suffer it. His next thought was to wonder why the girl was crying. It could not be over him. He was injured but would heal. It wasn't as if he were dying.

But what of Avelyn? Paen thought his heart might stop as he realized the girl might be crying because Avelyn had been hurt again . . . or even killed this time. His wife had suffered an unfortunate number of accidents from which she had managed to survive relatively unscathed, but her luck was bound to give out eventually.

"Where is Avelyn?" Colored with his worry, the question came out sharper than he'd intended.

Diamanda stopped weeping and turned a startled face his way, then slid off the window ledge and moved to the bed. "You are awake."

"Where is Avelyn?" Paen repeated. "Was she hurt? Is that why you were crying?"

"Oh!" The blonde's eyes widened as she realized what her crying had led him to believe. She quickly shook her head. "Nay. She is fine, Paen. Truly."

Paen relaxed back into the bed of furs, realizing only then that he'd half sat up in his worry. Grimacing over the pain all the movement was causing him, he sighed and asked wearily, "Then why were you weeping?"

Diamanda sat down on the edge of the bed with a sigh. "Because of what I have to tell you."

Paen waited, and when she merely sat there sniffling, asked impatiently, "What?"

Diamanda bit her lip, then stared at her hands and said, "You will hate me."

She wanted to be coaxed into telling him, he realized with a sigh. Paen really was not in the mood for such games. "Just tell me, Diamanda."

"I am the one who destroyed the tunic and braes Avelyn was making for you," she admitted unhappily.

Paen frowned. "Which ones?"

"Both sets," she admitted in a bare whisper. When Paen opened his mouth to speak, Diamanda rushed on. "Avelyn had blown out the candle in the tent. I deliberately relit it and used it to set the furs and clothing on fire. Then at Gerville, when she was nearly done with the second pair, I snuck some meat from dinner away from the table and rubbed it all over the tunic, then ripped it up and put holes in it before I used it to tease the dogs. I left it with them, knowing they would be blamed."

She was now shredding the linen in her hands. "I told Avelyn all this a little while ago and apologized. I told her I intended to tell you. She said I need not tell you, that the mischief had been made against her and so long as she forgave me——"

"She forgave you?" Paen asked.

"Aye." Diamanda nodded. "She was very understanding."

Paen stared at her with bewilderment. He was glad his wife was understanding, but *he* didn't understand at all. "Why did you do it? You hardly knew her when you burnt the first outfit, and she was kind to you when you unintentionally said those foolish things about your pregnant cousin after the wedding."

Diamanda made a face and admitted, "Actually, that was intentional. I was deliberately insulting, though I did not think to tell Avelyn that when I told her the rest."

"Why would you do all that to her?" Paen asked sharply, his confusion beginning to fade beneath a surge of anger on his wife's behalf.

"I was jealous," she admitted unhappily, then raised her face, revealing pleading eyes. "I love you,

Paen. I have always loved you. I came to Gerville knowing I was to marry Adam, but it was you I loved. You were always stronger and smarter and . . ." She shook her head helplessly. "I love you. And I was jealous that she got to marry you and would be your wife and . . ." She sighed. "I wanted to make her as miserable as I was, I guess. Or maybe make you see how useless and clumsy she was."

"Avelyn is neither useless nor clumsy," Paen said grimly.

"I know." Diamanda nodded. "Her cousins told me she was, and that just made me angrier because I thought she did not deserve you. But I have come to know Avelyn since then and I know she is neither clumsy nor useless. She is smart and funny and kind and I hope that I am half as good a wife someday as she is to you." She shrugged unhappily. "I came to like her. That is why I did nothing else to try to make her look bad in your eyes after arriving here."

She grimaced. "Of course, with the plague of accidents she has had since arriving here, I did not feel the need to bother, but even so, I do not think I would have done anything else. I do like her, Paen. And I am sorry."

Paen let his breath out on a slow sigh. The girl sounded sincere, at least about being sorry. He didn't believe for a minute that she really loved him. She had a child's infatuation for him, was all, and would get over it soon enough. Her behavior toward Avelyn had been appalling, however, and he wasn't sure what he should do about it.

"So Avelyn knows all this and forgave you?" he asked.

"Aye. She is very kind."

"I am surprised that you confessed all this to her," Paen acknowledged.

Diamanda grimaced. "She made me."

"What?"

Diamanda nodded, then frowned. "It was the oddest thing. Avelyn was angry and said she knew what I had been doing and had seen me. I thought she meant she had seen me either start the fire or ruin the second tunic and I confessed all, but it just seemed to confuse her. And then she asked me about being up on the parapet earlier, as if it were more important."

"Earlier today?" Paen asked sharply. "You were up on the parapet today?"

"Aye. I wanted to be alone to think about everything. I was feeling bad for the unkindnesses I had dealt Avelyn, and I could see you had come to love her, which only made me feel doubly bad." She shrugged unhappily.

Paen stared at the girl, his heart pounding. She could see he had come to love Avelyn? Nay, he did not love his wife. He might have some affection for her, but love? Paen swallowed and glanced toward the window, a myriad of memories running through his mind—Avelyn chattering before him on his horse; covered in quail eggs he'd knocked her into; telling him angrily that of course she'd thought he preferred the hard-packed earth to bedding her, else he would have been in their tent; her dejection over his not bedding her; her gleeful laugh as she beat him at chess; her earnest expression as she told him Samson was very smart; her brave face as she denied she was in pain after the boulder hit her; her passion-filled gaze as he made love to her; her clutching a bit of linen in front of her as if it would hide her nudity. . . .

Aye, he acknowledged. He loved her. He loved every last contrary bit of her. The woman was too kindhearted, too shy, too giving. She was just plain perfect . . . for him. He loved her. Damn, when had that happened?

"I thought I could be alone up on the battlements." Diamanda went on, drawing Paen's thoughts away from his love for his wife in time to see her grimace. "Of course, I almost did not go up when I saw Aunt Helen hurrying down, but I hid under the stairs and waited for her to pass and then went up." She sighed. "I was walking along the parapet and heard voices. I looked over and saw David helping Avelyn to her feet. She must have tripped or something."

She shook her head with amused affection. "As much as I like Avelyn, she truly is clumsy." Then she shook her head. "That fall through the floor nearly did me in. It scared me so much, and still she will not admit she is accident prone."

Diamanda sighed and peered at him. "Anyway, she must have seen me when I looked over the parapet. Avelyn was very upset that I had been up there at first, then just looked mystified when I explained I had been up there to think."

Diamanda stood now, then hesitated. "If you wish me to leave, I will. Avelyn said there was no need to and it was only small mischief, but—"

"No, no." Paen shook his head. "There is no reason for you to leave."

She let her breath out on a sigh of relief. "Thank you, Paen."

He blinked in surprise when Diamanda suddenly bent forward to kiss him on the cheek. She then straightened and moved to the door.

"Diamanda?" Paen asked as she opened the door.

Pausing, the girl glanced back.

"Where is Avelyn?"

"She went up on the parapet for something. Though she may be back now. Aunt Helen stopped in here looking for her for some reason, and I told her where she was, so she may have found Avelyn and brought her back down for whatever she wanted. I shall tell her you are awake if she is back in the keep when I go below. Avelyn will be glad. She was very worried. She loves you as much as you love her, you know."

Diamanda closed the door softly behind herself as she left.

Paen stared after her, his heart in his throat for several reasons. First, he had just come to realize that he loved his wife. Secondly, Diamanda thought his wife loved him too, and third, he very much feared his wife was in terrible danger at that very moment.

Paen's mind was working fast, putting all the pieces together. He'd thought his wife clumsy because of all her little accidents, but it seemed that some of them were not accidents at all. The fire in the tent had not been, the drowning had not been a drowning . . . what else might not be what it seemed? He had wondered about the fall through the hole in the floor, finding it hard to believe she could have missed seeing the hole. He still did, but he had never got to question her on it.

The chamber door opened, distracting him, and Paen glanced toward it as Runilda paused in the entrance. A bright smile lit her face as she saw he was awake. "Lady Avelyn will be happy you are awake. She has been worried."

"Wait," Paen said as she started to back out of the room, apparently to go find Avelyn.

Runilda paused, her eyebrows rising in question.

"Come here," he ordered, not wanting anyone passing in the hall to hear him.

Runilda stepped back into the room, closed the door and approached the bed. "Aye, my lord?"

"Did Avelyn ever talk to you about the fall she took the first day here? When she fell through the hole?"

Runilda hesitated. "Not really, my lord."

Paen was frowning over this when she added, "Though, when she first woke up, she did say something about being hit and falling through."

"Being hit?" Paen stiffened. "What exactly did she say?"

340

The maid thought for a minute, then said, "I think it was 'Someone hit me, I fell through the hole.' "

"Someone hit her?" Paen asked with disbelief. "Why did no one mention this to me?"

"Well, she was alone upstairs; who could have hit her? Lady Helen seemed to think it had just been something Lady Avelyn had dreamed while she was unconscious," Runilda added apologetically.

"Lady Helen did, did she?" Paen asked, recalling Diamanda saying she'd hidden beneath the stairs as Lady Helen had hurried off the battlements before she'd gone up onto the wall—which would put Lady Helen on the wall right about when the boulder had fallen from the battlement and nearly crushed his wife. Was Helen trying to kill his wife? But why? And why now? These more serious, deadly attacks hadn't started until they'd arrived here at Rumsfeld. Or had they?

Paen ran quickly through the list of events at Straughton and on the journey to Gerville.

Paen's thoughts paused abruptly as he recalled one odd event on the journey he hadn't put any significance to: the dead fox, the rabbit meat and the signs that someone had been sick in the woods behind his wife's tent. He hadn't connected the two things at the time, but what if they *were* connected? What if the meat had been poisoned and the fox had died after eating some of it?

"Did Avelyn throw a roasted rabbit leg behind the tent on the first night of our journey?" Paen

341

asked, making Runilda startle at the sharp question after such a long silence.

"I do not know," she said, then frowned in thought and admitted, "She may have. I know Lady Helen gave a roast rabbit leg to Diamanda to give to Lady Avelyn for sup." She shrugged. "I have no idea whether she ate it or not, but her stomach may have been bothering her after being ridden around camp across your horse like that, so she may have thrown it away rather than risk eating it and tossing it back up."

Or the ride around camp might have made her throw up the meat and saved her from being poisoned, Paen realized and sat up suddenly.

"My lord, what are you doing? You should not be getting up!" Runilda cried

"I have to get to the wall. Avelyn needs me," Paen growled, ignoring the pain ripping through his head as he gained his feet.

"Good afternoon, Lady Helen," Avelyn murmured. The woman had frozen when Avelyn turned, and for a moment her expression had been of such hatred that Avelyn was startled. Then—as if it had never been there—the expression was replaced with a smile, and she moved slowly forward. But Avelyn had seen the look and could not pretend she hadn't.

"Hello, dear. I thought it was you up here so I came to caution you. It is not safe to be hanging over the side of the wall as you were a moment ago. Accidents happen."

"Aye," Avelyn agreed, taking a step back along the wall. "And they seem to happen to me a lot."

"You do seem accident prone," Lady Helen murmured, continuing forward.

"Why?" Avelyn asked, refusing to play ignorance. The moment she'd seen her expression, she'd known Lady Helen was behind the attacks. She just didn't understand why. Surely not because Diamanda had an infatuation with Paen.

Lady Helen paused, her head tilting, and Avelyn knew she was debating whether to acknowledge what she'd been doing. Finally she sighed and took another step forward. "I bear you no malice, Avelyn."

"Judging by your expression a moment ago, I find that hard to believe."

Lady Helen grimaced. "It gave me away, of course. I am sorry. I fear it is just frustration that causes my irritation with you. Why will you not die?"

Avelyn had no idea how she was supposed to answer that polite question, so she simply took another step back.

Lady Helen mirrored her action. "Four times you should have been dead, and four times you have escaped harm. I—"

"Four times?" Avelyn interrupted with amazement. She only knew of two.

"You survived the poisoning twice, then the fall through the floor, and the boulder."

"Poisoning?" Avelyn gaped at her. "When?"

Lady Helen shifted with irritation. "On the journey from Straughton to Gerville. I powdered poison on the bit of rabbit meat I had Diamanda bring to you. It is very potent poison and should have killed you quickly, but instead of awaking to the shout that you were dead, I awoke the next morning to see you wandering back to camp after bathing."

Avelyn blinked as she recalled the meat the first night. Her tongue had tingled after her first bite, but she'd bitten her tongue at the same time and thought that the source. As she recalled, she'd also felt as if ants were crawling over her skin, but had been distracted by her stomach's revolt when she'd vomited the meat up. Avelyn had thought the rough treatment of her stomach when Paen had ridden her around on her belly had caused her stomach's refusal to keep anything in it. And it probably had, she realized. It had also saved her from dying that night.

"When that did not work," Lady Helen continued, taking another step closer. "I made stew the next night using Paen's inability to eat with his bandaged hands as the excuse. In truth, I wanted to double the dosage of the poison, but feared it would be too obvious on roasted meat. I hoped the stew would hide it." She shook her head with bewilderment. "But even with double the dose, you survived. All it did was make you tired."

It hadn't made her tired. Avelyn had made herself tired by sewing through the night. The poison hadn't worked because Avelyn hadn't eaten the stew either. She'd been full from the cheese, bread and apple Runilda had brought her. Once again, fate had saved her. She didn't bother to tell Lady Helen that, however. Instead she said, "And you did hit me with a plank, knocking me through the hole?"

"Aye. I had gone out to check the gardens, but came back when you told Diamanda you were to look for the servants above stairs. I stepped back into the kitchen and waited for Diamanda to go look into the matter of the well. Then once you were upstairs, I followed. Those stairs were tricky," she said dryly. "However, I managed them quickly and without scraping my leg as you did."

Avelyn didn't respond to the taunt, but simply waited for her to continue.

"I found the plank in one of the rooms and carried it with me. When I discovered you, you were leaning over, peering down the hole. Before I could hurry forward and push you, you started to back away from the hole, so I used the plank." Her mouth tightened. "But again you escaped death. Your skirt caught on one of the broken floorboards. I would have moved forward to free you to fall to your death, but Runilda was screaming to high heaven. I knew help would come quickly and I was afraid she might see me through the hole, so I hid in one of the rooms until Diamanda sent Runilda to fetch Paen and hurried upstairs to the room. Then I came in behind her as if I had just come from outside."

"I take it, then, that you did not prevent her

from trying to pull me up because you feared she might drop me," Avelyn asked dryly, taking yet another step back.

"Nay. She is strong and would have insisted I help, and the two of us might have saved you. I was hoping your skirt would yet rip and you would die ere Paen could get there to save you. But, of course, that did not happen."

"So you tried pushing the boulder on me next."

Fury flashed across her face; then she took a deep breath. "You are the luckiest of creatures."

"And that angers you," Avelyn guessed, recalling the expression of hatred she'd caught on the woman's face when she first spied her.

"I have taken great risks each time," Lady Helen pointed out shortly, then snapped with frustration, "Why will you not die?"

Avelyn took another wary step away. The woman looked ready to launch herself at her at any moment. This was not the kind, motherly woman she had come to know since her wedding day. She could hardly believe that the woman before her was Lady Helen, and she still didn't understand why the woman wanted her dead.

"Why?" she repeated her question of earlier.

"Why?" Lady Helen peered at her as if she were stupid not to realize the reason behind the attacks. "For Diamanda."

"For Diamanda?" Avelyn stared at her, thinking she must be mad.

"Do not look at me like that," Lady Helen snapped, taking two quick steps forward.

"Like what?" Avelyn moved warily back again.

"Like I am crazy. I am not crazy."

Avelyn wasn't willing to debate that. Instead she asked, "You would kill me because Diamanda has a child's infatuation with Paen?"

"Do not be ridiculous." Lady Helen looked impatient. "I would kill you because Adam died."

Avelyn blinked in confusion. "I do not understand."

"Adam was betrothed to Diamanda. This was to be their marital home according to the marriage contract."

Avelyn glanced around with surprise. This was news to her. No one had mentioned it, and it made her feel a bit bad that they were living there when it should have belonged to Diamanda and Adam. Avelyn then realized that Lady Helen had backed her to a section of the battlement where the inner parapet—the section of wall that kept soldiers from tumbling to their deaths in the bailey below during battle—was missing. If the woman attacked now, Avelyn would be swept off the walk to fall to her death. She continued to move backward, hoping to back herself to a section where the wall was still intact on both sides.

"But the fool went and got himself killed on Crusade. Paen would have been a fine substitute for Adam, but he was contracted and betrothed to you. But were you dead, we could force the Gervilles to honor the marital contract with Diamanda, with Paen taking Adam's place."

"But why do you even want to?" Avelyn asked

quickly, hoping to keep her talking until she reached a safer area. "Surely with Diamanda's beauty, you could find her another husband easily enough. She—"

"Beauty is next to useless without wealth behind it," Lady Helen snapped, following her. "Unfortunately, my brother is not nearly as successful a lord as our father before him. Though he had managed to keep it quiet, he had lost nearly everything but the castle itself by the time he contracted Diamanda's marriage. The betrothal share he used to secure Diamanda's marriage to Adam was supposed to have been mine. It was to go to my betrothed on my marriage, but he died young and my brother never bothered to negotiate another marriage. He did not wish to spend the money. Instead, I became a mother to Diamanda when her own mother died in birthing her. I had no husband, but she became my child."

Helen took a deep breath. "I raised her as my own. Tended her hurts and fixed any problem set in her path. I will fix this too. She is too good to be the wife of a minor baron, or to have to lie with a wealthy old one who has one foot already in the ground. I will not see it. She deserves a husband as strong, handsome and wealthy as Paen, and she will have him!"

On that note, Lady Helen lunged at her. Avelyn scooted backward, desperate to get to a safer section of wall, but Diamanda's aunt came after her like a valkyrie, her cape flying out around her as she charged. She hit Avelyn hard, sending her reeling backward, and for one moment, Avelyn feared she hadn't been quick enough, that she would fall through where the parapet was missing. But then she felt her shoulders strike the wall and she sent up a silent prayer of thanks. But, of course, Lady Helen could not stop now. Avelyn knew too much.

An enraged screech pouring from her lips, the woman grabbed her and tried to drag her away from the wall, apparently intending to throw her off the walk. Caught up in the struggle, Avelyn almost didn't notice the brush of something against her leg; then she glanced down. Much to her astonishment, Samson was wiggling between their moving feet, rubbing against first her, then Lady Helen.

Even as Avelyn feared that the baby pig would be crushed, Lady Helen glanced down and saw the creature. Avelyn found herself suddenly released. She sagged back against the wall in surprise as Lady Helen danced away with horror. Samson immediately followed, snorting and snuffling at her feet and sending the woman into a panic. Screaming in fear now rather than anger, Diamanda's aunt continued to scuttle backward, desperate to get away from the sweet creature.

Avelyn straightened and cried out as she saw Lady Helen backing toward the missing section of wall, but the woman was too panicked to listen. Avelyn watched with shock and horror as the woman set her foot back one last time, only to find empty air. Avelyn saw the realization and horror cross Lady Helen's face as she fell backward, arms open as if reaching, mouth wide on a scream of horror as she dropped out of sight.

Her legs suddenly weak and trembling, Avelyn let her breath out on a slow sigh and sank to sit on the walk. She would have been happy to stay there for a good long while. Avelyn had no desire to see the results of Lady Helen's fall. Nor did she have any eagerness to face Diamanda just then. In fact, she felt absolutely no urgency about leaving the walk at all.

Samson's snuffling at her knee through her skirt made Avelyn glance down. She picked up the small creature who had saved her life and cuddled him against her chest. "You saved me, Samson."

"Aye, he did."

Avelyn glanced up with a start to see Paen moving slowly along the walkway toward her. Pausing when he reached her, he bent and took her hand, helping her to her feet. He engulfed her in a huge hug, then stepped back. Paen glanced from her to Samson, a soft smile curving his lips as he reached out to pat the small pig's back.

"Good boy," he praised, and they shared a smile before his expression became serious. "I thought I had lost you. I could see her backing you along the walkway as I ran across the bailey to the stairs. By the time I was halfway up, she was lunging at you and I thought I would be too late, that she would throw you off the wall before I could get here. I thought I had lost you."

"She gave it a good try," Avelyn admitted. "She

was hoping that if she did, they could force you to fulfill the marriage contract with Diamanda in Adam's place."

"What?" Paen stared at her in amazement.

"Aye." Avelyn nodded. "It seems Diamanda's family has fallen on hard times and Helen feared they would not find her a suitable husband if they could not force you to it. But to do that, I had to be removed." She patted his chest soothingly as anger built on his face. "But she failed. Samson saved me."

"Aye." Paen let his breath out on a sigh. "And for that he will live to a ripe old age and need never fear ending up on the table." His voice was husky, and it was only now as the color began to return to his face that Avelyn realized how pale he'd been on first coming to her.

"Are you all right, my lord?" she asked with concern. "You took a bad head wound. Mayhap you should not be up and running about."

Paen ignored the question and took Samson from her arms. He set the piglet gently on the ground and ordered, "Go inside."

Much to Avelyn's amazement, the piglet immediately scampered along the walk to the stairs. Avelyn turned to lean over the wall and watch the stairs as he hopped down them.

"I did not realize he could manage stairs yet," she said with surprise.

"How do you think he got up here?" Paen asked.

"Oh." Her mouth was an "o" of surprise, and her husband grinned.

"You should not look so surprised. You are the one who has been telling me how clever he is."

"Aye." Avelyn smiled wryly and turned back to smile at her husband. "I am not accident prone and the fates have not been against me."

"Nay," Paen agreed. "I talked to Diamanda and Runilda, and from what I can piece together, you have survived at least three attempts on your life."

"Four," Avelyn corrected. "Two poisonings, the fall through the floor, and the boulder."

"Two poisonings?" he asked with dismay.

Avelyn nodded.

He shook his head. "And then there is this, her last attempt," he pointed out and said solemnly, "Rather than be against you, the fates would most definitely seem to have been looking out for you. You are very, very lucky."

"Aye." She grinned.

"And so am I."

"You?" Avelyn asked with surprise.

"Aye. I am lucky because I have the perfect wife."

Avelyn shook her head. "I am not perfect."

"You are perfect for me, Avelyn. You are intelligent, beautiful and capable. You *are* the perfect wife for me."

He kissed her, then pulled back and said, "I just wish I could make you see your value."

"I believe, my lord, that I am beginning to do so. But perhaps it is something I had to see for myself," she said gently, then explained, "With each

352

accomplishment I have felt better and better about myself."

"I am glad." Leaning forward, he pressed a kiss to her lips, then slid his arm around her shoulders and turned her to walk to the stairs. "Avelyn, in the future I think we should talk more."

Avelyn blinked. "*We* should?"

"Aye, Runilda told me that you claimed someone had hit you with something and knocked you into the hole in the floor. If you had told me that, I could have put this all together much more quickly. And I notice you did not mention that you had seen Diamanda on the wall after the boulder fell today. In future I would like you to be more forthcoming."

"Hmm." Avelyn didn't know what to say, since he was correct. She had thought he wasn't as forthcoming with her as he could be, but on the other hand, nor had she been. And she wasn't speaking up right now. He had told her that he considered himself lucky to have her as a wife, but she hadn't reciprocated. Nor had she yet told him that she loved him.

Clearing her throat, she said, "Husband?"

"Aye."

"If we are to be more forthcoming, I think there is something I should tell you."

"Aye?"

"I love you."

Paen stopped walking and turned to face her. "What?"

"I love you," she admitted, lifting her chin bravely.

"Not just with the dutiful love of a wife for her husband, but I love you . . . so much that it makes my heart ache at times just to think of you."

Paen stared at her. For several minutes he simply stood there, staring at her as if he thought he might never see her again; then he bent his head and kissed her in a way she had never experienced before. His kisses were usually hungry and passionate, but this one was gentle, achingly so.

When he lifted his head, Avelyn blinked her eyes open.

"I love you too, wife," he announced solemnly, then tucked her against his side and continued walking.

The CHASE
LYNSAY SANDS

Seonaid Dunbar was trained as a Scottish warrior, but fleeing to an abbey would be preferable to whacking Blake Sherwell with her sword—which she'll happily do before wedding the man. No, she'll not walk weakly to the slaughter, dutifully pledge troth to anyone the English court calls "Angel." Fair hair and eyes as blue as the heavens hardly prove a man's worth. And there are many ways to elude a devilish suitor, even one that King Henry orders her to wed. No, the next Countess of Sherwell is not sitting in her castle as Blake thought: embroidering, peacefully waiting for him to arrive. She is fleeing to a new stronghold and readying her defenses. This battle will require all weapons—if he ever catches her. And the chase is about to begin.

What
She Wants
Lynsay Sands

Earl Hugh Dulonget of Hillcrest is a formidable knight who has gotten himself into a bind. His uncle's will has a codicil: He must marry. And Hugh has just insulted his would-be bride by calling her a peasant! How can he win back her hand?

Everyone has advice. Some men-at-arms think that Hugh can win the fair Willa's love by buying her baubles. His castle priest proffers *De Secretis Mulierum*, a book on the secrets of women. But Hugh has ideas of his own. He will overcome every hindrance—and all his friends' help—to show Willa that he has not only what she needs, but what she wants. And that the two of them are meant for a lifetime of happiness.

- -

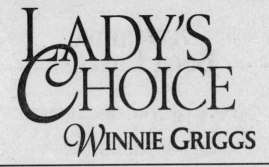

LADY'S CHOICE
WINNIE GRIGGS

Her preference? What a joke! She doesn't want any of them. Regina Nash's grandfather has sent a trio of men to Texas, along with a contract; and if she doesn't sign, agreeing to marry one of them, she risks losing custody of her nephew. To escape the trap, Reggie devises a plan: To be the worst prospective bride ever.

One man won't be tricked. Adam Barr. He isn't one of her three suitors, but he has delivered the contract for her grandfather and is charged with seeing it carried out. Using his charm and wit he has Reggie acting smart, compassionate, and funny. Trouble is, he's outsmarted himself. He isn't in the running—can't be—and yet he wants Reggie for himself. Can he become the lady's choice?

Carnival Pride℠
April 2 - 9, 2006.

7 Day Exotic Mexican Riviera Itinerary

DAY	PORT	ARRIVE	DEPART
Sun	Los Angeles/Long Beach, CA		4:00 P.M.
Mon	"Book Lover's" Day at Sea		
Tue	"Book Lover's" Day at Sea		
Wed	Puerto Vallarta, Mexico	8:00 A.M.	10:00 P.M.
Thu	Mazatlan, Mexico	9:00 A.M.	6:00 P.M.
Fri	Cabo San Lucas, Mexico	7:00 A.M.	4:00 P.M.
Sat	"Book Lover's" Day at Sea		
Sun	Los Angeles/Long Beach, CA	9:00 A.M.	

ports of call subject to weather conditions

TERMS AND CONDITIONS

PAYMENT SCHEDULE:
50% due upon booking
Full and final payment due by February 10, 2006

Acceptable forms of payment are Visa, MasterCard, American Express, Discover and checks. The card-holder must be one of the passengers traveling. A fee of $25 will apply for all returned checks. Check payments must be made payable to **Advantage International, LLC and sent to: Advantage International, LLC, 195 North Harbor Drive, Suite 4206, Chicago, IL 60601**

CHANGE/CANCELLATION:
Notice of change/cancellation must be made in writing to Advantage International, LLC.

Change:
Changes in cabin category may be requested and can result in increased rate and penalties. A name change is permitted 60 days or more prior to departure and will incur a penalty of $50 per name change. Deviation from the group schedule and package is a cancellation.

Cancellation:
181 days or more prior to departure	$250 per person
121 - 180 days or more prior to departure	50% of the package price
120 - 61 days prior to departure	75% of the package price
60 days or less prior to departure	100% of the package price (nonrefundable)

US and Canadian citizens are required to present a valid passport or the original birth certificate and state issued photo ID (drivers license). All other nationalities must contact the consulate of the various ports that are visited for verification of documentation.

We strongly recommend trip cancellation insurance!

For complete details call 1-877-ADV-NTGE or visit www.AuthorsAtSea.com

For booking form and complete information
go to **www.AuthorsAtSea.com** or call **1-877-ADV-NTGE**

Complete coupon and booking form and mail both to:
**Advantage International, LLC,
195 North Harbor Drive, Suite 4206, Chicago, IL 60601**